There was a throbbing pain behind his temples

For a few beats of the heart, Ryan slipped out of consciousness into the dark. Then he was sitting up, supported by someone's arm around his shoulders, still feeling sick, aware that he had another pain, a burning sensation in his good right eye.

"I think that he's back with us. Ryan, my dear fellow, can you hear me?"

Ryan's tongue felt as if it had been hand-knitted, five sizes too large for his mouth. "Hear you, Doc."

"You feel all right, lover?" Krysty asked.

"Fine."

But he knew that he wasn't fine. He was way short of fine.

To remove the blackness, Ryan had opened his good right eye. He knew that he had opened it.

But the blackness was still there.

**Also available in the
Deathlands saga:**

JAMES AXLER

DEATH LANDS®

Bloodlines

A GOLD EAGLE BOOK FROM

WORLDWIDE®

TORONTO • NEW YORK • LONDON
AMSTERDAM • PARIS • SYDNEY • HAMBURG
STOCKHOLM • ATHENS • TOKYO • MILAN
MADRID • WARSAW • BUDAPEST • AUCKLAND

This is for Angus Wells. He and I have ridden the same
trails in the past. We've both lived in the shadowed
valleys and climbed to sunlit peaks. Now we inhabit
different universes, but I'm pleased to say that we
are still friends.

First edition December 1995

ISBN 0-373-62529-4

BLOODLINES

Vampires don't exist! They have never existed. They are the product of fevered hysterics with far greater imagination than sense. There is no such thing as a vampire! Definitely. Then why do I cast such nervous glances over my shoulder when walking alone along a dark track?

—From *No Reflection in the Mirror*
by Barton B. Goode,
Elmore Press, Mapperley, Utah

Chapter One

The shouting had already faded into silence.

Ryan Cawdor and J. B. Dix, oldest and best of friends, hunkered in their limited shelter, their blasters cocked and ready for the inevitable attack from the natives.

By squinting around the corner of the control console, Ryan could see the first glow of dawn through the open doorway and the shifting wall of bright emerald green of the eternal forest.

"Won't be long," he said grimly.

The one-eyed man heard a faint clicking sound, like hot metal cooling, and glanced back at the pallid green armaglass walls of the gateway chamber. The matter-transfer unit could pluck you from here and send you instantaneously to there. Unfortunately everyone who'd understood the workings of the gateways had died in the worldwide nuclear holocaust of 2001, nearly a century earlier, taking with them the details and secrets of matter transfer.

So, when the chamber door was closed, triggering the "jump" mechanism, you had no way of knowing where "there" might be. It might be anywhere. The most recent jump had left the companions stranded somewhere in Central or South America, in the deeps of a dangerous tropical forest.

After a desperate and lethal adventure, Ryan and his friends had just reached the gateway unit, in a small predark military redoubt, moments ahead of the vengeful villagers.

Ryan's combat reflexes had told him that there was no choice. If they'd all tried to make the mat-trans jump together, they would have been dead meat, trapped in the hexagonal chamber, helpless as a hog on ice.

He'd ordered the others into the unit, while he and J.B., the armorer of the group, stayed behind to secure their safe retreat.

Now it was silent outside.

He wondered where the others had jumped and if they'd made the transfer safely. His thoughts dwelled particularly on his eleven-year-old son, Dean, who was tall for his age, strongly built, with the same curly black hair as his father, with dark brown eyes. Ryan hadn't even known of Dean's existence until a year or so earlier, long after the bleak death of the boy's mother, Sharona.

The other four who'd made the jump were all the closest of friends, though none quite as close as Krysty Wroth.

Easing toward her late twenties, Krysty was five feet eleven in her bare feet, weighing in at 150 pounds. Her eyes were like liquid emeralds, her hair a cascade of living fire. She had come from a ville called Harmony, where she had been taught mystic skills by her mother, Sonja, which included the force of Gaia that would give her unimaginable strength, but at a terrible toll on her health.

She and Ryan had been lovers since they'd begun traveling together through the blighted society that was Deathlands. Both of them hoped that the day would eventually come when they might be able to settle down someplace good and safe.

They hadn't found it yet.

The other woman in the group of companions was Dr. Mildred Winonia Wyeth. Five feet four inches tall and a stocky, powerful 136 pounds, Mildred was a black woman in her middle thirties, with beaded, plaited hair.

She had been born on the seventeenth day of December in 1964.

Less than a year later her Baptist minister father had been slaughtered in a firebombing of his church by a group of anonymous redneck butchers, concealed behind their white sheets and pillowcases.

Mildred had gone on to become a leading expert in the medical science of cryonics and cryogenics. Ironically, eleven days after her thirty-sixth birthday, Mildred had gone into the hospital in her home town of Lincoln, Nebraska, for minor abdominal surgery, which went terribly wrong.

And they had frozen her.

Only a few days later came skydark, the time when the heavens were filled with the shark shadows of nuclear missiles and over ninety-nine percent of the world died.

But the hospital that held her in a dreamless state of frozen suspended animation had its own peaceful nuclear generator, computer controlled, and it had kept Mildred alive until Ryan and his friends came along like latter-day princes and plucked her from the long sleep.

Now she was the partner of John Barrymore Dix, weapons expert and longtime comrade of Ryan Cawdor.

To survive for long in Deathlands it helped to have special skills.

Mildred had been the chairperson of her local pistol club and had represented her country in the free-shooting event in the Olympic Games, where she'd won the silver medal.

Now she carried a Czech-built target revolver. The ZKR 551 was a six-shot blaster designed by the Koucky brothers and manufactured at the Zbrojovka works in Brno. It was a beautiful weapon, with a solid-frame side-rod ejector and a short-fall thumb-cocking hammer, chambered to take a conventional Smith & Wesson .38-caliber round.

With it Mildred Wyeth could put a bullet up a gnat's asshole at fifty feet.

There were two men in the group that had made the jump from the forest.

One was a teenager, Jak Lauren, an albino with a shock of snow-white hair and eyes like smoldering rubies. Jak had become a friend of Ryan and the others a little later than Krysty, after a murderous adventure down in the bayous. He was sixteen years old, standing a hare five feet five, weighing in around 120 pounds. Jak was a brilliant athlete and acrobat, better at hand-to-hand combat than anyone Ryan and J.B. had ever seen. Though he carried a satin-finish Colt Python with a six-inch barrel, his weapon of choice was the throwing knife.

He carried a number of the leaf-bladed knives, with taped, balanced hilts, concealed about his person, and used them with a deathly accuracy.

Jak had been married for over a year, down on a spread in New Mexico. It had been a serene and happy time, but the long darkness had come grinning to take both his wife, Christina, and his little baby, Jenny.

So now he rode again with Ryan and the others.

A single long hunting arrow hissed into the control room, its barbed point digging a chunk out of the plastered wall, falling to the floor a yard from Ryan.

"Keeping us reminded that they're still out there," he said quietly.

"Good of them," J.B. stated, busily polishing his glasses on the sleeve of his jacket. His Uzi and the Smith & Wesson M-4000 scattergun lay at his side, ready for instant use.

Ryan glanced behind him again, thinking of the last of the vanished companions.

Dr. Theophilus Algernon Tanner was a Doctor of Science at Harvard and a Doctor of Philosophy at Oxford University. He'd been born in South Strafford, Vermont, on the fourteenth day of February in the year of Our Lord, 1868.

By some calculations, Doc Tanner was around 230 years old. He certainly looked like an old man, with a mane of silvery hair and a gnarled face. And his speech and most of his attire were undeniably Victorian: a frock coat that was slowly acquiring a patina of green over the glossy black material; knee breeches; cracked leather boots; and a gun that was originally popular during the War between the States, a beautiful, gold-engraved commemorative "Jeb" Stuart limited edition of the huge Le Mat handgun.

Like Jak, Doc had once been married, and there had been great happiness for Doc and his young bride, happiness compounded by the arrival of two adorable children, Rachel and Jolyon.

But life was holding snake eyes for Doc Tanner.

In the late 1990s the whitecoat scientists had been working under conditions of great secrecy on Operation Chronos, which was a part of the Totality Concept.

Time travel.

Their successes were infinitely small, and their hideous disasters enough to keep a special crematorium burning through the day and night.

However, they got Doc Tanner, plucking him from a crisp fall morning in November of 1896.

They brought him forward to a secret laboratory in Virginia in 1998. But the time jump had seriously and permanently affected Doc's mind, and he refused to do anything to cooperate, declaring his intention to do anything that he could to sabotage the evil whitecoats and their foul experimentation. He also made several determined efforts to reverse the "trawling" procedure and travel back once more to Victorian times, to rejoin his lost wife and his dear little children.

Eventually tiring of the recalcitrant old man, the leaders of Operation Chronos decided that Doc Tanner was more trouble than he was worth. In December of 2000, days before skydark and the beginnings of the long winters, they cut their losses and pushed him into the future.

Into Deathlands.

And there he had eventually met up with Ryan Cawdor and his companions.

Ryan sat cradling his Steyr rifle, wondering when the natives would gather their courage and rush the place.

He was crouched behind a computer control console with a polished black plastic surface, and his reflection glowered back at him, showing him to be a powerfully built man with thick, curly black hair.

A dark patch covered his left eye, the right gleaming with a vivid, cold blue. A scar ran from its corner down to his mouth, both injuries dating from his childhood.

The reflection revealed that he wore a long coat, trimmed with white fur, and a white silk scarf was tucked around his neck.

As well as the powerful rifle, Ryan carried a trusty SIG-Sauer P-226 blaster, a 9 mm automatic with a built-in baffle silencer that had seen better days. Balancing it on the opposite hip was a long panga with a honed eighteen-inch blade that ended in a needle point.

"You come up with part two of the plan, Ryan?" J.B. asked.

"Part two?"

"Part one was getting the others to make a safe jump so we didn't all get butchered in the gateway. I didn't quite catch you telling me about part two, which is where you and me also get to jump safely."

Ryan grinned. "Fair question. Guess I never got much beyond part one."

There was a sudden burst of yelling from outside the open sec door, guttural words in an alien language that neither Ryan nor J.B. had heard before they arrived in the emerald jungle.

Ryan risked a quick glance over the top of the console, but there was nothing to be seen. "Best I can come up with is that you cover me and I run for the door, throw the handle and hope that the bastard thing drops quick enough to keep them out. How's that sound to you for part two?"

"Like shit, Ryan." J.B. adjusted his dusty, stained fedora. "Then again, I don't have anything better. Real chance they'll pick you off from outside."

Ryan nodded. "Yeah."

He narrowed his good eye, sniffing. "You smell anything? It smells like—"

"Gasoline," J.B. concluded. "Looks like part two just got obsolete."

Chapter Two

"Doing to us what we did to those bastard ants! They're hoping to drive us out."

Life was measured in seconds.

There was no point now in trying to close the exterior sec door. The gas could be ignited in a heartbeat.

"Have to jump," Ryan said. "Now."

Keeping low, almost on hands and knees, the men splashed through the gasoline that had gushed into the area, reaching the closed door of the gateway chamber.

"Use the LD button," J.B. said.

"I know," Ryan replied irritably.

The one thing they'd been able to learn about mattrans units was that their control panels contained small black buttons marked with the trim white letters *L* and *D*, which stood for *last destination*.

It worked two ways. If you'd made a bad jump, you could press the LD control and you would be back where you were before. Or, in this case, if you used the button within thirty minutes of a previous jump, then you would go to the same place.

That was the theory.

If Ryan and J.B. could make it safely and trigger the jump mechanism, then they should arrive at the same destination as the others.

The Trader always used to say that when it was time to move, the breadth of a human hair could make the difference between living and dying.

Ryan looked behind him. The rifle was across his shoulder and the handblaster in his fist. Their movement hadn't been followed by a shower of arrows or spears, as he'd feared, which meant the natives out in the dense, sweating greenery were about to light the fire.

He reached up and threw open the door, gesturing for J.B. to roll into the chamber.

Now the natives saw that they were in danger of losing their prey.

There was a scream of rage, and an arrow struck the watery green armaglass only inches from Ryan's shoulder, bouncing off and landing with a splash in the gasoline.

The control panel was set at chest height in the frame of the door, and Ryan lunged for it, left-handed, aiming for the LD. button, hitting it.

Simultaneously, almost in slow motion, a burning branch was thrown into the gateway from outside, whirling in the air above the chattering consoles, the oxygen making the flames roar brightly.

It seemed to take forever for the fire to ignite the lake of gasoline.

Ryan grabbed the edge of the door and started to pull its great counterbalanced weight shut to trigger the mat-trans mechanism, his eye watching the torch.

The jagged branch landed, a ripple of blue fire running from it across the surface of the gasoline, turning it into a sea of fire.

"Dark night!" J.B. gasped, on hands and knees behind Ryan, holding the Uzi, ready to open up if the berserk natives came after them.

Ryan recoiled from the flaring heat that seared up at him, the hot yellow flames cut off by the closing armaglass door. The lock clicked shut and the mat-trans mechanism was activated.

The walls of the hexagonal chamber were immensely thick and powerful, but there was no way of locking or bolting the chamber to make it secure against an external attack. No doubt its original manufacturers, a century earlier, had never envisaged a time that it might be needed.

"Fire might keep them away," Ryan said, sitting quickly on the floor, avoiding the metal disks, leaning his back against the cool armaglass. He noticed in passing how all the smooth walls were smeared with patches of lichen and moss, laid there in the extreme humidity of the jungle since they'd first arrived a few days earlier.

The fire was visible beyond the armaglass, the smell of smoke filtering through. But there was no sign of any of the natives daring the heat to try to get to them.

J.B. sat opposite Ryan, the scattergun across his lap. He snatched a moment to take off the fedora and place his spectacles safely in one of his pockets.

The air at the top of the chamber was already filling with tendrils of whirling gray-white mist, and the disks in floor and ceiling were glowing brightly.

Ryan could feel the familiar nauseous feeling of his brain being swirled around inside his skull, as though the bony walls were expanding and the pinkish tissue was shrinking, smaller and smaller toward infinity.

"Here we go," he said, his voice thick, echoing inside his own head.

The darkness was birthing, spreading out from the depths of his own mind, swallowing all of his senses. Hearing went first, followed by speech.

At the last moment of sentience, Ryan thought he saw a dark group of figures, silhouetted against the bright fire, struggling to open the door of the chamber.

"Too..." he muttered.

IT WAS A BAD JUMP. There were times when the transfer from here to there was made with nothing worse than a sick headache and, occasionally a nosebleed, but with no sensation that every molecule and atom of your body had been dissolved and projected through space and reassembled at some distant point.

Other times, the jump fucked your head.

J.B. FOUND HIMSELF walking along a beach. The stones beneath his combat boots were of differing sizes, from duck egg to basketball. A thick mist drifted in from the gray sea to his right, which lapped at the edge of the beach with small, monotonous rollers, sucking at the shingle, rising and falling, advancing and withdrawing.

To his left he could just make out vast cliffs of smooth, polished granite, rising vertically, their tops out of sight in the lowering clouds.

The beach stretched ahead of him for about two hundred yards until it merged with the grayness. Behind him, the dreary vista was exactly the same.

Despite the chill, the Armorer was dressed only in a thin shirt and a torn pair of camouflage cotton pants. The air was bitterly cold and damp, and he shivered as he walked along. The sky was completely overcast, and he had no clue which direction he was taking.

The stretch of beach was completely deserted, with no seabirds wheeling above his head, no sign of life out to sea and not even the smallest crab clicking among the stones.

J.B. became aware that it was beginning to drizzle.

Suddenly, and seamlessly, he was inside the ruins of some vast building, filled with huge rusting pieces of machinery so archaic and corroded that it was impossible to tell what they might once have been.

Water dripped from the rotting ends of the roof timbers, splashing sonorously into great, dark weed-fronded pools that almost covered the stone floor.

And he was not alone.

Every time that J.B. took a few steps forward he caught the sound of someone—or something—following him. But when he stopped there was silence. And when he spun there was nothing to be seen.

The way forward led him deeper into the maw of the ancient building. His glasses were covered in condensation, but when J.B. tried to wipe them clean he found that it formed a sticky film, like spilled honey.

A strange, bitter smell hung in the cold air, like blood poured over molten iron.

The passage ahead of J.B. became more narrow, the ceiling dropping lower.

A rusted iron door with a massive handle blocked the passage. J.B. hesitated, glancing behind him. Above the slapping noise of the waves outside the building, he could hear steps moving closer, stumbling and unsteady, sounding like a recently revived corpse. A pale sun broke through holes in the roof and walls of the passage, penetrating in spears of jagged light.

Unarmed, J.B. had to go on.

The handle wouldn't move, though he thrust at it with all of his strength. The red-orange corrosion was sharp and jagged, and blood began to flow from his palms, dripping from the ends of his fingers onto the concrete floor.

The steps were closer, so close that the Armorer no longer dared to turn to face what was pursuing him, in case the sight of it drove him staring mad.

At last the handle moved, creaking open.

J.B. darted through the narrow gap and pulled the door shut behind him, slamming home a pair of well-oiled bolts. He glanced around to make sure he was safe and found himself in a box of stone, six feet high, five feet lengthwise and four feet across. Solid concrete with no window, yet there was an odd filtered, phosphorescent light inside the chamber that enabled him to see a polished steel grille set in the center of the floor.

The room was filled with the scent of the ocean.

Water began to rise through the grille, slowly and silently, icy cold. It had a thick consistency, more like molasses than water, and was flooding inexorably into the small cube of stone.

Whatever the horror waiting outside, it couldn't be worse than a hideous and lonely death by drowning.

J.B. tried to open the bolts on the door, but they were utterly immovable.

The liquid had reached above his knees.

He reached down, locking his fingers in the bars of the grille, using all his strength to try to pry it open. He realized he'd have a glimmer of a chance if he could force himself down into the oily water and swim out against the advancing tide.

But the grille didn't move.

J.B. straightened, panting for breath, fighting against crippling panic.

The liquid was above his waist.

He stood as tall as he could, rising on the tips of his toes, pressing his head into the angle between ceiling and wall.

Rising higher, the water was to his shoulders, then brushing his chin.

J.B., hanging stubbornly on to the last shreds of survival, lifted his mouth and nose into the tiny pocket of air that still remained.

The liquid covered his mouth, filling his nose as he took a long, deep breath.

A long, last breath.

There wasn't even a chance to scream.

IT WAS A BAD JUMP.

Ryan lay in a hammock, stretched between a pair of sturdy old oaks. Around him were all the sights and scents of the fall in New England.

Beyond the bottom of the flowering garden he could see the rolling hills, dappled with the fiery hues of red, yellow and burning orange, the startling beauty of death in life, as he'd once read.

Dean knelt on the cropped turf a few yards away, puzzling over a chessboard. "Black to play and mate in three, Father?" he asked.

Krysty was there, wearing a long print dress, her feet bare. She lay on a pile of Turkish cushions, the material decorated with tiny shards of mirror that caught and reflected the brightness of the noon sun.

"Don't ask your father," she said. "You know the only way to learn is by solving problems yourself."

The boy grinned. "Sure. Think I'm going in for a spell. Practice my viola."

He walked across the lawn toward the half-timbered house, past the mullioned windows and in through a heavy iron-studded door, moving with an easy coltish grace.

Ryan watched him go, his heart swelling with pride at the beauty of his son.

Krysty stood to join him, pushing the hammock so that it swung gently from side to side. She leaned over him, her right hand brushing over his naked chest, lower, caressing him through the thin material of his cotton pants, smiling at his instant reaction to her.

"Seems like you have a diamond cutter down there, lover," she whispered. "Perhaps we should do something about it."

Ryan glanced toward the house, worried in case they were being watched. But a massive purple buddleia, its fronds attracting dozens of beautiful butterflies, kept them safely concealed from prying eyes.

"Why not?" he said.

Though he wasn't aware of either of them taking off their clothes, they were both naked. Krysty had gently tied his hands to one end of the hammock, his ankles to the other.

"Heighten the pleasure, lover," she whispered, dropping her head and feathering his erection with a long, slow kiss.

She sat firmly astride him, his penis jutting from the flames of her brilliant crimson pubic hair, while she leaned forward and kissed him sweetly on the lips, gripping his thighs with her heels.

"Put it in," he said hoarsely as she straightened, the movement making the hammock sway again.

"Soon, lover," Krysty replied, throwing her head back and laughing. Her mane of sentient hair was tumbled across her shoulders, her teeth showing white in the sunshine, her nipples peaking with desire, hard and firm.

"Now," he insisted, pushing his hips up against her. "Now, lover."

Krysty laughed. "Be patient. Have to take my own special pleasure first."

The sun went in, and a cold wind blew up the valley from the sheer walls of Queechee Gorge.

Ryan shivered.

Leaves fluttered from the trees, landing silently on the dead grass.

Krysty reached into her flame-bright hair and plucked out a number of long steel needles, their points glittering coldly. They were about six inches long, each tipped with a perfect pink pearl.

"Have to take my own special pleasure first."

"No pain," Ryan said, tugging at the silken bonds, unable to shift them.

The red-haired beauty laughed in delight at his futile efforts to escape her.

She lifted herself up, then lowered onto him, building him inside her with her left hand, giving a sigh of contentment and wriggling from side to side.

Despite the horror of the situation, Ryan found that he was still rock hard inside her.

"Where shall we start with the acupuncture?" she whispered, leaning over him, her breath on his face, rotten with the stench of corruption. As she opened her mouth, a small white maggot wriggled from between her lips and dropped onto Ryan's chest, close to his left nipple.

"Please," he breathed.

"Naughty little worm," she said with a giggle, lifting one of the needles and poking it through the maggot, pinning it to Ryan's chest. She worked the end of the needle until the point slid sideways, piercing the nipple in an explosion of pain.

"Just starters, lover," she said. As Krysty spoke, she used her internal muscles on him, keeping him erect, milking him, bringing him racing toward a climax.

The needles darted in front of him, sticking into the other side of his chest, so deep that he felt the point grating off one of the ribs. Another ran into the angle of the elbow, exquisitely painful, and a fourth went in and out and in and out across his stomach, as though the woman were doing invisible embroidery.

Ryan bit his lip until he felt blood flowing warm over his chin.

Krysty saw it and dropped her head again, licking at the fresh-flowing crimson. "Good."

The woman carefully worked two of the needles through both his lips, one of them from the bottom and one from the top, quieting his moaning. Another slender sliver of steel pierced his nose from side to side.

She rubbed her hand over the pearls, sending waves of white pain through him. "Pain is good, lover," she breathed.

Krysty's skin was like parchment, her eyes a milky, scumming green.

He blinked his good eye, aware of tears streaming from it, across his stubbled cheeks.

"Oh, does my hero weep? I see that he does. And I have only used about a quarter of my needles. I have to find amusing places for all the others." She was moving quicker, rising and falling, and he knew, through the fog of agony, that he was nearing a climax.

Her gnarled hand, gripping a long steel needle, rested on his salt-slick cheek. The point, blurred in his vision, moved back and forth across his eye.

"One eye good. No eyes better," she murmured. "You move into darkness, so you need only see darkness."

Ryan blinked his good eye shut, feeling a tiny prickling as the point of the needle probed at the closed eyelid.

"Open up, lover," Krysty said. "Want to get the timing just right. Feel you come inside me at the same moment that I stab out your eye."

But it was no longer Krysty who straddled him in the wildly swinging hammock. The woman was unbelievably old, her skin sweating with ancient evil, her rheumy eyes glistening down at Ryan's agony, her straggling, matted hair lying lank across the yellowed, goatlike skull.

"Not her, lover. Never was her. That flame-haired bitch with her Gaia powers and her fucking Mother Sonja!"

Ryan closed his eye again, but the crone was pinching at his face, squeezing his good eye between finger and thumb, forcing it open.

He was forced to look up at the needle as he sped the last seconds toward a pounding orgasm.

Ryan didn't even have time to scream.

It was a bad jump.

Bad.

Chapter Three

Ryan recovered first. He rolled onto his side and retched violently, bringing up threads of yellow bile and clotted lumps of food, congealed from his last meal.

His head hurt, with a band of steel clamped around his temples. Slowly and with infinite caution, Ryan lifted his right hand toward his closed eye, his good right eye, touching it with fingers that trembled.

He blinked it open and saw armaglass walls of a dull, dark brown, showing that they had successfully jumped somewhere else. The disks in floor and ceiling had ceased to glow, and the mist near the top of the gateway had almost vanished.

He felt terrible, his brain still being chewed around inside his head. The slightest movement produced murderous vertigo that led in turn to violent sickness.

Ryan decided to lie still for a while, until his body recovered from the shock of the jump.

He could still taste the burning gasoline that had given them the flaming send-off. He remembered the relief that the natives had failed to get at them, though his last sentient memory was of dark figures, silhouetted against the flames, struggling to wrench open the gateway door.

Ryan blinked again, lifting a hand to rub at his eye with his sleeve.

He was right. There *was* something lying just inside the door of the chamber. Some kind of small animal.

Whatever it was, Ryan decided that it was no threat to him. It had the unmistakable stillness of death. Perhaps some little creature had been sheltering in the gateway and had been caught by the speed of the second jump.

He crawled a few inches closer, peering at it, then heard J.B.'s voice, sounding frail and weak, from behind him. "It's a hand."

"A hand?"

"Yeah. Hand."

Ryan squinted, realizing that the Armorer was correct.

It was a human hand, dark skinned, with the end joint of the middle finger missing from an old wound. Three thin bracelets of woven hair encircled the wrist.

Ryan took a single deep, slow breath and risked sitting up, steadying himself against the cold armaglass wall. He got a new perspective on the severed hand, seeing that it had been cut off a few inches above the wrist, halfway toward the elbow. It was a startlingly clean wound, with very little blood, the two ends of bone showing as white and clean as if a massive guillotine had been used on them.

"Looks like the poor bastard got the door open just as the jump was taking place," J.B. said, sniffing, removing his glasses to polish them. "We brought his hand with us. Rest of him must've stayed and bled back in the jungle.''

"Fireblast!" Ryan looked across at his old friend. "You look worse than I feel."

J.B. tried a fragile smile but didn't even get close to it. "I feel about twice as bad as you look, and you look three times as bad as me."

"Not the best jump. You have bad dreams?"

The Armorer replaced his spectacles, looking around for his fedora and tugging it on at a jaunty angle. "Seemed like I was drowning in a small, sealed room under the sea. Too realistic for me.''

"I was being fucked and murdered at the same time by..." He hesitated, holding back a part of the nightmare. "By this evil old slut."

"Dark night!" J.B. had tried to stand, using the shotgun as a crutch, but his strength failed him and he dropped back to hands and knees.

"Think the others have had such a bastardly bad jump?'' Ryan asked.

"Hope not. For their sake. Might've been something to do with the mat-trans being used twice so close together. Or the equipment might have malfunctioned.''

Ryan looked around, feeling the nausea retreating. "Think we've reached the same place?"

J.B. wiped sweat from his forehead. "Find out soon enough. I'd have thought they might have been letting us know they were here by now."

"Yeah."

There could be any of a hundred reasons why Krysty and the others weren't already opening up the heavy door and greeting their safe arrival.

But the most likely and the most menacing was that they'd somehow jumped to a different destination. The LD button might have failed to work.

But as the Trader used to say, there was plenty of time to worry about things you could control and understand without bothering about anything else.

"Feel up to moving?" Ryan asked.

J.B. cleared his throat. "Pretty up and walking good. Ready when you are."

"Sure?"

"Yeah. Long as I don't have to run or fight or do anything more than a gentle stroll, then I'm your man, Ryan." He pushed a hand against the walls and stood, rocking from side to side, eyes pinwheeling behind the lenses of his glasses.

"Sure?" Ryan repeated.

"Let's do it."

Ryan drew the SIG-Sauer, checked that the Steyr was snug over his shoulder, then opened the door a few inches and kicked the severed hand out of the way.

He saw the usual small side room that stood between the actual mat-trans chamber and the main control area. It was about ten feet square, bare of furniture, with a couple of empty shelves on the wall to the right.

Through the open doorway beyond it Ryan could see the rows of desks, computers and monitor screens that typified that section of the military redoubts.

He stepped out of the chamber, J.B. right at his heels, and sniffed the air, finding it had the arid and flat taste typical of most gateways.

The redoubts had mostly been built during the last years of the twentieth century, mainly in out-of-the-way places in the wilderness regions of the country. Despite the bitter and fruitless objections of the powerful conservation lobby, these often happened to be in national parks.

The redoubts had been powered by the most sophisticated nuke plants, designed to run on carefully planned comp programs without any human interference. This meant that after the megakilling of skydark, many of the surviving redoubts carried on running themselves, ignorant of the fact that their human masters were already dead or dying of rad sickness.

So the stabilization procedures involving cleaning, security and air-conditioning were still working in most of the redoubts.

A faded piece of pink paper on the wall was tacked to the off-white plaster.

Ryan checked it out before going on to examine the rest of the gateway complex. It was already obvious that Krysty and the others weren't in the immediate vicinity.

"What is it?" J.B. asked.

Ryan read it aloud. "Says 'Redoubt 47's own theater group invites you to their January production, *Whip It Out and Wipe It,* a revue written by Officer

Jim Laurens. Take your mind off the troubles. Monday thru Friday, 1900 hours.' That's all.''

The Armorer screwed up his eyes, peering at it. ''Must've been just before skydark. The intensity of the military situation would've been the troubles it mentions.''

''Wonder if the show ever took place?'' Ryan looked at the notice. ''Guess it doesn't matter much either way. Let's go check out the rest of the place.''

THE MAIN CONTROL AREA WAS in excellent shape, with no sign of any structural damage or electrical failure. The banks of controls showed flickering lights and whirling dials, giving off the faint distant hum of the operating machinery.

''No clue anyone's been here for a hundred years,'' J.B. said, running a finger along the top of the nearest desk, showing it to Ryan, completely clean.

''Main sec doors are closed.''

''Yeah.''

Ryan stood still, sniffing at the air. ''I reckon I can just about smell sweat.''

''Sure you're not imagining it?''

''Mebbe.''

''They have to have come this way.'' J.B. shook his head, pushing back the fedora.

''Why didn't they wait?''

The Armorer looked around, considering the question. ''Too many possible answers to that, friend.'' He hesitated. ''I reckon I can smell sweat, as well.''

"Better get the sec doors open. See what lies behind them. If Krysty and Dean and the others aren't there, then we can start doing some serious worrying."

The green lever at the side of the vanadium-steel door was in the down "locked" position.

"Usual," J.B. said, taking hold of the lever. "Stop it after a few inches."

"Right. Soon as I give you the word."

Ryan gripped the P-226 blaster in his right hand and crouched on the floor, slightly to one side of the door.

"Ready?"

"Go," Ryan said.

Nothing happened.

He glanced sideways, seeing that the Armorer was wrestling with the green lever, trying to move it upward.

"Nothing," J.B. panted. "Like the mechanism's totally jammed."

"Means that they're somewhere on the other side of it and it jammed after they left this area." He paused, thinking aloud. "Or it could also mean that it's been jammed for countless years and they never jumped here. Fireblast! Why can't things take an easy turn for once?"

"Manual override?"

"Is there one? Not always one."

"Sure. Small panel at the side here."

The handle that could be used to wind up the sec door was only six inches long, folded back out of sight. To lift the enormously heavy weight of the massive bombproof door, it had to be linked into an intricate system of gears and counterweights.

J.B. flicked open the lid of the panel, unfolding the brass handle and setting it carefully in place. He gave it an experimental couple of turns, and the door trembled and moved upward a fraction of an inch.

"Looking good," Ryan commented. "Take it away."

"Brilliant machinery," J.B. said as he started to turn the handle. "Makes you wonder at the wonder of it. Some things they knew how to build in those days."

Ryan flattened himself on the floor, ready to squint out beneath the slowly ascending door. If this redoubt was like the majority of others that they'd visited, there would likely be a passage outside that would ultimately lead into the rest of the redoubt and then on into the open air.

Raising the sec door by hand was immensely slow and laborious. After thirty seconds it wasn't much more than an inch off the concrete floor.

Ryan held the SIG-Sauer ready, laying his face flat, squinting under the door with his one ice-blue eye— staring straight into a pair of dark brown eyes, less than a foot away.

Chapter Four

"You stupe kid! I might've put a full-metal-jacket round through your damn-fool head!" an angry Ryan gritted after J.B. had finally raised the door and the companions were together again.

Dean Cawdor shuffled his feet. "Sorry, Dad. It's just that as soon as the door started to move, we all figured that it had to be you and J.B. there."

"Suppose it had been one of those Japanese samurai guys we ran across a while back?"

"Well . . . I didn't think—"

"Right. You didn't think. Might have had a sword blade through your eye, Dean."

"Suppose so. Sorry, Dad."

"Come on, lover," Krysty said, putting her arms around Ryan, hugging him tightly. "Main thing is that we're all safe together. What happened back there?"

J.B. answered the question, holding hands with Mildred. "Tried to burn us out. Flooded the complex with gasoline. Didn't quite make it. We jumped."

"Both look dreadful," Jak stated, running his long fingers through his mane of stark white hair. "Bad jump?"

"One of the worst." Ryan shook his head. "Still feel like I've been run through the wringer."

"The natives didn't get in after you?" Doc asked. "After we deprived them of their godhead, there was some serious grief. They seemed unusually persistent in their efforts. I believe that the poor wretches would gladly have given anything to have laid a hand on you."

Ryan laughed. "Well, they came close to laying a hand on us, Doc. But that was all. Just one hand, and it's lying out by the gateway door."

BOTH RYAN AND J.B. were still weak from the effects of the jump, and they elected to wait in the control area for an hour or so until they felt better.

Dean was eager to explain how they'd opened the sec door while waiting for Ryan and the Armorer to come along. It had worked perfectly well that time, and everyone had gone out into the corridor beyond.

"Then we all heard this harsh snappin' noise, like a half-track breaking, you know? And the whole door started to move on down."

"Falling?"

"No, Dad, not like free-fall. That would've been a real triple-hot pipe. Start a quake clean across Deathlands if it had crashed down."

"So it came slowly?"

The boy sniffed. "Not real slowly. More sort of not fast. I don't know the right words for it."

"Well, when you've gotten some learning, then you'll know all the right words, son."

"Sure. I know that. Anyway, the control lever, the green one, didn't work it and there was no override outside in the passage. So we was fucked."

Krysty had been listening. "That's not the right thing to say, Dean."

"Sorry. You mean saying 'fucked,' Krysty?"

"I mean that. Partly. Also, you shouldn't say that we 'was fucked.' Bad grammar. Say we *were* fucked."

Ryan grinned. "Better still, don't say fucked at all, Dean. Not until you're a little older."

SINCE THE CONTROLS WERE so obviously shot, Ryan decided that it was safest to leave the sec door raised three-quarters of the way toward the ceiling.

"Someone could get in at the gateway," Mildred warned, "leaving us in deepest ordure."

"Have to take that chance." Ryan sniffed the air. "Still smells like nobody's been in here for a hundred years. You didn't find anything interesting?"

Krysty answered him. "Never got to do any exploring. Like Dean said, the door came down too quickly. Good job that you and J.B. stayed behind. If we'd all been together, we'd have been trapped on the wrong side of making another jump. And we don't have the nuke-missile power to blast the sec door open."

"You feel any signs of life anywhere else in this redoubt, lover?"

She shook her head, her mane of fiery hair dancing across her shoulders. "Nothing. Be surprised if I'm wrong. Like Uncle Tyas McCann used to say back in Harmony ville, feels deader than a beaver hat."

Ryan whistled softly between his teeth. "Then we might as well get moving, friends. Let's go ahead on orange and we'll see what we see."

Orange meant having the option to draw your blaster if you wanted. Red meant there was no choice.

Even on green it didn't mean you walked free as air without paying attention.

You never moved carelessly in Deathlands.

Ryan led his friends out in a casual skirmish line, leaving the gateway behind. The passage was fifteen feet wide, with concrete walls that rose vertically and then curved in toward the arched ceiling, at least twelve feet above their heads. There were sections of neon strip lights at intervals, casting a ghostly pallor over everyone. About one in four had failed over the years, but there was still plenty of light in the tunnel.

Every forty or fifty yards small sec cameras were fixed at ceiling height, some with tiny ruby lights showing that they were still dutifully obeying their programmer's instructions and sending pictures back to some hidden control center.

The setup they found was similar to many of the other redoubts that they'd visited. The gateway was located at the farthest end of the line. To the left of the sec door the corridor ran along for less than fifty featureless yards before ending in a wall of solid stone. There was the familiar feeling of being deep below the earth.

Ryan strode along to the right, his boot heels clicking on the cold stone. Krysty was second, followed by Dean. Doc was fourth, his knees creaking at every step, while Jak padded silently at his heels. Then came Mildred, walking together with J.B. at the rear.

There was no sign of life anywhere in the redoubt.

The farther they went along the featureless passageway, the more lights had failed. But there had been no side corridors or doors on either side.

The corridor seemed to wind ceaselessly around to the right and to climb slowly.

"It's like being inside the shell of a snail," Dean observed. "Been walking miles."

"About a mile and a quarter," J.B. corrected him, checking his wrist chron.

"Certainly going up and up and around and around." Jak shook his head. "Where we finish up?"

"Inside our own rectal orifices if we go around many more times," Mildred commented. "I swear that I'm starting to get dizzy. This layout remind you of anything, Doc?"

"I don't believe so. Though the simile proposed by young Master Cawdor was unusually accurate. Around and around the little wheel goes, and where it stops, nobody knows. What does it remind you of, Dr. Wyeth?"

"Place in New York. A big art gallery called the Guggenheim after the guy who paid for it. Got the same kind of shape. You go up to the top and stroll down and around." She stopped walking for a moment. "Thoughts like that are bad, aren't they? Brings back a tiny part of what was lost. Last time I went there with my Uncle Josh, Dad's younger brother, they had a beautiful exhibition of paintings by Chagall.''

Everyone else rested for a few moments while the black woman recovered her composure, blowing her nose noisily on a white handkerchief.

''You feeling all right, Mildred?'' J.B. asked. ''Want to take five?''

''I'll be all right. Guess it must be that time of the month again. Always get a little weepy.''

''Wait till you reach my time, madam,'' Doc said, baring his startling white teeth. ''Someone once said that old age is an island surrounded by death. I vow that there are days when I feel that I am slipping off that island.''

Mildred smiled at him. ''Know what you mean, Doc. You and me, we're the only people in all Deathlands with such long pasts. Gets hard at times, knowing that everyone you ever knew has been dead for years.''

''Well over a hundred years, in my case. I sometimes dream, you know, friends. Dream of my beloved wife. And sometimes of my children. Of Rachel and beaming little Jolyon. Oh, he was such a merry little fellow.'' Tears gathered in the corners of Doc's pale blue eyes, breaking free and trickling through the silvery stubble on his cheeks. ''I dream that they are full grown with their own children. And grandchildren.''

''They probably lived good lives, Doc,'' Ryan said, trying to cheer up the old man.

''Perhaps. But they are still so long dead.''

THEY FOUND THE PLAN of the redoubt at a junction about 350 yards farther along. It was bolted to the wall, behind a Plexiglas screen.

They gathered around, peering at it in the semidarkness, as five out of the twelve overhead lights had blown.

"There's the mat-trans unit," J.B. said, pointing to the bottom part of the layered map. "And that's this corridor."

"And this must be where we are now." Ryan traced the circling corridor with his finger until he reached the first junction. "Looks like the gateway has its own entrance. Get in and out without having to go through the rest of the redoubt."

"Doesn't give us any clue where we are, does it?" Krysty said, scanning the map.

"They never do. Just the number at the top. Redoubt 47."

"It seems to have had an unusually large laboratory complex," Doc commented. "I wonder what fresh evils the whitecoats were up to there?"

"Since we can't seem to get up there, I guess we'll never know," Mildred stated.

"Probably stripped bare, anyway." Krysty looked again at the plan. "This corridor sort of winds upward and around and around, kind of on the perimeter of the main part of the redoubt."

Dean had wandered off on his own, checking out the side passage, returning with the news that it ended abruptly in a closed sec door.

"Locked shut, Dad. And there's no kind of control panel or lever or nothing."

"Anything," Krysty said, automatically correcting him.

"Mebbe it could only be opened from the inside." Ryan scratched his chin. "Or they could've had some kind of automatic device. Like they used to have on garage doors."

"Sure there's no way of opening it?"

Dean turned to Jak. "Go look for yourself. There's nothing there. Plain walls."

They stood for a moment, undecided what to do.

Ryan looked ahead of them, referring again to the map. "Well, if we can't get into the rest of the redoubt, we might as well head straight for the exit. Least we can find out where we've ended up."

THEY WALKED PAST three more side corridors, but each was blocked off by vanadium-steel sec doors, firmly and immovably locked shut.

"Unusual this," Ryan said as they paused for breath. "Wonder why the gateway section is so carefully isolated from the rest of the redoubt?"

Krysty looked about her. "Has it occurred to you, lover, that it might be the other way around?"

"How do you mean?"

"That it's the redoubt that's been isolated from the mat-trans section. That huge laboratory section— never seen anything like that in any of the redoubts that we've jumped to, have we? It's a new one."

"Yeah, could be."

Doc was entranced with the idea. "Those devilish whitecoats!" he spit. "Their fearsome experiments behind the safety of locked doors and screened units. Highest sec clearance anywhere. Who knows what frightful mischief they might have been up to in those last weeks, before the nukecaust revealed the utter futility of all research."

"Less we know, less we worry," Jak commented. "Be good taste fresh air after this weak recycled shit. How much farther?"

J.B. considered the question. "Nor more than another quarter mile," he replied. "Been climbing all the while, but it's finally starting to level off some."

"I'm hungry, Dad."

"We're all hungry, Dean. Something about jumping that makes you feel sick and hungered, all at the same time. Long as the main entrance sec door can be opened, we'll soon be out in the good air and do us some hunting."

"Right now I could chew on a mutie's skull and drink a bowl of stickie's blood."

Doc shuddered theatrically. "Drink blood, my sweet imp! There is nothing more profane."

The boy grinned. "Well, better than rat piss."

Ryan ruffled the boy's hair. "Let's get to the entrance first and see what we can see."

Chapter Five

It was obvious that they hadn't found the main exit from the whole complex. There were no extra security points, and the passage hardly opened at all. It was just wide enough for a single wag to drive through.

"Got the standard number-code control panel," called Dean, who'd been given permission by his father to go along ahead of them. There wasn't any likely danger with the air tasting the way it did, along with Krysty's strong feeling that there was no kind of life anywhere within the redoubt.

Ryan looked at the others. "Might as well go out straightaway. Nothing to gain by waiting. You agree?" Nobody spoke. "Well, you don't disagree. On condition red. Dean, punch in the usual code and see what happens."

"But be ready quick stop," Jak reminded him.

"Sure," the boy snapped. "I know I don't know much about using the right word and all that shit, but I know what to do with redoubt sec doors."

The albino shrugged, holding out his hands, palms showing. "Back off, Dean," he said quietly. "Stick your fingers down bear's throat and get bit off."

"That a threat, Jak?" Dean stood by the control panel, his body as tense as a drawn bowstring.

Ryan took a half step toward his son. "Enough," he warned. "Time for fighting among ourselves. But this isn't one of them. Press in the code."

"Three, five and two," Dean said.

"Right."

Ryan crouched again, ready to peer under the rising sec door and give a warning of danger. The others were ranged in a rough half circle close behind him, everyone with a blaster at the ready.

The buttons clicked loudly in the oppressive stillness. Five. Three. Two.

This time there was no problem.

The monstrous weight began to lift. Ryan squinted into the opening, but didn't order his son to stop the process, not calling a halt until the door was about eighteen inches off the ground.

Dean pressed the single button that held the sec door in position, waiting for the word from his father to continue.

"Humid again," Mildred stated, breaking the silence. "Hope we're not back at the village."

"It *is* humid, lover. And got the same kind of green taste as before."

Jak dropped to one knee beside Ryan and peeked out cautiously. "Smells like swamps to me," he said. "Smells to me like home."

Ryan nodded. "Bayou smell. More rotting vegetation than the last jump. Not so hot. Not so wet. Least we can breathe this air all right."

"Louisiana?" J.B. said. "Think we're back down in the southeast again?"

"Could be." Ryan turned back and looked out under the door again. "Can't see very much. Gray-green trees, dripping with Spanish moss."

"Always reminds me of the rotting wedding dress of some dead duchess in a Jacobean tragedy," Doc mused. "A kind of faded decadence."

Mildred nodded. "Must be getting soft in the head, Doc. Here I am agreeing with you again."

"Take it up all the way, Dean," Ryan ordered. "Unless... You don't feel any threat, do you, Krysty?"

"Feel a lot of life, but nothing that close and nothing personally hostile."

Dean pressed the release, and the mass of dull metal began to ascend again, reaching up to the ceiling before it stopped with a faint hydraulic hissing.

Now everyone could see out past the entrance to the redoubt, see the tall trees, festooned in the Spanish moss. There was an open space of overgrown tarmac, surrounded by the vegetation, but no sign of any kind of trail.

"Air smells wetter than last time. Sort of gray, colder wetness. Kind strikes through to the heart of your bones," J.B. said. "I'd lay money on the bayous again."

"We exploring some, lover?" Krysty asked. "Hunt us up some food?"

"I'd be interested in trying to get at the main entrance to the redoubt." The Armorer looked around. "Got to be something special to have labs that size."

"I cast my vote against that suggestion," Doc said, his voice ringing out loudly.

"Why?"

"Because, John Barrymore Dix, I have more knowledge of the whitecoats than any of you." He bowed slightly to Mildred. "Even more than you, Dr. Wyeth. And I have found them universally evil psychopaths."

"I'll go with that," Mildred said with a nod. "Some good doctors, but when you get to the experimenters... Needles into the eyes of kittens and electrodes that probe directly into the brains of week-old monkeys. No, that's not for me."

"Could be something triple interesting in there," the Armorer insisted.

"I believe that's what Pandora said before opening her box and releasing every plague and wickedness into the world." Doc stared challengingly at J.B. "And, forget not, my friend, that the cat was slain by curiosity."

J.B. glanced at Ryan. "What do you think? Might not get a chance like this again."

Ryan swatted a persistent wasp away from his face. "I honestly don't know, J.B."

"There might be some kind of predark virus just waiting to leap out and start chilling all over again," Krysty said. "I'm with Doc and Mildred on this. If there are any dogs sleeping up there in the main lab complex, then leave them sleeping.''

''Three to one against going in,'' Ryan stated. ''How about you, Jak? And you, Dean?''

The younger boy waited for the teenager to answer. Ryan would have laid a wagload of jack that his son was going to go along with whatever Jak decided.

''Doc's double right,'' Jak said. ''Where whitecoats step, grass dies.''

''Dean?''

The boy looked at his father, brushing a curl of dark hair from over his eyes. ''I reckon J.B.'s the one who's right. Wouldn't do no harm, and it might be a real hot pipe to find what they were experimenting with. Could be monsters.''

Ryan grinned, glad that he had never had a wagload of jack with which to wager.

The Trader used to say that you couldn't trust anyone. Not anyone. But you very *specially* couldn't trust any women, animals and children.

''Four to two,'' he said.

''How do you vote, Ryan?'' the Armorer asked. ''Just like to know.''

Ryan considered refusing to answer the question. But that would have meant backing off, and he had never liked backing off anything for anyone.

''I say there has to be a risk of some bug still being around. Place that size was working for the military. Wouldn't have been making raggedy dolls, that's for sure.''

J.B. took off his glasses and gave them an extra polish. "Five to two. Real solid majority. Still doesn't make it right. Trader said that a man who turns his back and walks away from a closed door'll never get rich."

Ryan laughed. "You cunning son of a bitch! You know that Trader didn't say that."

"He didn't?"

"No, J.B., he didn't. He said that a man who turns his back and walks away from a closed door'll never get himself chilled. Kind of different."

"Guess so." J.B. put his spectacles back on. "We going to recce, or do we stand here jawing all day?"

WHEN THEY LOOKED behind them, once they were clear of the lowering weight of the sec door, the main surprise was that the redoubt was almost invisible.

"It's all buried," Dean said.

As on previous occasions, Ryan was awed by the extent of the labors of the predark government. To build anything remotely similar in Deathlands would be impossible. The man-hours and technical expertise involved were mind-blowing.

The redoubt, from the map, had to have been over a mile in diameter and have a total depth of more than a thousand feet. Like an iceberg, most of its unimaginable bulk was buried out of sight below the swampy ground.

He looked at the complex. Apart from the open sec door, looking like a toothless mouth, the place was amazingly well concealed. It had been covered in layers of earth, and time and weather had sown and nurtured seeds of all sorts of plants and trees, so that it was now hidden beneath an impenetrable layer of vegetation.

With the doors shut, you could probably have walked right by it and never noticed it was there.

"Big," Jak commented.

"No sign at all of anyone trying to break into it," J.B. observed.

Doc was staring around him. "There appears to be a narrow trail over to the right. Perhaps we could begin our exploration in that direction"

Ryan nodded. "Sure. Dean?"

"Yeah, Dad?"

"Punch in the closing code. Let's leave it secure. Particularly as we couldn't close the entrance into the gateway."

The boy ran to the small panel, concealed by a section of camouflaged rock, and entered two, five, three, watching as the heavy vanadium-steel door slid slowly and almost silently back down to close the entrance.

Ryan sniffed, looking up at the gray sky, with occasional streaks of blue. "Let's go, people."

THE PATH WOUND SLOWLY downhill, getting muddier as it went. Judging from the pools of water lying in the ruts and hoof marks, it had rained heavily within the past hour or so.

When they reached a large clearing, J.B. took out his minisextant and got a bearing on the pale sun, checking his readings carefully.

"Where are we, John?" Mildred asked.

Everyone jumped as a bird exploded out of the screen of flowering bushes to their right, making its way skyward with long, slow movements of its powerful white wings.

"Snowy egret," Doc said. "One of the most beautiful creatures in God's own aviary. Vain and stupid women thought so, too, so they sported the feathers in their silly hats. In the early part of the last century there were only a dozen or so birds living. I suppose that it was about the closest a species has come to extinction, without falling clean off the edge of the world. There was an active policy to save the snowy egret and, miracle of miracles, it was successful. By the time I arrived in the future, there were more than a hundred thousand birds. The Lord alone knows how many more of them there might be by now."

J.B. took his reading again, nodding. "Right about the bayous," he said.

"Where?" Jak looked at him intently, not hiding his eagerness.

"Close to your home," J.B. replied, putting away the sextant. "South of Lafayette, from what I recall of the maps. More south of Baton Rouge. Some way west of Norleans. Probably not all that far from the Gulf of Mexico."

"Heart of swamps," the albino said.

"Looks that way. Unless there's been some big climate alteration the last couple of years. It happens." Ryan stared at the vegetation around them. "Doesn't seem like there's been too much change. Just classic swamp."

"Cajun country," J.B. muttered. "Place where you get a sore neck from having to look behind you all the time." He cleared his throat and spit in the mud. "Dark night, Ryan! Mebbe we should get right back into the gateway and jump out of here. Swamps mean trouble."

"Have another jump like the last one?"

"Might be better this time. Couldn't possibly be a whole lot worse, could it?"

"Mebbe not. Still reckon we'll take a look around. See if we can find any food. The trail winds on ahead over there."

Other than that single magnificent snowy egret, they had seen no wildlife at all.

THEY WERE STILL HEADING gently downhill. Ryan's guess was that they'd soon be running into some serious water.

It was Jak who spotted something off to the right of the track, a half mile after their stop.

"Folks around about," he said, pointing to the skeleton of what looked like a good-size deer. It had been stripped by the predators, large and small, from the swamps. A few ants were still marching busily around the jumble of bones, picking out the last shreds of decaying meat from the darkened carcass.

"Just look at what chilled it," J.B. said, walking closer and dropping to his knees to see it better.

His right hand pointed to the arrow that protruded from between the xylophone of ribs, its shaft split and broken halfway along. It wasn't like an arrow you'd normally see anywhere around Deathlands.

It was close to five feet in length, made from a bamboo shaft with dark goose feathers at the end. The point seemed to be made out of hand-carved bone, and faded strips of colored silk were scrolled neatly at regular intervals around the peculiarly long shaft.

"I recognize that," Doc said quietly. "I would think there is no doubt that it once belonged to one of our Oriental friends."

"The samurai?" Jak asked, looking behind him at the stunted bushes and the thick mud that lay all around them. "Think it belongs to them?"

"*Belonged* to them," Ryan corrected him. "Been here some time. Must've hit the deer and not killed it outright. So it ran and died here. It hasn't been butchered for cooking and eating, so the man never found his arrow."

Some months ago they had heard the first whispers of an odd band of slant-eyed strangers roaming through Deathlands. But it was a time of rumor and fantasy, and they hadn't taken much notice of the stories.

For one thing, the tales put these Oriental mercenaries all over the place: up in the Darks and down on the Keys, out in the western islands and drifting through the high plains, in too many places, too close together.

Nobody traveled that fast.

Unless they were using the gateways.

More recently Ryan and the others had been given irrefutable proof that a gang of Japanese killers had definitely been making mat-trans jumps. Indeed, there had been a confrontation with them that had left one of the samurai warriors dead and another badly injured.

Now here, in the bayous, was further proof that they were active within Deathlands.

"How long ago?" Mildred asked.

"Months," Jak replied. "Probably at least two months. Might be three."

"So there's no danger," Krysty said.

"No danger," the albino agreed.

As they all turned away from the dead deer and the broken arrow, the ground around them seemed to erupt and a dozen or more screaming creatures leapt at them, attacking with short stabbing spears.

Chapter Six

It took Ryan a single heart-stopping moment to realize that their attackers were muties, some kind of radsick devil's crossbreed of scabbies and swampies.

They had to have spotted the outlanders coming along the path, between the densely packed trees, giving themselves enough time to prepare their assault.

The muties used a similar trick to that practiced by the Chiricahua Apaches of the deserts. Where the Apaches would dig a shallow hole in the dry dust and conceal themselves beneath it, the swampies would scoop out a grave for themselves in the soft, clinging mud, and wait there, naked and hidden until their unsuspecting prey came within reach of the ambush.

At first glance, they were all male, scrawny bodies streaked with mud, dappling their putrefying skin like animals that have been at the wallow.

The nearest swampie stabbed at Ryan with the short-hafted spear, giving him no time to use the blaster. All of the seven friends had holstered their guns while they stopped to examine the samurai arrow.

It had been careless, and in Deathlands, carelessness cost.

Ryan parried the thrust with the edge of his right hand, moving to one side, finding that the ground beneath his combat boots was slippery and dangerous, giving a natural advantage to the screeching swampie in front of him.

The jostling throng of yelping, screaming muties outnumbered Ryan and his friends by at least two to one.

A taller swampie, armed with a pair of predark cook's knives, had joined his comrade with the spear. He grinned at Ryan from a toothless and lipless mouth, his face pitted with running yellow sores, which brought the idea of scabbies to mind.

The muties were poor tactical fighters, eager to strike the chilling blow and with no idea of team fighting. A halfway decent pair of average sec men from a midsize ville would have had Ryan down and dying by now.

But the swampies constantly got into each other's way, cursing and pushing. Their deep-set eyes were almost hidden behind flaps of gangrenous skin that had peeled off their foreheads. They had only one ear between them, and one mutie had lost its nose from the racing, flesh-eating rad cancer, with only a rotting hole in the center of its face where porcine, snot-smeared hairs bristled outward.

Ryan snatched at a moment when the muties were snarling at each other to draw the panga from its sheath, swinging the razored eighteen-inch blade in a murderous blow, aiming at the nearer mutie's groin.

The creature tried to pull back, squealing as the panga's edge opened up a deep gash along the top of its right thigh, blood running thickly down past the knee and puddling in the dirt. He staggered away, hopping on one leg, dropping both of his knives.

Ryan was just able to bring the panga back in time to block the lunge with the spear from his second opponent. The steel cut into the ash shaft, nearly slicing it in two. The mutie tried to strike again at him with the damaged weapon, but Ryan kicked out, snapping it into two useless pieces.

Now there was time to draw his SIG-Sauer, but he wasn't the first to manage to get at a blaster.

Doc had been near the back of the group and had used the precious extra second this gave him to draw his rapier from its ebony sheath. The needled point darted out like the head of a striking Western diamondback, pinking the shorter of his attackers in the throat with a wounding, but not a killing thrust.

Doc was getting better and better with the swordstick. He turned his wrist to lunge at the other mutie, who was already falling back from the fray, trying to defend himself with a clumsy ax. The blade danced past the awkward weapon and pierced the mutie through the center of his ulcer-covered chest, sliding between the ribs and cutting open the pumping muscle of the heart.

"¡No me saques sin razón, no me envaines sin honor!" the old man panted as he sheathed the Toledo steel, quoting the motto that was engraved along

the blade: "Draw me not without good reason, and sheathe me not without honor."

The Le Mat was in his fist, cocked, while Doc glanced around for a suitable target. He spotted three of the mud-streaked swampies pressing Dean against a thorny bush, gibbering and giggling at him as he stood helpless, trying to dodge the thrusts of the hunting spears that all three muties held.

The hammer on the commemorative gold-chased Le Mat was set over the single shotgun chamber.

Doc leveled the gun and squeezed the trigger, staggering a little with the impact of the huge 18-gauge round. He blinked through the cloud of powder smoke to see that the shot had starred out across the twenty feet or so and knocked down all three of the muties, leaving them writhing and screaming in the dirt.

That single shot was the turning point of the entire firefight.

The noise of the explosion was deafening in the small clearing, and every one of the hideous muties broke off from the fight to look around at their stricken companions.

From that moment on it was like shooting fish in a barrel.

Ryan took out the weaponless mutie, then put a second 9 mm round through the forehead of the man with the slashed thigh.

Jak had already taken out one of the swampie-scabbies with a throwing knife, but he used the stunned silence caused by the shuddering concussion of the Le Mat to draw his own .357 Magnum blaster, chilling one of the muties that was armed with a hatchet, then going on to waste the three screaming victims of Doc's archaic weapon.

J.B. had already chilled one of his attackers with the heel of his hand, jamming it up under the residual, ragged nose and forcing the splintering bone and cartilage up into the unprotected front part of the brain.

Krysty and Mildred had been fighting back-to-back, both of them having a moment to draw thin-bladed knives, but the pressure on them from the slobbering, disgusting muties had been growing almost overwhelming.

Until Doc and the Le Mat entered the fray.

Krysty was a nanosecond ahead of Mildred, snatching out her double-action Smith & Wesson 640 and firing twice at the swampies, the big .38 rounds drilling through their upper chests and knocking them both over.

Mildred fired only once with the ZKR target revolver, shooting the oldest of the muties in the middle of the forehead, the bullet angling upward and lifting out a chunk of skull the size of a baseball. The fringe of thin, lank hair drifted in the still air as the round slice of bone and poxed scalp circled like a nightmare Frisbee disk, eventually landing nearly twenty yards away from the twitching corpse.

Silence surged in after the burst of shooting and dying.

One of the wretched muties was still alive, gut shot, moaning in pain, head rolling from side to side, its swollen purple tongue protruding between its rotting lips. Both arms and legs were covered in open sores, many of them large, crusted pits of corruption. One eye was missing, the raw socket weeping clear liquid over the scarred cheek.

"Going to question him, Dad?" Dean asked. "Might give us news about any villes. Or food."

"Waste of time," Ryan replied.

"Dying scabbie's no better than a break-backed scorpion. Can't trust either of them. Just cut its throat and watch out it doesn't try and bite you. Trader used to reckon that a mess of muties all had rad-poisoned teeth that could kill you."

"Sure."

Ryan took the panga and approached the dying creature. The scabbie tried to grab at his ankles with its blood-stained clawed fingers. The one-eyed man dodged easily, feinting to the right, then quickly switching the eighteen-inch blade to his other hand, cutting down at the exposed throat of the mutie.

The sharp steel sliced through a nest of deep sores along the side of its neck, before cutting open the carotid artery, spilling the blood in a pattering fountain of crimson.

The sound of applause made everyone swing around to the left side of the dreary, blood-sodden clearing, confronting the lone man who had crept silently up on them under cover of the brief and savage firefight.

He was tall, well over six feet, but skinny as a lath. He had long blond hair tied back in a kind of pony-tail with a scarlet ribbon. His neatly trimmed beard and mustache were both white. The man's complexion was pink and rosy, setting off his piercing blue eyes.

He wore buckskins, fringed across the shoulders and down both arms. Riding boots, dappled with fresh mud, reached almost to the knee.

"I swear it's the ghost of Buffalo Bill Cody," Doc whispered.

Ryan noticed that the stranger was wearing a beautiful pair of matched Navy Colts, with flashy mother-of-pearl butts. A brass-hilted cavalry sword trailing on the left hip completed the dazzling ensemble.

He had been gently clapping his gauntleted hands together. Now, with everyone looking at him, he stopped. A fawn Stetson sat on his head, and he swept it off with an actor's flourish, bowing to Ryan and the others.

"An excellent performance, ladies and gentlemen. If only I had my cameras with me to record it all for posterity, I could have toured it for many a long year. Such courage. Such grace under pressure. Allow me to introduce myself. My name is Johannes Forde and I make films."

Chapter Seven

The campfire crackled brightly, sending a curling pillar of gray-white smoke circling into the evening air, filling the stillness with the scent of apple and cherry wood. An old black caldron hung on a tripod in the heart of the flames, its contents steaming and bubbling.

The fight with the muties had been only a hundred paces away from an overgrown two-lane blacktop that ran roughly from east to west. Alongside it were the remnants of an orchard, with fallen trees everywhere.

Johannes Forde had led them to it, through a screen of alders to where his wag waited, a pair of bay mares chewing quietly at the long grass. His name was emblazoned on the side of the canvas, advertising his trade: Maker of Films for Every Occasion.

A rare occupation in Deathlands.

He explained while they waited for the gator stew to cook that he had found an enormous cache of 16 mm cameras with lenses and miles of film stock, with several projectors and screens.

"It was in a tumbled barn, a country mile or so to the south of old Interstate 20, a good distance north of us here, in a small town that no longer had a name. Streets of tumbled tar-paper shotgun shacks. Several houses looked like they'd once belonged to the pre-dark wealthy.''

He got up and stirred at the stew with a ladle. The mix of vegetables and white strips of meat was simmering gently, its delicious aroma rising from the pot.

"You have old films?" Mildred asked. "The big stars like Clint and Kevin and Macaulay and Claudia?"

Forde shook his head, the shadows playing across the sharp planes of his cheeks, dancing off the bright blue eyes. "No, Dr. Wyeth. Most of that had been converted to video, and it's almost impossible to find working players these days. Last vid I saw that was nearly complete was..." He calculated on his fingers, lips moving. "Must be fifteen years ago, up near Richmond. It had some wonderful stars in it. Jack Nicholson. Bruce Dern. Harry Dean Stanton. I have read much on the ancient movies, and they were three of the finest. About a gang of bikers. Never knew the title as the lead ten minutes was missing, but I can lay my hand on my heart and say without hesitation that it was one of the worst movies that I have ever seen.''

"You actually make what used to be called 'home movies,' do you?" Doc asked.

"Yes, I do. I still have dozens of hours of film left and the equipment for developing and editing and projecting them.''

"Who pays?" Ryan asked, picking at his teeth with a long thorn off of a wild brier rose. "Barons from villes?''

"Yes.''

Doc snorted. "Those who can afford the jack for it. Like the painters of the eighteenth and nineteenth centuries. Most of them did dull portraits of even duller people. The nobs. Those who could afford the fees."

Forde nodded at the old man. "Good to meet up with someone with a passable education. All of you got reading and writing?" Everyone nodded. "That's fine to know. Average ville has about a dozen readers and writers and counters. If that. Some places there's only the baron and his family. And their tame priests."

"You got films we can see?" Jak asked.

"Guess so. Y'all be interested in my doing some filming of you? Won't cost much. Or we can trade. See some of the finest blasters I ever laid eyes on."

"Not bad weapons yourself," J.B. commented. "Looks like you've had them pair of matched Navy Colts rechambered for a .38."

"Right. Sharp eyes, Mr. Dix. Would weaponry be your specialty, by any chance?"

"It would."

"And you're in the trading and the traveling line, you say?" The question was asked by Forde with a wry grin that showed his disbelief without actually calling Ryan's short explanation into doubt.

"That's what we say." Ryan stared at him, waiting until the elegant stranger dropped his gaze. "Anything beyond that falls into the box marked Our Business."

Forde shrugged, holding out his hands like a traveling huckster. "Fine, fine. Forgive me for asking.

Never been down this part of the world before. Sorry if I gave offense.''

Jak answered his apology. ''Bayou folks keep open eyes and closed mouths.''

Forde nodded. ''I understand, Mr. Lauren.''

''Call me Jak.''

''Of course. And I am Johannes...'' He paused a long moment. ''To my friends.''

''Good to meet you...'' Ryan allowed his pause to stretch to more than match Forde's. ''Johannes.''

The filmmaker laughed. ''I'm sure that the stew's ready for eatin' right now. Let's get to it.''

JOHANNES FORD WAS a first-rate cook. The alligator tasted like the finest corn-fed chicken, tender and flavorsome. The mix of vegetables, including potatoes, collard greens and delicious mashed rutabagas, was scented with a variety of herbs and spices, including some nutmeg that Forde measured out of a tiny glass vial as carefully as if it had been gold dust.

''Can't get it these days,'' he said. ''Always on the lookout for a predark grocer's, but I haven't found one untouched for six years. And I've been looking real hard.''

''Unusual to find a man who likes cooking,'' Krysty commented, ''and who's good at it.''

''Lady, I never had the time,'' Ryan replied, offering his earthenware dish for a second helping. ''Though I gotta admit it's good.''

Forde was leaning his back against one of the big wag wheels, lighting up a small black cigar. He blew a smoke ring, sighing. "Life is good at times like this. To meet fellow outlanders and travelers. Men and women who know the main roads and the thin blue highways of Deathlands."

"How long've you been riding along the blacktops?" J.B. asked.

"I first saw the light of day in New Haven. Poppa was a fisherman. Caught the last boat west when a giant devil crab bit him in half. I was . . . let me see . . . I was about twelve when that happened. Momma liked company, after he was gone. Mebbe before, as well. Male company. Her only son found himself in the way, so he lit out running and never stopped. That'll be twenty-five years ago come the equinox."

"And you've been doing this filming all this time?" Mildred asked.

"Lord save you, no. It was only a few years ago that I stumbled upon the filmmaking material that has been my salvation. Before that I was lost and godless, a man who lived by the turn of a card or the roll of a dice." He paused, blowing another perfect smoke ring. "Or the quickness of my finger on the trigger. Surviving was mistakes not made."

Ryan nodded understandingly. "And you got hopes of doing some filming in the villes around here?"

"That's the idea, friend Cawdor. Any of you know this part of the world? Be there monsters here?"

"There be monsters everywhere," Doc replied. "And most of them walk tall on two feet."

"Very true. By God, but that's true."

Jak cleared his throat. "I was borned ways from here. Don't know any big villes. No powerful barons. Not since Tourment bought farm."

Forde extinguished his cigar in the dirt, making sure it was properly, safely out. "Never heard of the man. All I heard of is of a big old house close by. Family lives there and they have some power over their neighbors." He tugged at his neat beard. "But it was odd...strange."

"What?" Dean asked.

"Strange, the behavior of most of the folks that told me on the road. Warned me away, you might say. Wouldn't meet my eyes. Stared at their boots like they might find the mystery of the ages writ there. I'd have said they were scared."

"They say what they were scared of?" Jak looked around at the circle of darkness that surrounded their fire. Twice they'd seen the golden eyes of some nocturnal predator glinting back at them, but the menace had passed on.

"No. One old woman crossed herself like this." Forde demonstrated, using small pecking gestures. "Said to sleep with my windows closed and to face the north."

"You know what she meant?" Ryan was considering whether a third helping of the stew would be excessive, consoling himself with the thought that it would probably go to waste if it wasn't all eaten. He ladled out another generous helping.

Forde shook his head, the flowing hair, the color of Kansas summer wheat, catching the red glints of the flames and reflecting them, as though his skull were covered in a dancing array of tiny fireflies.

"No idea. I've come across isolated communities where they were frightened of shadows. Frightened by seeing three magpies together in a field. Seeing a ginger cat turn twice around, widdershins. Broken a mirror or spilled fresh-boiled milk. Deathlands is filled with taboos and totems, isn't it?"

Ryan nodded. "Most of them are aimed at outlanders. Watch out for blacks or redheads or white hairs or tall or short or fat or thin. Anyone who looks kind of different from other people. That's the fear."

"Deviation from the norm," Doc stated in his deepest voice.

"I'm heading for the ville tomorrow," Forde said. "You're more than welcome to come along."

"Know its name?" Jak asked.

"I believe . . ." He tugged once more at his goatee. "Bramton, I think."

"Not know it," the albino teenager said. "Most my early life didn't go far from home. Must be hundred villes around bayous don't know."

"We could walk along with you." Ryan looked around the circle of companions. "Nobody vote against that? No? Fine. Yeah, Johannes, we'll come to Bramton with you."

BEFORE RETIRING for the night Forde delved inside his wag and emerged red faced and triumphant, flourishing a dusty bottle. "This will aid sleep and bring the sweetest of dreams to us all."

"What is it?" J.B. asked. "Some kind of home brew?"

"Bathtub hooch," Doc suggested.

"Predark gin," Mildred added. "Used to come in earthenware bottles like that one."

Forde swung himself off the wag's tail, grinning broadly. "Wrong. Wrong. Wrong. Zero from ten for all of you. I would stake a mile of 16mm film that none of you has ever sampled anything like it."

"What?" Ryan took the bottle from the stranger, wiping at it with his sleeve, discovering that it lacked any sort of label. "We give up."

"Samphire liqueur," Forde said.

"Never heard of it," Dean told him. "You greasing our wheels, mister?"

"Samphire is a sort of herb," Doc explained. "The name originally came from France in old Europe, a corruption of the herb of Saint Pierre. I have never heard of anyone making a drink from it." He licked his lips. "But if it complements your cooking, friend Forde, then it should hit the spot."

The man was sitting down again, cross-legged, working with an antique Swiss Army knife, hacking away some metallic foil around the cork.

"Ah, there. Now, care is needed. I have known corks to break in the neck of the bottle and... Ah, here it comes."

There was a faint popping sound, and the air filled with an elusive and delicious aroma.

Another journey into the back of the looming wag brought a number of small shot glasses, emblazoned with the name of Stovepipe Wells. Forde handed them around the group, glancing at Ryan before offering one to Dean.

"Sure. Small drink never harmed nobody," Ryan said.

"Anybody, lover. Never harmed anybody." Krysty shook her head. "How can you expect the lad to ever learn anything when you set him such a poor example?"

"Sorry. I reckon Dean should be even more pleased at the chance of getting himself some good learning. Specially when he sees the problems his old man has."

Forde poured out eight measures of the samphire liqueur. "I'd like to propose a toast," he said, lifting the shot glass. "To new friends that might one day become old friends."

"I'll drink to that," Doc responded, sipping at the dark green liquor. "By the Three Kennedys! But that is a taste of paradise. The flavor of tropical ice overlaid with arctic fire."

"Prettily put," Forde said. "I was taught the secret of preparing the samphire by a wise old woman who lived up on the high plains. Only a dozen miles from the scene of the Little Bighorn battlefield."

"The place where the ghosts walk in the midday sun," Doc said, holding out his glass for a refill.

"It's delicious," Mildred said. "Got a fresh tang to it."

"Burns when it starts getting down into your belly." Dean finished the contents of his shot glass, shaking his head at the offer of a top-up from Johannes Forde.

"Can we see some films tomorrow?" J.B. asked, also rejecting a second glass of the richly scented liqueur.

"Don't see why not. Fact is, you can see them better in the darkness."

Krysty glanced sideways at Ryan. "How about it, lover? Couldn't we...?"

"I don't think so. Been a tiring day, what with the muties and all. Could be a big day tomorrow, visiting a strange ville. Specially one with a reputation. Best we all get some sleep now. Mebbe see the vids tomorrow."

"They're films, not vids, friend Cawdor," Forde said. "Common mistake."

"Bed sounds good." J.B. yawned even as he said that, putting out a hand to touch Mildred affectionately on the arm. "How about you?"

"Yeah, John. Least the weather's decent."

"If any of you would like to use the bed of the wag...?" Forde offered.

But they all agreed to sleep in the open, at the center of the circle of nodding trees. Ryan considered placing a watch, but there didn't seem to be any feeling of danger.

He slept dreamlessly.

Chapter Eight

Daylight came late, a sullen sun reluctantly appearing from a bank of heavy, dark gray cloud to the east of the clearing. The air felt cooler, with a hint of rain riding in the teeth of a fresh norther.

Ryan blinked his eye open, his hand reaching automatically to check that his weapons were still secure. The Steyr rifle lay at his right side, the barrel pointing toward his feet. The SIG- Sauer was close to the rolled-up coat that had been his pillow for the night. And the panga was still snugly sheathed on his hip.

Like the rest of the group, Ryan hadn't undressed for the night, simply loosening the laces in his steel-capped combat boots.

Krysty was very close to him on the left side, her firm buttocks pressed against his groin and the tops of his thighs, so that the lovers lay together like two spoons, laid neatly in a cutlery drawer.

She sensed his waking and opened her bright emerald eyes, her arms stretching, muscles creaking, above her head. Ryan noticed that the coils of sentient hair were curled tightly and defensively against her nape.

"All right, lover?" he whispered, not wanting to wake the others.

"Sure. You?"

"Slept great."

"The samphire drink didn't give you any good dreams, did it? Like Johannes promised."

He sighed, brushing a dried sycamore leaf from his chin. "No. Just sleep. How about you, lover?"

She lifted herself onto an elbow, turning to smile down at him. "Gaia! But I love you, Ryan," she whispered, lowering her face to his, kissing him on the lips.

"Love you, too," he said, when they broke apart. "But tell me about your dreams."

She looked around the clearing. The pair of bay mares were standing contentedly still, heads close together, their breath just visible in the cool of the morning. There was no sign of life from the canvas-topped wag, nor from the hummocked bodies that circled the fire.

"Dark dreams," she said.

"Nightmares?"

"Kind of."

"Remember them?"

Krysty nodded, lying down again and cuddling up to Ryan for warmth. "Course. Nearly always remember my dreams. They were coiling and dark."

"Tell me."

She laughed quietly. "No. Nothing more boring than listening to someone else's dreams."

He nudged her. "Tell me before I beat it out of you."

She smiled. "Mmm, that's an interesting thought. Long as I can beat you back."

"The dream?"

She hesitated a moment. "When I was a young girl, up in Harmony ville, Mother Sonja would get me to tell her all my dreams. Every night."

"You tell her the truth?"

"Course!"

"Always?"

"Nearly always, Ryan. When I was going through puberty, there were some dreams that were so odd and embarrassing that I never told her. Never told anyone."

He squeezed her hand. "You can tell me. Here comes the smut, lady."

She giggled. "Not even you. Just say that some of them involved horses, dogs and piles of soft cushions. All kinds of weird stuff. But I never dreamed anything quite like last night."

"Go on."

"It was mixed-up. We were all in it, but we were in this huge building, like an old office tower from the big predark cities. Hundreds of floors and we were separated." She paused. "I was near the top, above the clouds."

"Yeah?"

One of the horses whickered softly, and both of them turned to look. Ryan's right hand dropped to the cold, slightly damp butt of the powerful blaster in case the animal was giving them an early warning of some potential danger. But the deep silence remained all around them.

Krysty continued, whispering.

"I kept sleeping, sleeping inside my dream. I was a thousand feet high, and I dreamed I was dreaming. You ever had that happen, lover?"

"Funnily enough, yeah, I have. I once dreamed all my teeth had fallen out. Put my fingers in my mouth and it was all bloody gums. In my dream I yelled out and woke up. Got out of my bed and walked to a big mirror that stood against the wall. I recall feeling so relieved that it was all a dream. Stood in front of the mirror and opened my mouth. And saw nothing but bloodied sockets and gums and no teeth! I remember that I shouted out loud, screamed and *then* I woke up."

"That's a bad one." She returned the squeeze of fingers. "Mine wasn't nothing... anything like that. In this building, it was a strange kind of half-light, like just before dawn or just after dusk. And there were these people." She swallowed hard. "There were these people, trying to get into the building at me through the big windows."

"A thousand feet high? They have wings?"

"No. That's the point, though lover. They were flying. I saw the wind through their robes."

"Robes? What kind of... ?"

"Okay, they were more like loose clothes. Gray. They all wore gray."

"How many of them?"

"Give me time, will you? This is my dream, Ryan. Five or six, with more women than men. Mostly old. Quite beautiful. And they wanted me to go outside and join them."

"So, they were friendly?"

"No. They *seemed* friendly. They were pretending to be friendly. But there was something unspeakably old and evil about them. Like they were..." Krysty struggled for the word. "Unclean. Unwholesome. They were pissed because the glass had a power to keep them out and away from me. They scratched at it with long nails." She shuddered. "It really was triple-shit horrible. I can still hear the sound of their nails on the glass. And they kept showing their fangs when they faked these smiles."

"Fangs."

She laughed quietly. "Well, long white teeth. Mebbe fangs is putting it a bit strongly."

"Then you woke up?"

Krysty sat up, and Ryan saw in the dawning light that she was unusually pale. "Not quite. Someone joined them. Younger. Someone who looked like Dean."

FIFTEEN MINUTES LATER the camp was up and stirring. The embers of the previous night's fire had been revived with some dry kindling that Forde fetched from the wag. The horses were fed and watered, and some coffee was boiling away on the flames.

Everyone was bustling around.

Everyone except Dean.

The boy had opened his solemn brown eyes and blinked up at his father when Ryan had shaken him awake.

"Oh! Hi, Dad," he mumbled. "Time to get up already? Only just fell asleep."

"Been in the sack for long enough."

Ryan had been busy helping to get the fire going again, as well as washing himself and using some hot water from Forde's battered iron kettle to shave. He'd never bothered to check if Dean was up.

"Looks like the lad had himself a late night," Forde said, grinning. "If I didn't know better, I might have thought he'd been out getting his coals hauled at some nearby gaudy. But there isn't one and he hasn't."

When Ryan looked across he saw that Dean was fast asleep again.

He lay on his side, his hands delving between his thighs for warmth, knees up to his chest for the same reason. His eyes were tightly shut.

"Hey, come on, son," Ryan said loudly, kneeling on the wet turf and shaking the boy again by the shoulder. "You waiting for breakfast in bed?"

"Is it time to get up already, Dad?" The words were slurred and barely audible. "Seems like I only just got into bed. Feel triple tired. Can I have a few more minutes?"

"No!" Ryan replied loudly, and with more than a passing touch of anger. "You can't."

Krysty had been walking by, carrying a copper pot of water from the small pool that lay just beyond the fringe of trees. She paused and laid down her burden. "He looks pale, lover."

Ryan hadn't really noticed. In the first light of dawn, most people tended to look pale and slightly soiled, their skins sagging and waxen from the night.

"Suppose he does." He touched Dean on the forehead with the flat of his hand. "Doesn't feel fevered."

"Seems like I've just run ten times round a plowed field," the boy moaned.

"Get up and have something to bridge the gap between backbone and belly," Mildred suggested, kneeling beside Ryan, staring intently into Dean's face.

"Yeah," the boy replied, managing something that started off as a smile, then sort of lost its way on the road.

With an an obvious struggle Dean sat up, swaying from side to side as though he had an ague. Mildred put an arm around his shoulders to support him.

Forde joined the group, his cavalry sword trailing in the wet grass, his boots damp to the tops. "Got an invalid, have we? Can't have that."

"Sorry, Dad," Dean said. "I . . .'spect I'll be better once I'm up and had some food." Ryan helped him to his feet, holding him firmly just below the elbow. "You know I had a triple-sick dream last night."

"What was it?" Krysty asked quickly.

"Sort of like being wrapped in a . . . big blanket of fog. But I couldn't breathe properly. And I was growing smaller and smaller. The room I was in was getting bigger, and the window with the moon behind it...was getting farther away. There was someone or something behind the window that was dangerous to me. Next thing I knew was you shaking me, Dad.'' The boy took a slow, deep breath. "Feeling better now. Think you can let me go. Yeah, definitely better.''

Ryan took a cautious step away from his only child, watching him with continuing anxiety. He glanced across and caught a similar look of concern on Mildred's face, which did nothing to make him feel better.

The woman moved to stand close to Dean, making him open his eyes wide, telling him to put out his tongue and cough a couple of times.

The boy obediently did what she told him.

"You haven't got any nasty pains anywhere, have you?'' she asked.

"Bit of a headache and I feel a bit sick. But I'm sure I'll be all right.''

Ryan noticed that Mildred was checking both sides of his throat with some interest, as if she was looking for some specific symptoms.

Finally she patted Dean on the shoulder. "Just growing pains, I guess. Go sit by the fire and take it easy until we get on the road again.''

They all watched him walk away a little unsteadily and squat by the fire, holding out his hands to warm himself.

"Well?'' Ryan said to Mildred.

"Well, nothing. Can't find anything wrong. No swollen glands. No temperature. Pulse is a little bit slow, but he's only just woken up.''

"Why were you looking so carefully at his neck, Mildred?" Krysty asked.

"Checking his glands. Mumps. Glandular fever. That kind of thing."

"Was that all you were looking for, Doctor?" Doc pointed the ferule of his swordstick accusingly at her. "I beg leave to call that statement into question, if I may."

"What're you on about, you old peckerwood?"

"Were you not looking for marks on the lad's throat? Perhaps for bite marks?"

"Maybe I was. But there weren't any."

Forde straightened. "Vampire bats that had been sucking the lifeblood from the boy?"

Mildred sighed. "All right. Everyone's a smart ass, it seems. Yeah, something like that was a possibility. No more than that. But there are no marks so it's not that."

They all broke up to go their separate ways. Jak and J.B. hadn't been a part of the conversation and were both coming back from the trees together.

"Sky's clearing," the albino called.

While everyone else went about their business, he sat by Dean, who had rolled up his sleeve and was peering at a small mark in the crook of his elbow.

"What's that, Dean?"

"Don't know, Jak," the boy replied. "Looks like something must've bit me in the night."

Chapter Nine

After a bowl of steaming-hot vegetable soup, Dean seemed to recover some of his natural vitality, though Ryan still insisted that his son should ride in the bed of the wag driven by Johannes Forde.

"Rest of us'll walk," he said.

"I can walk," the boy protested.

Ryan pointed at him, his face stern. "This doesn't come under the heading of something we can talk about, Dean. You ride. Probably not far to this ville of Bramton."

THE TRAIL WOUND between bayous, passing unbelievably ancient mangroves, draped in the veils of Spanish moss. The water was still and a muddy brown, lapping at the edges of the embankments that carried the road.

The rig went first, Forde sitting relaxed on the seat, Dean at his side. The filmmaker allowed the boy to take the reins of the pair of bay mares, while he leaned back, the gentle wind tugging at the fringes of his jacket, a skinny black stogie helping to keep away the mosquitoes.

Ryan walked behind the high canvas-topped wag, with Krysty at his side. J.B. and Mildred brought up the rear of the group, with Doc and Jak in deep conversation between them.

"Like to watch his movies," Krysty said.

"Me too. All my life I haven't seen that many. Most of them were bits of vids, played on battery-powered machines that was like watching the pictures at the bottom of a deep well."

"When we reach the ville?"

"Hope so."

"You never been to Bramton?"

Ryan shook his head. "Nearest I came was when we first met up with Jak."

"AND YOU NEVER VISITED this community when you lived close by, Jak?"

"No, Doc. Gotta remember there's Cajuns and Native Americans and trappers and all sorts. Not many big villes after skydark. Travel's often tough. So you stay close by where you're birthed."

The old man nodded, glancing around him, just catching a splash of movement on the far side of one of the swampy pools to their left. "Upon my soul! What was . . . ?"

The albino smiled, showing his teeth between pale lips. "Brother gator."

"There are many of those creatures around the swamps, are there not?"

"My father once told me that anywhere around bayous you're likely less than twenty paces from big gator."

Doc patted Jak on the shoulder. "Well, thank you for that splendid piece of information, my dear Ganymede."

"Dear what?"

"Classical allusion, Jak."

"Like a trick?"

Doc frowned. "What do...?" His face suddenly brightened. "No, not an illusion. An *allusion*. Means a sort of reference." He saw the teenager's bewilderment. "But let it pass, Jak. Just let it pass on by."

"IT COULD EASILY be some sort of alien virus that the boy picked up at our last jump."

"You worried, Mildred?"

"A little, John. His pulse was definitely very slow, and his skin was cold and slightly moist. He looked as white as a sheet when I first saw him this morning."

"Kid usually bounces with energy," J.B. said. "Must be something wrong if he won't get up."

Mildred looked up. "Weather's still brightening. Look at those hummingbirds, high up."

"Probably a bees' nest. Honey attracts them."

"At least it wasn't vampire bats, John."

"You sure?"

"Not a mark on his throat. It isn't likely that even a sizable flight of bats would kill a healthy person. Danger comes from them being notorious carriers of rabies. But there's none of the symptoms of that with Dean. Just one of those things, I guess."

THERE WAS VERY LITTLE sign of human life.

At one point the trail became a moss-covered two-lane blacktop, carrying them along at a good rate. That ran into an elevated section, riding over the placid water on cracked and stained concrete piles.

"Good traveling," Forde called. "If only all the highways of Deathlands were so easy."

"Don't speak too soon," Krysty warned. "Back in Harmony ville Uncle Tyas McCann used to say that life was always checks and balances."

Sure enough, a half mile farther on it was obvious that there had been some serious quake activity, almost certainly during the geoturbulent months that followed skydark and the beginnings of the long winters. Volcanoes and massive earthquakes became commonplace, changing the face of the country forever, turning deep valleys into lava-puking mountains and serene islands into bottomless lakes.

The elevated highway had presumably been rocked by such a quake, bringing it down into the surrounding bayous. But someone had taken a lot of trouble to build up a causeway of packed earth that enabled the team to carefully draw the loaded wag down onto another dirt trail.

"Sign ahead," Dean said, pointing. "Past the ruins of that gas station."

The sign was tilted sideways, as though one flank of it was sinking slowly into dark ooze. A small shotgun shack of unpainted wood sat just beyond it, which also leaned to one side, as though it had become too much of an effort to remain vertical.

"Bramtown," the boy read slowly. "That the place we're looking for?"

Forde had reined in the team. "Seems like it. What's the sign say on that hut?"

Dean peered at it, shaking his head. "Writing's too clumsy and daubed. Paint's run, as well. I can't make it out. What's it say, Doc?"

The old-timer strode to the front of the wag, leaning his hand on the splintered sides, shading his watery eyes. "Totems and items for sale." He laughed. "Short and to the point. I admire that in a sign painter. Though I confess that I have precious little idea what it must mean."

"Mebbe religion," Jak suggested. "Used to be lots voodoo in bayous. Totems is what you buy keep safe against things of dark."

"Voodoo?" Mildred shuddered theatrically. "Cutting the throats of chickens, walking dead, needles stuck in dolls? Like Haiti? Zombies?"

The albino nodded, his hair clouding forward to conceal his long, narrow face. "Yeah, Mildred. All of that. All of that and much more."

Ryan glanced up at Forde. "Think it's best we go ahead and take a look."

The man put his head on one side, smiling at Ryan, though the smile never got close to his hooded blue eyes. "Now would that be a suggestion or an order, friend Cawdor?"

"You heard the words. Meaning that you put on them's up to you. Just that I've some experience of the swamps. Man can get himself some nasty surprises."

Forde pushed back the Stetson, squinting at the sky. "Fairly said. I'll stay here and pick up the pieces of your ass, Cawdor. Or back you, if you need that."

"Dean, stay here with him."

The boy opened his mouth, ready to make an automatic protest, then saw the look in his father's eye. "Sure, Dad."

The rest of them walked forward.

As they got closer to the shack, they could see that the township lay beyond it, in a swampy dip in the trail, a couple of hundred paces farther down the line. Thirty or forty small houses were scattered on both sides of the rutted track, as well as the burned-out ruins of what once might have been a church.

The place was deserted.

There were the remains of a peach orchard behind the shack. The trees looked as if they last gave fruit before the long winters. A solitary hog with only three legs hobbled around a cramped, muddy pen out back. Somewhere, they could just hear the faint barking of a dog, and there was the faint smell of cooking fish in the still air.

Ryan signaled for everyone to spread out.

"They throw a blanket and it covers us all," he growled.

Everyone had blasters drawn and cocked, ready on a red skirmish line.

The hog scented them and looked up, limping toward the far corner of its compound, giving a plaintive, almost human cry of warning.

Ryan noticed that the mud-splattered, three-legged beast also lacked an eye.

Doc also spotted it. "Is the kine kin to you, my dear friend, Ryan?"

At that moment the front door of the shack barged open on frayed rope hinges, and a stout, middle-aged woman lumbered out, smoking a corncob pipe and carrying a filthy 12-gauge under her right arm.

"Who fuck you?" she grunted. Her greasy jowls, covered in bristling clusters of thick black hair, dropped almost to her hunched shoulders.

"She kin to the kine, as well?" Doc whispered, making Mildred giggle nervously.

Ryan half turned toward them, narrowing his eye, the angry expression on his face reducing both Mildred and Doc to instant silence.

"You outlanders? Must be. Know every fucker from Bramton and miles around. What you want?"

"Name's Ryan Cawdor. These are some of my good friends. Passing through. Saw the sign saying you sold totems." He pointed to it with the four-and-a-half-inch barrel of the big SIG-Sauer.

"Fancy blaster don't mean shit. Musket ball from a self-make can chill you just as quick an' easy."

"You won't find any of us arguing with that," J.B. said, taking off the fedora, his glasses twinkling in the watery sunlight that had broken through the clouds. "Might I point something out that could be of interest?"

Ryan wondered why the Armorer was copying Doc's old-fashioned way of speaking, guessing that J.B. had figured it might impress the thuggish woman.

"What fuck you talkin' about?"

"Just felt you should know, lady, that one barrel of your scattergun's blocked with mud."

The woman stared at him with eyes that were as warm and friendly as a week-dead cod. "Lotta mistakes. I ain't no lady. Not my scattergun. My old man's. He's not here. Out catfishin' in swamps. Last thing is that it ain't fuckin' mud in the blaster. It's from where I stirred the dog stew with it last night. So, you don't know fuck. Probably have to use both hands to find your shrimp-limp dick."

"Homecoming queen from charm school," Jak muttered, standing at the back of the group.

Doc stepped forward to chance his arm against the slatternly harridan.

"We are but poor strangers who make our way toward the eternal city."

"If you mean Norleans, then you're a fuckin' long way off the trail, you stupe old goat."

It crossed Ryan's mind that the best, quickest and cleanest thing to do might be to put a bullet through the brutishly low forehead and then move on.

But some of the other houses in the scattered ville were close by, and he knew how intensely tribal the Cajuns were against all outlanders. He didn't fancy being hunted through the swamps by a gang of keen-eyed raggedy men. It had happened to him before and the memory wasn't pleasant

"You sell totems?" Jak asked.

"What the fuck happened to your hair, sonny?"
She bellowed with laughter at the albino. "Somethin'
scare you to death? Come look at what I got inside.
Might have some dye for your hair. Make you look
like a fuckin' man again."

"You got a name?" Ryan said.

"Sure. Madame Maigris. Folks call me Mudchuck
behind my back. Not to my face."

She spun and went back inside. Ryan saw she was
wearing men's work boots under the trailing, torn hem
of her ankle-length dress.

He shrugged his shoulders and led the way inside,
Krysty at his heels, the rest of the group following
them into the shadowed, musty interior.

The cold voice from the darkness stopped everyone. "No stupe moves. Nobody hurt."

Chapter Ten

"Put your fucking pistol away, you triple-stupe old idiot. Now! Before I ram it up your skinny ass and pull both triggers. These are outlanders, interested in buying a totem or two."

"Sorry, angel heart."

Ryan's eye had adjusted quickly to the dim light inside the store, focusing on the old man who was sitting in a wheel-backed rocking chair, to one side of a cobwebbed window, holding a double-barreled flintlock pistol in both his bony hands. At first glance he looked like he might be around a hundred years old.

"Man could easy get himself shot, doing something foolish as that," Ryan snarled, conscious of how close he'd come to blowing the old man away. Part of his anger was directed inward for having walked so carelessly into the shack without taking some elementary security precautions.

"He don't mean no harm, mister." The arrogance and foul-mouthed hectoring vanished in a heartbeat. "Baptiste's my fourth husband. Kind man, most times. But he got caught badly by..." She hesitated, carrying on along a different tack. "Never been the same since. Repeats hisself a lot. Lost his idea of what fuckin' time of day or night it is. Shadow of the man he was."

"Rare blaster," J.B. commented. "Mind if I take a look, Madame Maigris?"

"Baptiste, show the outlander your pistol."

"My precious blaster..."

"Show him or I'll take the quirt to your chicken balls! Right now!"

The old man offered the pistol with trembling fingers. The Armorer took it and held it angled to the light that came through the open doorway, rubbing with his thumb at a dark, silvered maker's plate.

"Dated 1815," he said. "William Parker. Gun maker to His Majesty and the Honourable Board of Ordnance. Two thirty-three, High Holborn, London."

"Nice," Ryan said.

J.B. sniffed. "Was once. Give me a week in a decently equipped workshop and I could make it good." He balanced it in his right hand. "Not charged with ball." He peered at it. "Flint and powder, but no bullet."

"Gimme my precious pistol," the old man moaned, grabbing it from the Armorer and pointing it at Ryan. "Bang, you're dead. Bang, you're undead. They're all undead and we're all dead. Forever and ever. Oh, man!"

Madame Maigris reached down and slapped him across the cheek, making his false teeth rattle. "Enough," she said, then smiled at Ryan and the others. "Shadow of the fucking man he was."

"What are the undead?" Mildred asked.

The woman turned and offered a broader smile, marred by the dreadful state of her teeth and the nervous tic in one corner of her mouth. "Tales of old women. The buried ones who walk again. Slaves to the voodoo masters."

"I seen them," Jak said. "When little. Worked for baron with power. Died in fire."

The woman looked toward the door, making a halfhearted attempt at crossing herself. "Don't listen to those old men's tales. Satan uses lazy tongues to spread his mischief. Look, since Baptiste gave you all such a nasty moment, least I can fucking do is make it up."

"No need," Ryan said. "Best we move on, anyway. We're with a friend whose wag . . ."

But Madame Maigris wasn't paying much attention to him. "Place is in such a shitting filthy state. Still got some nice totems. Look around the place. Pick what you like. Free jack to you all."

While old Baptiste sat in the corner and mumbled, smiling at his fingertips, Ryan and the others looked around the cramped little shack.

It was hard to know what most of the stuff was. Everything was covered in a layer of dust that felt oddly sticky to the touch, making you want to wipe your palms on your pants after holding anything.

Jak moved to stand by Ryan. "Lot voodoo stuff," he whispered.

"Seen crucifixes."

"Sure. Some upside down. Chickens' claws. Rabbit feet. Vials dried blood. Glass eyes. Candy skulls. Corpse candles. All kinds stuff I remember."

"Good quality, ladies and men," the woman said, pushing her bulk between them, picking up beads and ribbons from trays, holding them out in her beefy hands.

"I don't really see anything I fancy," Krysty told her. "No offense."

"None taken. Wouldn't like to sell or trade your hair, would you, my dear?" She ran her fingers through it, making Krysty shrink from her. "Lovely, lovely color. Worth a fortune in some of the villes north and east. Or in the gaudies of Norleans. Do you a good deal on it."

"Thanks, but no thanks," Krysty said, moving away and wincing as Madame Maigris was reluctant to let her go and tugged at the fiery hair.

"Who runs the ville?" Ryan asked, edging toward the door of the fetid little hut.

"The Family," the old man said in a surprisingly clear, firm voice.

"What family?"

"Just called the Family," Madame Maigris replied. "Live in the big house to the north of the ville."

She turned to Jak. "Fact is, youngster, I wondered if you was a cousin or something similar to that. Some of them got that snow hair and white skin. But I see you fuckin' ain't."

"Did you say you'd give us a present?" Mildred asked. "Pretty little cross here."

"Take it an' welcome, dear lady. Solid gold and proof against any evil of day-stalking or night-creeping."

The crucifix was on a slender chain that Mildred suspected was closer to brass than gold. But it was nicely worked and held a tiny figure of Christ.

"Well, thanks, Madame Maigris. I'll take it."

"Much use as tits on a bull," Baptiste shouted, aiming the flintlock pistol again, waving it around dangerously close to J.B.'s face.

"Ignore him, please. Nothing else any of you would like as a memory of Madame Maigris?"

Krysty had a tiny crystal pendant on a silver chain, holding it to the door, watching the way that it seemed to glow with a yellow-green light.

"Fire opal," Madame Maigris said. "Supposed to have come from a land to the far south, beyond the edge of the known world. Whatever the fuck that means."

"I believe that it might mean *Terra Incognita Australis,*" Doc ventured. "Or Australia, as it was more commonly known. A small mining town called Coober Pedy was one of the centers of the opal trade."

"It's unusual."

"Take it. Go on. Don't want nothin' for it. Supposed to have power against witches and all."

"You do much trading here?" Ryan asked, helping Krysty to fasten the catch of the pendant around her neck. "Doesn't seem too lively."

"Some says we do and some says we don't. I calls it a matter of fucking opinion."

Baptiste cackled with laughter. "The rest of the world says we don't and she says we does. If you call such a matter of shitting opinion."

"Shut it," his wife said, but there was no venom in her voice and she seemed to have become suddenly tired and bored. "You got what you wanted, out-landers. Mebbe you should be hittin' the trail again."

"Be interested in meeting this Family you talked about," Ryan said, standing between Baptiste and the door.

The woman sniffed, wiping her nose on her sleeve. "You see the Family and they'll probably be real triple happy to see you. And your friends."

"Get many strangers?" Jak asked.

"No. Off the main highways."

"Guess it'd be like a lot of villes." Mildred was admiring her crucifix in a fly-specked mirror with a round pewter frame. "Some welcome new blood. Some don't."

There was a sudden stillness in the shack, as though the angel of death had swooped by, low overhead.

The woman stared at Mildred, her eyes wide, jaw gaping. She half lifted a hand to point, then let it drop. Her husband had half risen from his chair, waving the blaster around in an uncontrolled, spastic movement.

"Blood," she stammered.

"What'd I say?" Mildred looked quickly around at her friends, the rows of beads knotted into her hair whispered and clicking like the far-off sound of billiard balls.

"You been sent? That it? You all been sent by the Family?"

Baptiste nodded at his wife, a thread of spittle drooling from his parted lips. "You got it woman. They be spies for the Family. Sent here!"

"Nobody sent us." Ryan's hand had dropped to the butt of his SIG-Sauer P-226. Something had happened that he didn't understand, but the shotgun shack seemed brimming with a strange, hesitant, unspoken menace.

"So you fuckin' say!" The woman took a couple of steps toward the door, her head turning from side to side like an enraged walrus, peering out into the morning. "You brought other Family spies to take us into that dark house."

"We've never seen the Family," J.B. protested. "Never been here before."

"Let's go," Ryan said to the others. "Best we leave before there's blood spilled."

"More blood speech," the old man screamed in a hoarse, cawing voice.

Madame Maigris was skipping from foot to foot as if she were in a child's game. "You get out. Tell nobody nothing and nobody does nothing."

"We're going." Krysty reached out a hand. "Sorry if we've upset you."

But the fat woman drew back with a horrified expression on her face, as if Krysty had offered her a white-hot branding iron to embrace.

"Get the fuck away, fire bird!"

There was a sudden disturbance toward the back of the shop as Jak knocked over one of the trays of totems. As it fell, a corner ripped away a length of filthy curtain behind it, showing a crude wall painting.

A naked man had been nailed upside down to a cross, patches of red daubed on his hands and feet and over the genital area of his body. Hooded figures stood around him, one of them kneeling by the bottom of the crucifix, holding a copper bowl in one hand and a sharp silver knife in the other. Its edge touched the man's throat, opening up a torrent of crimson that was flooding into the bowl.

Everyone stopped moving and stared at the fresco, held by its animal power, by the atmosphere of brutish violence and terror that emanated from it.

"Sorry," Jak breathed, the single word hanging in the silence like a forgotten promise.

Madame Maigris stared at her own right hand, watching the fingers crabbing across the countertop toward the filthy scattergun.

"It's obscene," Mildred whispered. "Sort of a mix of senility and childishness."

"Shouldn't have seen it," Baptiste said, his face now seeming completely sane and wise.

"Leave the blaster," Ryan warned, his own automatic now clear of the holster.

But the fingers kept moving, while the woman looked down at them, face blank, as though she were observing someone else's hand.

"Let's get out of here, lover," Krysty said, touching Ryan on the arm. He noticed out of the corner of

his good eye that she had drawn her Smith & Wesson
640. "Seriously bad feeling here, lover."

"Sure."

JOHANNES FORDE had become tired of waiting and
had left Dean to watch the team. He moved silently up
to the tumbledown shack, drawing both his Navy
Colts, the sunlight glittering off the mother-of-pearl
grips.

He jumped straight in through the doorway, landing with a jingle of spurs. "First man to reach for his
shooting iron gets on the fast track to meet his
Maker!"

The shout and the sudden appearance of the
stranger gave the striking mechanism of total chaos the
feather's-weight push it needed.

Madame Maigris snatched up the shotgun, pointing it toward Krysty.

Ryan squeezed the trigger once on the SIG-Sauer,
but he was pushed off-balance by Baptiste and he
knew instinctively that he'd missed the woman.

He swung a hasty punch at the cackling old dotard,
glimpsing the double-barreled flintlock pistol very
close to the side of his head.

There was a burst of dazzling light as Baptiste fired
the blaster, the flash in the pan sending grains of fire
into Ryan's right eye.

Into the good right eye.

Things got dark.

Chapter Eleven

The darkness was total, and no dreams invaded Ryan's unconscious mind, no characters from his past who rose gibbering from their temporal graves and clawed their way into the heart of his blackness.

There were colors, swirling around like gobbets of oil paint dropped into a basin of clear spring water, and specks of diamond brightness. But the patterns were displayed against an enveloping shroud of sable velvet.

"...coming around..."

The voice was somehow being projected from the top of a sky-scraping, star-toppling cliff that fell stark and sheer into a mighty cavern.

Ryan could hear it echoing inside his skull, bouncing from bony wall to bony wall.

"...me, lover...?"

A riding wave of nausea forced stinking bile into his mouth, making him cough.

"Help him to sit up, or he might choke before he comes around properly."

It was Mildred talking. Ryan recognized her voice. What he couldn't work out was what had happened to him. There was a throbbing pain behind his temples that seemed to have its source above and behind his right ear.

"Is he all right? Those scorch marks..."

For a few beats of the heart, Ryan slipped back out of consciousness into the dark. Then he was sitting up, supported by someone's arm around his shoulders, still feeling sick, aware that he had another pain, a burning sensation in his good right eye.

"I think that he's back with us. Ryan, my dear fellow, can you hear me?"

Ryan's tongue felt as if it had been hand knitted, five sizes too large for his mouth. "Hear you, Doc."

"Might be concussed," Mildred said. It wasn't a question, so Ryan didn't need to speak.

"You all right, lover?"

"Fine."

But he knew that he wasn't fine. He was a long way short of fine.

To remove the blackness, Ryan had opened his good right eye. He knew that he'd opened it.

But the blackness was still there.

Chapter Twelve

"A deserted house."

"Where?"

"On the edge of the ville."

"Who knows we're here?"

"Nobody."

"Sure nobody saw us?"

"I'm sure."

"Feels cold and damp."

"It is. But most of the roof is on, and it looks like someone lived here for a while. Some of the broken windows have been shuttered, and the back and side doors have both been barricaded. There's remains of a fire."

"Don't light it!"

J.B. patted him on the arm. "Relax a bit, Ryan. We aren't virgin stupes."

"Yeah, I know that . . ." There was a long, long silence between the two old friends. "Just that . . ."

"I know, Ryan."

"Mildred there?"

"Up the stairs. Keeping watch."

"How about food?"

The Armorer cleared his throat. "Jak and Dean are going out scavenging a little later."

"Tell them to be careful and..." He laughed qui etly. "Being blind makes you stupid," he said. "Course they'll be careful. What's the time?"

J.B. rolled his sleeve back to check his wrist chron. "Closing in on three, near as I can figure it. Light's still good."

"Not for me." Ryan sighed. "Fireblast! Swore I wouldn't say that kind of shit, and here I am pouring it out all the rad-damned time."

He heard feet moving down the stairs, recognizing the footfalls as Mildred's.

She entered the room where he was lying on an old mattress that smelled of cat piss.

"How's it going, Ryan?"

"Like you'd expect."

"Tough?"

"Yeah."

"How's the eye feel?"

He was aware that she had knelt by him, studying him. It accentuated the feeling of helplessness, and he half turned his face away from her.

"Still sort of burns."

"No sight?"

"Kind of speckling lights, like miniature jewels scattered on a black rug. But they keep moving. Can't focus on them. Can't see a bastard thing."

"Freak accident," she said.

Ryan didn't know that his son was also in the room. The boy had been keeping very still and silent. "Paid the bastards for doing it, Dad."

"I know."

Despite the pain from the blow on the head and the white agony of his damaged eye, Ryan's combat reflexes were still functioning in the totem shack.

He'd heard the scream from Krysty, riding on the heels of the explosion from the flintlock pistol; the angry, freaked voice of the woman, crying out against her husband; the unmistakable thunk of one of Jak's leaf-bladed throwing knives finding its target in the throat of Baptiste, the old man; the sharp crack of the Uzi, firing a single round; a yell of shock and pain and the muffled sound of the sawed-down, filthy shotgun; blood fountaining from the severed carotid artery in Baptiste's neck, pattering on the greasy floorboards; the woman going down, kicking and thrashing, trying to scream, but the 9 mm bullet had done its work, striking her in the upper chest, the angle of the round drilling through both lungs. She died quickly, drowning in her own blood.

After that, Ryan remembered only the silence, for what seemed an eternity.

Then the disbelieving realization of the disaster that had struck at him.

MILDRED HAD EXAMINED HIM with a scrupulous care, giving a running commentary as she did, so that he knew exactly what the damage was.

"Skin blackened and scorched around the eye. Extensive burning of the hairs on the eyebrow and the lashes. Pitting with some powder impregnation to outer surface of the forehead and the top of the nose, as well as all around the eye and down onto the cheek.

All of this is superficial and gives absolutely no cause for medical concern, though it should be carefully and thoroughly cleansed as soon as possible."

That had been the end of the good news.

Ryan had picked up on the change in the doctor's voice as she examined the damage to the eye itself.

"Not so good. The impact from the blast from the flash in the pan has obviously been serious. The lid of the eye is badly swollen and tender. Until this has subsided it's impossible to give a definite diagnosis. Also, I don't have any proper ophthalmic instruments to check deep damage. But I think there's scarring of the cornea and also injury to the surface of the eye."

"You mean I'm fucking blind!"

"Yes." She squeezed his hand. "No point in bullshitting you, Ryan."

"For good?"

Mildred hadn't answered him for a while, and Ryan could almost feel her gathering herself together. "I truly can't tell you."

"But?"

"It was a bad burn, and it was very close to your good eye. If only you'd been facing the other way."

"Then I'd have needed a new patch."

"Right. Truth is, the odds aren't good."

"But there are odds?"

"There's always odds, Ryan."

"Tell me what they are. Fifty-fifty? Sixty-forty? Ninety-ten? What?"

He had heard her shaking her head. "Not like that. This sort of injury sometimes gets better as the eye slowly heals itself. If the damage is too deep, then . . . then it doesn't ever get any better."

"How long before we know?"

"About a week? If your sight's recovering by then . . . If not, then it likely won't come back at all."

"Thanks." He still held her hand, squeezing it and holding it tight.

"IS IT NIGHT?"

Krysty had been sitting by Ryan, watching while he fell into a deep sleep, his body trying to patch itself up after the clinical shock.

"Nearly, lover. How's it feel?"

Ryan sat up, aware of how totally helpless he was. Even the act of moving brought a kind of vertigo that made his head swim. He reached out, grabbing at Krysty's shoulder, making her gasp with pain.

"Not so hard!"

"Sorry. Just trying... I want to say it right now, and you can tell everyone else. Don't keep asking me how I feel. I feel like I'm *blind*. If I get any fucking hint that my sight might be sneaking back, then you'll all know about it. Until then I'd rather not get asked."

Krysty didn't respond.

Time drifted by, the silence finally broken by Ryan.

"Smell burning."

"Jak went back to the store with Doc a half hour ago. Said he was going to fire it. Thought that it would be less suspicious if any of the locals went there and found the corpses. Fire covers it all up."

"Good idea. I should've thought of that."

"There's no sign of any life. This place is up a road off the main drag of the ville. Forde spotted it from the height of the wag seat. The trail was overgrown, and we dragged some brush across it."

Doc spoke, making Ryan start. "So, we have closed off the road through the woods, and now there is no road through the woods."

"Made me jump, Doc. Didn't hear you come in. Mebbe the blast of that flintlock made me deaf as well as blind."

"I have been here for some little time. There is an old chaise longue that fitted itself to my angular frame with surprisingly small discomfort. From its design and fabric I suspect that it might be almost as old as me."

"Anyone carried out a recce of the ville?"

Krysty shook her head automatically, then realized how pointless that was. "No, not yet, lover. Soon as it's dark, then Dean and—"

"You already told me that," Ryan said.

He lay down and within a couple of minutes had dropped off to sleep.

"EASY AS TAKING small jack from a young child," Dean boasted.

He and Jak had returned an hour after dark, bringing two gunnysacks loaded with food and drink. They unloaded them together in the room where Ryan lay in his darkness, the boy giving his father a running commentary on their expedition and its results.

"Bramton's oddest ville I ever saw. Only just gone dusk, but it's locked up tighter than a gaudy slut's heart. Not a place that wasn't locked and bolted, and only masked lamps showing through gaps in their drapes."

Jak supported him. "Almost taste fear."

"But no guards?" Ryan asked, wrinkling his forehead as he tried to puzzle it out.

"Not one. Also, dogs shut up in houses and barns. Few scented us and began barking. Not soul showed nose out doors."

"Fires?"

"Indoors," the albino replied.

"Then how did you get the food and stuff?"

"Mostly in sheds out back. Brain-dead lemming could've broken locks."

Dean recited what they'd taken.

"Two chickens, ready-plucked. Three parts of a big smoked ham. Some dried fish. Jars of preserves. Cherry and strawberry. Boysenberry."

Mildred took it from the boy. "I think that I prefer boysenberry more than any ordinary jam," she said, waiting for a moment as if she expected a response from the others. But none came. "Let it lie," she muttered.

"And there's a couple of jugs of home-brew beer and one of whiskey," Dean said.

"Bread, cheese and crock-salted butter. Milk. Fruit. Apples and pears."

"Right feast," J.B. said. "You did well."

"Yeah," Ryan agreed, a beat late. "Good. Real good."

EATING HAD BEEN a more humiliating experience than Ryan had imagined. Despite his efforts, with everyone else studiously ignoring his clumsiness, he finally had to give in and ask Krysty to help him.

"No sweat, lover. You want me to just cut it up and leave you to it?"

"No," he replied, almost choking on his own voice. "Even with a spoon I still can't get a fucking handle on it. Sort of slips away." He took a deep breath. "Can you feed me, Krysty?"

"Sure."

"Just for tonight. I'll get the hang of it in the end, I guess. But for now..."

KRYSTY HAD LED HIM by the hand out back to where the bathroom still stood. There was a copper-sheathed rain barrel, and she used an old pan to scoop up some of the water, carefully washing his food-splattered face with it, avoiding the burned part around his right eye.

"Messy eater," he said.

"You wouldn't know it now. There. Clean and smart again. Go back inside?"

"Not yet."

"Want to catch some fresh air?"

"Yeah. Feels overcast."

Krysty looked up at the cloudless sky, seeing the sprinkling of bright stars. "You're right," she said.

"Dull and dismal. Ten-tenths cloud cover. Looks like it might rain later."

Ryan smiled for the first time since the blinding. "I could feel it."

"Stay awhile longer?"

"I need a piss."

"Sure. Least you don't need me for that. Though I'd be very happy to grab hold and . . ."

"Just point me away from anything, lover. Don't want to do it on my boots."

"Right." She watched him in the filtered moonlight.

"You can see all right? In the dark?" he asked.

"Just about. Go ahead."

Ryan did it safely, the stream of liquid, silver-black in the moon, splashing against the trunk of a tilted alder, running into the dirt.

RYAN FELL ASLEEP QUICKLY, his body wanting to close down and shut off the horrors of one of the worst days of his life. Krysty had placed their mattress in the upstairs back room. J.B. and Mildred were sleeping in the next room, while Doc, Jak and Dean each had an attic. Johannes Forde had elected to sleep in his wag in the overgrown cottage garden.

The Armorer had discussed with Ryan whether he thought they needed a watch placed. But it was agreed that, as the house was well hidden from the rest of the ville of Bramton, they could reasonably take a chance and go without.

Ryan dreamed that he could see.

He had once known a severely disabled young woman who told him that she dreamed herself whole and well, running through fields of flowers. And she described the cold chill of the waking to grim reality.

He had never quite appreciated the sheer deathly impact of that.

It felt like the small hours and he nudged Krysty, his eye open, seeing only blackness.

"Is there moonlight?" he whispered.

"Yes, there is, lover." A note of hope entered her voice. "Can you see it?"

"No." He turned over and tried to get back to sleep.

Chapter Thirteen

Ryan woke several times during the slow, sweating eternity of night. He was aware that his sleep was painfully shallow, plagued with tedious anxiety dreams. He found himself standing beside one of the ancient predark interstates, somewhere in the flatlands of Missouri or Kansas.

The wheat fields had been cropped short, leaving only charred stubble stretching from north to south, from east to west. It was featureless land beneath a sky of unbroken gray with no hint of sunlight.

Ryan was waiting for something. He suspected that it was a war wag that was running hours late. It had been due to pick him up sometime in the previous day or so, but it had failed to arrive. And there was still no sign of it.

In the endless, turgid dream, Ryan had paced back and forth, his feet dragging through soft gray dust. Every now and again he would stop and look around the arid landscape, shading both his good eyes with his right hand, looking for the war wag.

Each time he woke up, Ryan had a strange moment of total disorientation, wondering where he was and what was wrong. And why it was so totally black.

Then he'd remember and turn over, rubbing at his sore right eye, wincing at how tender it felt. The memory of the dull dream would slowly ease back to him, and he'd turn over again, shaking his head.

But each time he fell asleep again, Ryan found himself back in the same place, where the interstate was crossed by a country road, still waiting for the wag that was going to come along and take him away.

TO HIS DISMAY, Ryan found the blindness seemed to have snatched away his sense of time. Normally he would wake up and know, instinctively how much of the night had passed and how much still remained.

Now that was gone.

He lay still, aware that his pulse was faster and more shallow than usual, indicating the stress he was going through. He could hear Krysty sleeping calmly at his side, her breathing slow, steady and regular.

For a moment Ryan almost woke her up, envious of her peace. He wanted a piss, so that could've been a good enough excuse to get her to help him.

But he stayed still and silent, eye closed, trying to use the meditation tricks that Krysty had taught him to ease away the worst of the tension.

Sleep came again.

This time Ryan had a road map in his hands, showing the interstate and the maze of smaller highways that danced around it. The colors were exceptionally bright, making him squint against the dazzle. The big map didn't have a heading to show which state it was, nor were there any names printed of counties or villes.

As Ryan stared down, the colored lines began to move. Slowly at first, like a sun-warmed cottonmouth, then faster, the dark green winding around some of the thin blue highways and choking them out of existence. It was like watching a kaleidoscopic maze of shifting patterns.

Ryan crumpled it angrily into a ball of crushed paper and dropped it in the dirt by his combat boots. But it unfolded itself, crackling noisily, lying flat on the ground before taking to the air like a multihued magical carpet, soaring high over his head on its own mystery tour.

"You can't look back, son. Not when you're moving on." The voice belonged to Ryan's father, Baron Titus of Front Royal ville, one of the most powerful men in all Deathlands.

But there was nobody there, just a scarecrow standing foursquare in the center of the north forty. It was around 150 paces away from the crossroads.

Ryan looked toward it, hunching his shoulders against a cold blue norther that had come sweeping in over the prairie. The voice had come from the direction of the scarecrow.

He began to walk toward the crucified figure, hearing the charred stubble crunching under his boots, filling the air with the sour smell of burning.

A lone crow had been circling for some minutes, gradually swinging lower. It swooped past Ryan's face, cawing, close enough for the rancid wing feathers to brush against his face. It perched on the shoulder of the scarecrow, pecking at some of the loose yellow straw that was leaking from the junction of head and body.

Ryan stood less than twenty paces from the scarecrow. It wore black rubber boots and a suit in a light brown check. The white shirt had a ruffled lace front, and the tie was maroon silk. A large black hat with a drooped brim, like a circuit preacher's, concealed the face.

The wind tugged at the clothes, making them flap on the wooden skeleton.

"Better to have died yesterday than to live tomorrow," Baron Titus's voice said again.

Suddenly Ryan didn't want to go up and look to see the face beneath the hat.

Over the years Ryan had watched the tattered loops of old vids and carefully read the crumbled shards of predark comics. And he had come across horror stories.

Even though he knew that he was dreaming, it didn't make the cold fear any easier to bear.

The face of the scarecrow might be his father's, or one of his brothers' or Krysty's.

Perhaps it might even be his own face. That would be the ultimate terror.

The crow sat perkily on the broom-handle shoulders of the tatterdemalion figure, head on one side, yellow beak ajar, bright eyes locked to Ryan's face.

"Come on then, pretty boy. See the show, my pretty boy. Who's the pretty boy?" The crow sounded hideously like a trained parrot or cockatoo.

Ryan was only a yard from the scarecrow, the shadow of the large hat still falling over its visage. The wind was freshening, and it suddenly gusted and blew the hat off.

The face wasn't anyone particular. It was a pumpkin, with a toothy smile neatly carved out and two small holes gouged for the nostrils, as well as two larger sockets to hold the succulent purple grapes that had been pushed in to represent the eyes. Strands of long straw had been stapled to the top of the round orange skull.

The crow hadn't moved, watching the approaching man through its perky, polished eyes.

As Ryan stared at the hewn face, the bird hopped on top of the head and lowered its beak, neatly plucking out both the grapes, leaving dark-rimmed sockets, raw and naked, brimming with purple juice that trickled across the orange cheeks like fresh blinding blood.

The bird looked at Ryan. "Blind as a bat," it squawked. "Though bats see fine at night. Fine at night. I see you, you don't see me. *Sí, sí,* amigo. I scream, you scream, we all scream for ice-cream." It gave a braying laugh and suddenly launched itself into Ryan's face, it's brass beak aimed directly at his one good eye.

RYAN WOKE UP, trembling, soaked in sweat. He lay still for a few moments, his right hand fumbling automatically tor the butt of the SIG-Sauer. It took only a second for him to locate it, though the cool slick metal felt oddly unfamiliar to the touch.

Once he had the blaster secure and cocked in his fingers, he lay still, trying to relax, fighting to slow his breath and steady his heartbeat. He realized in a few seconds that Krysty was no longer lying at his side. With her sensitivity to mood changes she would immediately have been aware of his distress.

He wondered where she'd gone, what the time was.

Cautiously Ryan lifted his right hand over his good eye, cupping it as he made sure that the eye was open, feeling the lashes brush against the skin of his palm, confirming movement. Then he slowly moved his hand away again.

"Anything, lover?"

"Fireblast!"

"Sorry. Didn't mean to make you jump. I know what you said, but I came in and saw you... experimenting. Guess there's still no glimmer of light."

It was a simple flat statement with no hint of a question to it.

"Nothing," Ryan said, the single word as abrupt and harsh as a handful of dirt thrown on a coffin lid.

JAK AND J.B. HAD BEEN OUT together on an early-morning recce. It was obvious that Ryan couldn't have gone out with them on a potentially dangerous mission, but it still hurt him that the Armorer hadn't, at least, gone through the motions of consulting him.

But he said nothing and listened intently as the pair reported back to the others over a breakfast of cold chicken and ham, with bread and cheese and a variety of the preserves that had been stolen the previous evening.

Johannes Forde was knocking back the whiskey, moaning constantly at the taste. "Worst I ever knew. Got to have me another chugalug just to make sure it's as hideous as I thought on the first drink." He had another swig, then sighed as he wiped his mouth and beard with his sleeve. "God damn Judas and all the little devils! I reckon it's worse than I remembered it. Guess I should have me another sip." After a pause he added, "Worse every time I try it. Anyone want to join me in getting rid of this catamount's piss?"

Ryan heard Doc's voice, the only one in the group to answer. "I will force down a drop or two. I have always said that there is nothing like good drinking whiskey." Doc choked, then let loose a spluttering cough. "By the Three Kennedys! This is *nothing* like good drinking whiskey!"

"Ryan, care for some?" Forde asked.

"No. Thanks."

J.B. spoke. "I was starting to tell you about Bramton. Sign called it Bramtown, but the store calls it Bramton. And the ruined church was the First Tabernacle of the Fishers of Men of Bramton, Louisiana."

"See anything of this Family we heard about?"

"Nothing, Ryan," Jak answered. "There's trout farm other side of the ville. Seems main source work.

Also logging. River runs through place. Goes off east through high bluffs. Could be big house there."

"Seemed normal," the Armorer added. "Reckon there's about two hundred or so men, women and children in the ville." He hesitated a moment.

"Go on," Ryan prompted.

"Something kind of off kilter the way they walked. Not the usual kind of chatter of women doing washing in the stream by the mill. Children seemed listless. Kind of halfhearted in their playing."

"Dogs ran quiet," Jak said.

"Watched from the screen of trees." J.B. sniffed. Ryan knew from long experience that the diminutive figure of his oldest companion had taken off his spectacles and was wiping the lenses clean, using the action to try to get his thoughts collected before he spoke again.

"Leave the glasses and get on with it," Ryan growled.

"Sorry..." J.B. sounded thrown by the interruption. "We hung around a half hour or so. Well, twenty-eight minutes by the wrist chron. Nobody came near us. Seemed like everyone knew precisely what they had to do and when they had to do it. Almost like robots in a predark vid."

"What kind of weapons they have?" Dean asked. "Messed-up scatterguns like the fat bitch in the voodoo store or the old flintlock that blew away...?"

"Blew away my eye," Ryan said, aware of how loud his voice sounded in the echoing old house. "Don't have to worry about saying it, son. Always tell it how it is."

"Still early days, Ryan," Mildred remonstrated, her fingers playing nervously with the small golden crucifix. "Early days."

"Yeah, sure." Ryan hated himself for the bitterness, overlaid with self-pity, that he heard in his own voice.

J.B. coughed. "Pass me another slice of that smoked ham, will you, Krysty? Thanks. You asked me about what kind of weapons they had, Dean?"

"Right."

"Didn't see much weaponry. Couple of Kentucky muskets, bound up with baling wire, looking like they were last fired in anger in the revolutionary wars."

Ryan was surprised at how honed and heightened his other senses had become since the blinding. He could actually hear J.B. turn toward Jak for confirmation.

"Most had long knives or axes. Workers. Saw one revolver. Holstered. Mebbe .38."

"Surprisingly little blaster power for a couple of hundred souls," J.B. observed.

"Bows?" Ryan asked.

"Didn't see any. Jak?"

"No. Some animal skins drying on stretchers outside one house. Probably hunted with arrows."

"Not samurai arrows," Krysty said.

J.B. gave a short, barking laugh. "No. Not a sign of those bastards around here."

"Some strips gator meat drying." Jak cut another slice of the bread. "Funny no guards. Must've missed food."

"Yeah, right, Jak." Ryan sat cross-legged on the floor, a piece of bread spread thick with gooseberry preserve in his left hand. "Reckoned they'd have been on double red after losing the chicken and stuff last night."

His eye was sore and he rubbed at it, vaguely admiring the bright patterns that whirled and drifted across the retina.

Forde stretched and belched loudly. "Sorry for that, ladies and friends," he said. "Still, better out than in, as my dear old silver-haired mother used to say. I was wondering whether the fair ville of Bramton might appreciate a showing of some of the finest 16 mm films in the whole florid history of Deathlands?"

"They might," Ryan said. "Only one way to find out. Let's go ask them."

Chapter Fourteen

"You're going to offer to take films of the people of the ville?" Dean asked. "And then you sort of process them and show them the next day?"

"More or less, son," Forde replied, half turning in the seat of the wag. "You sat comfortable back there, Brother Cawdor?"

"Could do with something solid to hang on to. Never realized that having to travel with eyes closed brought on a swimming sickness!"

"There's some boxes of film stock there. Can you sort of wedge yourself in?"

Ryan wriggled around, hands held out to try to fashion himself a kind of nest in the bed of the wag. "Think this is a bit better."

"Just don't lean too hard on the big case marked Acme Film Processor. There's a good man."

"How am I supposed to see any writing, you triple stupe!"

"Sorry." But Forde didn't sound all that sorry to Ryan, who sat with knuckles clenched bone white, hearing the man click his tongue to set the team walking forward again.

THE USUAL QUICK planning meeting had been odd and strained. Ryan still perceived himself as the leader of the group of friends, but it became immediately obvious that not everybody shared that opinion.

He had suggested that Jak and Mildred should ride along with him and Dean in the wag, while Johannes Forde drove the rig into Bramton.

The Armorer had immediately argued against that idea, pointing out that they'd seen no shred of evidence that the people of the ville were at all warlike, and they seemed sadly lacking in any serious armament.

"No point in coming in like an armed posse. You and the boy ride safe in the wag, and the rest of us'll walk along with it. Keep our hands close to our blasters, obviously. Stay on orange."

"Come to a strange ville and you go in on red! Didn't Trader teach you a bastard thing?"

He heard the faint chittering of the tiny beads in Mildred's plaits, he guessed that she was making some sort of conciliatory gesture toward J.B.

The Armorer had taken an audible long breath before replying. "Trader taught me to take care, like he taught you, Ryan. But he also used to say that you didn't fire off both barrels of a 12-gauge to chill a mouse."

That was the end of the argument.

Now they were moving toward the ville at an easy walk, and blinded Ryan Cawdor rode helplessly in the back of the two-horse wag.

"BE MY EYE, DEAN," he whispered into the blackness. "Tell me what you see, hear and feel. Show me the ville like I was looking at it myself."

The boy leaned toward his father, his voice low, barely audible above the jingling of the harness and the clattering of the hooves on the packed dirt of the road into the ville.

"Poor place. Not as bad as some frontier pestholes, but still poor. Sacking over some windows. Shingles missing and doors hanging crooked in their frames. Bushes untrimmed in gardens. Nobody noticed us yet and... Yeah, there's a young girl who spotted us. Took awhile. We're already well on past the first of the outlying houses. Almost in the heart of the ville."

"What kind of state are these buildings in? The main structures?"

"Kind of falling down, just about repaired, Dad. Know what I mean?"

"Sure. Any sign of anyone carrying decent blasters around the place?"

Dean hesitated, and Ryan guessed that the boy was looking all around the slow-moving rig.

"Like Jak and J.B. said. One man closing on forty, with a beer gut, wearing a handblaster on his hip. From the shape of the butt I'd say it might be something like a real old Navy Colt. Another man's got a long single-shot musket with a wire-bound stock slung over his shoulder."

"They don't seem all that surprised to see strangers," Forde noted. "Not excited. Not scared. Not nothing at all. Sort of odd."

"Some women coming out now, Dad."

"Many?"

"Eight or nine of them. Clothes look well worn but clean. Ragged bottoms to skirts. Muddy shoes. Most long-haired. Look all right."

Ryan heard the sound of a dog barking, but it was a halfhearted effort, quickly subsiding back into silence. It was the lack of noise that freaked him. Over the years he'd ridden into hundreds and hundreds of frontier villes, and there'd always been noise, sometimes welcoming and sometimes threatening.

But always noise.

He heard Forde reining in the team, bringing the wag to a swaying halt.

The man's voice boomed out into the morning stillness. "This the way you welcome outlanders to Bramton?"

Doc was standing close by the canvas side of the rig, and Ryan heard him mutter, "Not so much as a bang as a whimper. Truth be told, there's not much of a whimper, either."

"We don't see that many outlanders here in Bramton," a man said. "Mebbe you're right, and we've gotten out the way of being hospitable. But you're welcome. All of you."

"Thanks," Forde replied. "Need stabling for the animals and some kind of hotel or boardinghouse for the rest of us. Point us in the right direction?"

"Surely. Livery's down a ways on your right. Past the Clanton Corral. You'll see the sign unless it's fallen down again. Does that when it's a mind to. Hotel's called the Banbury. Like I said, don't get many strangers so you won't find it up to big-ville standards. But give awhile to get the roaches out the beds and the rat out the water tank and you can be snug as snug."

Forde laughed. "Glad to meet a man with a sense of humor in town."

"Name's Winthrop. John Winthrop. Don't catch your meaning about me having a sense of humor."

"Saying that joke about all the roaches and the rats," Forde said.

"Oh, that." The voice was as flat and featureless as a Kansas prairie. "That weren't no joke."

FORDE DROVE THE TEAM a little farther down the main street of Bramton, with Dean perched at his side and giving a running commentary to his father, who sat uncomfortably in the back of the wag.

"More folks coming out. Women wiping their hands on aprons. Man with bloodied hands and a big cleaver. Butcher, I guess. Or a slaughter man."

"No more blasters?"

"Nothing to worry about. Lot of knives. Axes. That kind of stuff. Not many children, Dad."

It was something that Ryan had encountered before. Villes with few young ones tended to be bad news.

"Stable's coming up," Forde announced. "Folks don't look to be either welcoming or outright hostile."

Ryan heard Krysty's voice. "Get the horses fixed up, Johannes. Rest of us can head for the hotel."

She addressed someone else. "Get us a wash there?"

John Winthrop spoke. "Sure can. But they'll want some time to pump up the water and get it heated."

"Go with them, Dean," Ryan said.

"How about you, Dad?"

"Make my own way."

"But—"

"Don't fuckin' argue—"

Forde's voice cut him off, checking his sudden outburst of temper. "Don't take your blindness out on the kid, Ryan. There's a good man. I'm going to be occupied in the livery for a good half hour or so. Makes plenty more sense for you to go to this hotel with the others."

Ryan bit his lip, feeling the throbbing rage subsiding. The movie man was correct. He knew that. But it still came triple hard to him.

"Right," he snapped. "Dean?"

"Dad?"

"Give me a hand out over the tail of the rig."

"Sure."

"And," he added, swallowing the last remnants of his anger, "sorry about shouting at you like—"

"That's okay, Dad. Shout all you like, if it helps you at all."

Which, if anything, made Ryan feel a good deal worse than before.

THE BANBURY WAS A SORRY run-down establishment. It was doubtful that it had ever seen better days, but if it had, they'd been long ago.

Ryan didn't need his eyes to tell him what kind of a hotel the Banbury was. He could smell it. Damp overlaid everything else—the damp of mildewed cellars and lofts with rotting, damp beams, where large gray rats scampered among the old water-tanks; the damp of men living alone in rooms with pee stains on their underwear; the damp of unwashed clothes and moist bedding and carpets; the damp of a building that had never, ever been either warm enough or dry enough.

And there were the drafts that blew in every direction, knifing around corners and along hallways as though they'd come from the wilderness of the Kamchatka Peninsula in farthest Siberia.

The owner of the Banbury introduced herself as Zenobia Simpkins.

From the sound of her speaking, Ryan put her someplace in her eighties, with a croaking voice that told of too many cigarettes and too many glasses of bathtub gin. She had the clipped tones of a hardy New Englander, overlaid with a Southern drawl.

"Haven't had so many outlanders arrive all at once for nigh on five years now. Stretches the limits of the Banbury's hospitality. How many rooms'll you all be needing?"

Ryan started to answer her, but J.B. had gotten in first.

"Need two doubles, and then enough beds for five others. Three or four rooms is all."

"Who looks after the blind guy? We sure don't have the facilities to watch him day and night."

Once again Ryan felt the familiar throbbing of the vein in his forehead, but Krysty put her hand on his arm, gripping him tightly, warning him.

She spoke quickly. "My husband has only just lost the sight of his one eye, but we believe it will soon come back again."

"I never heard of it."

"Well, you have now," Mildred snapped, anger riding clear at the front of her voice.

"Heavens to Betsy! No need to take on so. Talking to you strangers is like stirring your fingers through a nest of peppered scorpions."

"Baths and beds," J.B. said.

"And quick," Ryan added, not allowing all control to slip away from him.

Krysty led him across a thin carpet, past a bowl of flowers that were past their best, and up a flight of eighteen stairs, broken at the halfway point by a right-angle turn, along a corridor of bare boards, past the transient warmth of a half-open window, then stopped.

"This is the first double," Zenobia said. "Nearest the facilities so it'll be best for the... For your husband, my dear. Rest of you follow me along a mite farther, and we'll see if the other rooms are in a fit state.''

Ryan heard a handle turn, and Krysty led him into the enclosing walls of a small, cribbed room that smelled even more strongly of the pervasive damp.

The door closed again.

''Double bed with a brass frame that looks like it was last cleaned around the time Noah was building his ark. The one window overlooks the back of the building and there's a fire escape. Can't believe anything this wet would ever burn. Small chest of drawers in the corner. And that's it. Picture on the wall of Elvis Presley dressed as a gunman.''

Ryan felt for the bed, wincing at the sticky contact with a greasy bedspread. He sat. '' 'Welcome to the Hotel California,' '' he said, quoting from an old song that was on a tape owned by the Trader.

Krysty sat beside him, her arm around his shoulders, her breath soft and sweet on his cheek. ''Just give it time, lover,'' she said. ''Mildred said it would take time.''

''Time,'' he repeated bitterly. ''Well, lover, that's one thing that I seem to have plenty of.''

Chapter Fifteen

Ryan felt unaccountably on the edge of tears.

Johannes Forde had arranged with Winthrop to put on a movie show in the darkened back room of the local butcher, later that afternoon.

The rest of the group, with Dean the most enthusiastic, had been eager to share this rare opportunity. Even Krysty had come bursting into their bedroom to tell Ryan the news of the film show.

"Johannes says he'll show some real old movies he found that go back almost to the days of the long winter. And he'll take some new stuff of the ville and mebbe of us. Process it tonight and we can watch it tomorrow."

"Terrific."

Krysty was so excited that she missed the bitterness first time around.

"Yeah, lover. I can hardly wait."

"I don't mind waiting."

This time the red anger coated every syllable, unmistakable and out in the open.

Krysty had closed the door softly behind her, coming across the small room to sit beside Ryan on the narrow bed, laying her hand on his stubbled cheek.

"Want me to shave you, lover?"

"No!" The silence stretched for a dozen heart-beats. "Yeah, all right."

"I'm real sorry, Ryan. It was stupe of me to go on about this film show. I'll stay here with you this afternoon."

That was the moment that Ryan felt closest to tears. Not only was he washed in his own self-pity because he wouldn't be able to see the precious movies, but now the person he loved most in the world was offering to miss them on his behalf.

"You don't have to stay away," he mumbled. "No need for us both to not see them."

She kissed him, arms around his neck, holding him tight. "Stupe of me, lover," she whispered.

"No, it wasn't. I know Mildred says that the sight could come back in a few days but…but I can't build my hopes on that. Trader said a man who wouldn't face facts was a man who wouldn't face up to living."

"What did Trader know about the problem you have?"

"Trader knew plenty about plenty, Krysty. And he was right. I'm blind. Sure, there's a long shot it might go. Like it might snow in New Mexico in July. Doesn't happen often. So, the sooner I face it, the better for all of us. I'll come to the vids and you can tell me what's going on. All right?"

"All right."

FRESHLY SHAVED, Ryan stepped out into the bright afternoon air, pausing on the porch of the Banbury Hotel.

"Is it just my imagination. or is the vile smell of damp going away a little?" he asked Krysty, who was holding his arm.

"Your imagination. When I pulled on my boots this morning I could swear there was already mildew growing in them. You could farm mushrooms in the corner under the bed."

Ryan turned his face, staring up into the sky. "Sunny?"

"Some. Patches of high cloud. Signs of thunderheads over to the west. Could rain later."

Ryan opened and shut his "good" eye, trying to distinguish some difference. But there was none. Other than the now-familiar brightly colored floaters, his vision was as black as a sealed kiva at midnight.

"Looks like most of Bramton's going along to the show. Dozens of them."

Ryan nodded. "Not surprising. Frontier ville like this, way out in the boonies, probably don't get much in the way of visiting entertainment."

"True enough. No sign of anybody who looks like they might be linked to a baron or this mysterious Family that we heard about. Just plain folks."

"How far's the butcher's?"

"Close. You could almost spit one end of the main street to the other."

FOR RYAN, IT WAS AN HOUR or more of almost total boredom. He would have given a handful of top jack to have been able to see the scenes that Krysty whispered to him, above the whirring of the 16 mm projector and the oohs and aahs of the packed crowd.

Oddly his strongest memory of that film show was of hot, fresh-spilled blood.

The butcher had been slaughtering that very morning, and the carcasses of a half dozen sheep, some calves and a couple of roe deer were hanging on steel hooks from the ceiling, eviscerated and dripping blood.

The screen was a near-white sheet that Forde had unfolded from the back of his rig, setting it up on one wall. Benches and chairs were brought from all over the ville, but Krysty told Ryan that a lot of people were still standing, packed at the back of the airless, stinking room.

The films rolled by.

Ryan could tell from the reaction of the audience that some of them were fairly amazing.

"Gaia! This one must have been made at the end of the long winters. It's in black-and-white, not color. Shows banks of snow around the edges of some real big city."

"Duluth," Johannes Forde said from the middle of the room, where he was controlling his precious projector. "Tin was labeled, else I'd never have known. Frozen sea is one of the Great Lakes. Not sure which."

"It is most likely Lake Superior," called out Doc from close by Ryan.

"People look rad sick and raggedy," Krysty breathed. "Faces all waxen and lined and dirty."

Dean sat on the other side of his father. "Never seen such poor folk," he said.

Ryan could tell from the catch in his son's voice just how bleak and affecting the films had to be.

Next came a color film of a chem storm.

"Must be real early, as well," was Krysty's comment. "You can see all sorts of space junk burning up and coming down through the lightning."

Ryan had often seen a similar spectacle, though it had definitely decreased in frequency in the past few years. The detritus was largely the residue of the ill-fated Star Wars element of the Totality Concept, bits of missile launchers, tracking devices and laser guns blown apart during the brief holocaust of skydark, circling Earth in their own eccentric orbits, dropping lower and lower, until they flared through the atmosphere and burned back again.

Again, the effect on the audience was spectacular. There was calling, yelling and cheering, with one or two of the oldsters trying to explain that their mothers and fathers had lived through these times, passing on their tales to anyone who'd listen.

It was the first time that Ryan had been aware of any reaction from the people of Bramton. The only ones he'd heard speaking had been John Winthrop, who turned out to be the ville's mayor, and the owner of the hotel, Zenobia Simpkins. There was something that they were both holding back, an oddly guarded manner of speech, as the others had noticed about the rest of the ville.

While she was shaving him, Krysty had said they reminded her of people who'd committed some dreadful crime and were fearful of being found out. They were definitely scared, glancing over their shoulders and starting at shadows.

The third of Johannes Forde's films was a herd of wild mustangs that Krysty described running through the stark landscape of Monument Valley.

"Freedom, lover," she said with a sigh. "Looks like it was filmed from the back of a pickup wag. Now they're going through a river crossing, between trees. Sun and spray and shafts of bright light. Magnificent."

Gradually Ryan lost count of the movies that Forde was showing, losing touch with the subject matter. It was as though his blindness had somehow affected his short-term memory.

After the old films, some of them going back the better part of eighty years, there was a lot more modern stuff. Some Pueblo rituals and a gunfight in a frontier township, ending with a close-up of crimson blood seeping into yellow sand. "Proud of that," Forde commented. "Nearly got to catch the last train west myself. Bullet glanced off the camera tripod."

Young women, dressed in their finest, smiled shyly as they paraded through a town that Mildred identified as being Omaha, Nebraska.

A game of baseball was played between a team of young norm children and some muties, in a frontier pesthole that J.B. said he thought was somewhere around the southern edge of the Darks. But he couldn't be sure.

"This is the kind of film that I could make here in Bramton, if everyone is agreeable," Forde said. "This is a small ville close to the headwaters of the Missouri River that I took a month ago. Start with a general shot, panning all the way around. Then the main street."

"Everyone's grinning at the camera," Krysty said. "Look like a load of apes, escaped from a zoo and dressed in their keeper's best clothes."

A burst of laughter was quickly quieted. Ryan nudged Krysty. "What happened?"

"Fat guy, in a suit two sizes too small for him, walked toward the camera."

"Full of piss and self-importance," Mildred interrupted. "Striding along, thumbs in his watch chain, like he owned the whole town."

"Looked like the fabled Akond of Swat," Doc suggested. "Living proof of pride coming before the fall."

"He fell over, did he?" Ryan asked, grinning in readiness at the joke.

"Eventually," Krysty said, giggling. "After he trod in the biggest cow flop you ever saw."

The film had been rolling on.

Forde had talked over the whispered conversation of Ryan and his companions. "Here's the whole town in a single shot. Watch that kid with buck teeth on the left. Now the camera's moving slowly to the right. And look who's on the right-hand of the line, seeming like he's a little out of breath.''

''Kid with buck teeth,'' Ryan said quietly, the burst of laughter confirming his obvious guess.

''Happens in nearly every ville I visit,'' Forde stated complacently.

Ryan was almost overcome with stultifying boredom. Part of him desperately wanted to see these marvelous films, some of them showing a Deathlands that was gone forever. Life expectancy in Deathlands was around forty for men and in the midthirties for women, plagued with birthing deaths, which meant that the hideous horror of skydark, at the beginning of the new century, was lost to everyone except the extraordinarily old. And Deathlands didn't have many of them.

''Now I want to show you some movies I've made with a few special effects. Folk appearing and vanishing miraculously and stuff like that. Could be a bit midnight scary. So, if you've got a nervous disposition, hold on to your partner's hand. If you don't have a partner, hold on to someone else's partner.''

The joke went down like a lead balloon.

Ryan felt the short hairs prickling at his nape at the sudden certainty that something had changed in the butcher's back room.

''Lover,'' Krysty breathed, her fingers tightening on his hand. ''Feel that?''

''Yeah.''

There was a whispering silence, a stillness in the air, as if everyone was instantly frozen into immobility.

The loudest sound was the clicking of the projector, the film slotting through the gate.

Forde was conscious that he'd mysteriously lost the attention and interest of his audience.

"What's wrong, folks? Someone died in here? Only kidding, of course."

"What?" Ryan whispered. "Tell me what the fucking film's showing now!"

Krysty hesitated a moment. "Old ship, alongside a dock. Ruined ville behind it. Loads of rats pouring off the vessel. Close-up of some of them. They've got a double layer of teeth, Ryan. Needle pointed."

"Go on."

"A man appeared. Could be Forde himself. Wearing a weird wig that makes him look bald."

Doc recognized the allusion in the last reel of film. "Nosferatu, the vampire," he muttered.

But it was a crudely edited and jumpily shot scene, the camera seeming to be operated by an oddly inexpert hand.

Forde kept turning and leering campily at the screen, though at least twice he was clearly calling out orders to whoever worked the camera.

Then the tricks started—clumsy and unsophisticated compared to the amazing special effects Doc had seen just before they gave him his time push into Deathlands from December 2000.

But the audience in the slaughterhouse in Bramton acted as if they'd never seen anything like it before. There was shrieking from women, men yelling and children bawling. To Doc's right someone stood up and then slumped down to the blood-slick floor in a dead faint.

"Only a film!" Forde called out, trying to hang on to a semblance of order.

"Too little and too late, my old chum," Doc said to himself, watching as bodies jerked across in front of the white swathe of light, turning into capering, distorted shadows for a few delirious seconds.

"Don't panic! No need for this. I'll switch off the film. There."

The flickering images vanished from the sheet, being replaced by a stark-white rectangle of dazzling light that spilled over and showed the disemboweled corpses of the animals, swinging from their hooks.

Doc actually considered for a moment the possibility of fighting his way to the front of the panicked throng and making shadow shapes of camels and crocodiles and bunny rabbits with his fingers.

But he sat again as a bizarre figure appeared in the core of the light, as sudden as a pantomime demon, holding up both hands for silence.

"Everyone sit down," said the cultured, gentle voice from the young man.

"Who the fuck's that?" Ryan hissed.

"I think we've just met a member of the Family," Krysty replied.

Chapter Sixteen

"Six feet three. Weighs... Be surprised if he tipped the scales above one-ten. Slim build. Long white hair and pale face. Looks quite a bit like Jak. Black suit, beautifully cut. And a... I guess it's a cloak across his shoulders. Black satin, lined with scarlet silk. From the quality of his clothes, the Family must be seriously wealthy."

"Age?"

"Difficult, lover. Around the late twenties, into the thirties."

"Weapons?"

"Nothing I can see. No obvious bulges under the arm or at the hip. His clothes are cut too well and too tight to let him hide a blaster."

The panic in the audience had subsided instantly at the appearance of the young man. Everyone turned and looked for their seats, and those who had fallen were helped to their feet by their neighbors.

Forde was fumbling with the controls of the projector, eventually finding the control that switched off the powerful halogen bulbs, plunging the blood-scented abattoir back into total blackness.

"Dean, would you switch on the lights on the wall by the door where we came in?"

Ryan felt his son move away and was aware of a stab of something that he guessed was fear.

He felt for Krysty's hand and held her tightly. "Things all right?" he whispered.

The voice that answered came from a dozen feet away and slightly to his right, where he knew the movie screen had been. "Everything is perfectly all right, Mr. Cawdor. The alarm is over."

"So I hear. You have me at a disadvantage, Mr....? You can see me, but I don't see you."

"Seeing and not seeing are merely the opposing sides of the same coin."

"Can't say I believe that. And I still don't hear your name."

"I'm Elric Cornelius. I am one of the members of what is known locally as 'the Family,' I believe. And you and your friends are welcome to Bramton."

"Thanks."

"Oh, the taint of blood in this room is quite overwhelming. Can I suggest we all move outside into the afternoon sunshine before I am overcome by the smell."

His voice was languid and gentle. Ryan had a strange and sudden vision of an elegant snake, coiled on a warm stone, when the man talked.

But his words had an immediate effect on the villagers of Bramton.

Chairs tumbled over again as they almost fought to get out of the butcher's back room, pushing and jostling. Ryan sat where he was, still holding Krysty's hand. He heard J.B.'s voice rise over the bedlam and the sound of a single round from the Uzi, fired into the ceiling.

"Cut out the panic! Door's plenty wide enough for everyone to get out safe and unhurt. Now, calm down and shut the noise, all right?"

"Well said, Mr. Dix." Cornelius hadn't moved during the brief hubbub. "My family sometimes puzzles at the way good, honest, decent, sensible folks are moved to behave like headless chickens. It is a puzzle wrapped in a mystery."

"Shrouded in an enigma," Doc added. "You left that part out."

"Indeed, I did, Dr. Tanner. And you were right to reproach me for it."

"Wasn't a reproach, young man. Much more of a small jog to your memory for quotations."

"I stand corrected, Doctor." There followed a meaningful pause that Ryan could almost see. "It is a rare experience for any member of the Family to be corrected."

Ryan wasn't sure if Doc recognized the cold anger that lay behind the gentle words. But to his heightened senses, it sounded like the crack of a lash across the face.

There was the noise of everyone leaving the room, muted and subdued.

"Who's left?" he whispered to Krysty.

"All of us. Winthrop and Cornelius."

Once again he heard the bored voice, revealing that Cornelius had preternaturally sharp hearing to have picked up the breathed words from Krysty.

"And Mr. Winthrop will be leaving to join the rest of his flock, Miss Wroth."

"Yeah, I'm on my way. Stayed behind in case you wanted... Thought you might need me to... Nobody to be picked for today, though? Not time."

The words from the mayor of the ville tumbled nervously, one over another.

"For pity's sake, Mr. Winthrop," Cornelius said, betraying the first hint of emotion. "You must allow your brain to function before you operate your mouth. Think before you speak, man."

"Sorry, Mr. Cornelius. Sorry about that." Feet moved quickly over the sticky floor, the door opened and then closed, so quietly that Ryan could barely hear it.

"Seems to me..." Krysty began, hesitating, then remaining silent. Ryan guessed that this was because of the uncannily sharp hearing of the Family member.

"I assume that you are staying at that wretched flophouse, the Banbury. That pit of fleas. That inhospitable abscess on the face of the ville. That sodden excuse for a hotel. That absurd and miserable—"

Ryan interrupted him. "Yeah. We're staying there. And most of what you say about it is right enough. But it's the only game in town."

The young man laughed quietly, a sound like a pair of black velvet gloves brushing together in a dusty room. "Then you shall be the guests of the Cornelius Family. Outlanders are rare as hen's teeth in this place."

"They check in but they don't never check out," Mildred said. "Like they used to say about an insect trap called a Roach Motel."

"An amusing comment, Dr. Wyeth. Your knowledge of predark Deathlands is unusual. Other members of the Family might be fascinated to talk with you. Now, Mr. Forde, about your film show that I so rudely interrupted."

"Doesn't matter," the man replied. Ryan noticed that Johannes's voice had gone up an octave, a sure enough sign of nervousness. "Seemed like my ghosty horror movie worked better than I'd thought it would."

"Fools!" Cornelius said, snapping his fingers dismissively.

"How long has your Family been the barons around here?" J.B. asked.

"Barons? Yes, others have called us that, Mr. Dix. We never see ourselves in that role. We have always been here. Ever since then and beyond that yesterday. We do not rule as barons or kings rule. We guide the people. We teach them and show them how best to serve themselves. And also serve us. That is how the Family operates, Mr. Dix."

"Believe that's called being a benevolent despot," Doc suggested. "Not many made that work through history. Catherine the Great and Elizabeth of England. And now there's the Cornelius Family."

Ryan heard the note of gentle barbed mockery in the old man's voice and hoped that Cornelius didn't hear it, as well, his feeling growing all the time that this was a dangerous man and it would be better not to cross him.

But there was no reply.

Ryan waited, locked in his blindness, wondering what in the dark night was happening. He sensed discomfort, but nobody was speaking or moving.

Suddenly Jak broke the silence.

"We look alike, but not Family."

"We had been told of you, Jak. Hair like snowy silk. Face as pale as the finest porcelain. Eyes like the embers that smolder in a dying fire. How can it be that you are not one of us?"

The white-haired teenager answered the question without any hesitation. "Because know *not* Family like you. I'm just me. Not you. Not like you."

Ryan heard a sound like someone licking his lips, which was puzzling as there was no food there. Except for the raw, butchered meat on the hooks.

The door opened, and Cornelius said, still placid and calm, "Come to our house on the bluffs above the river to the east. Ask anyone for directions. I can safely say that every living soul in the ville knows where our house is. Come for an evening meal. We can find rooms for you all. I will expect you at six, just as the sun begins to sleep and Mistress Moon awakens herself."

The door closed, and Ryan was aware of a collective loosening of breath from the others.

"Gaia! That was something over and . . ."

"Rad-blast it!" the Armorer said. "Wouldn't care to meet him in a dark alley behind a pesthole gaudy. Or any other time and place, come to that."

Jak sounded genuinely upset. "Just because has white hair and skin thinks like me. Wouldn't lick blood like that. Not me. No."

"Lick blood!" Ryan exclaimed. "When did...? Right at the end, there was a few moments when..."

Doc answered him. "By the Three Kennedys! I thought for a second or two that blindness can have its advantages, my old and dear friend. The albino fellow was standing near a slaughtered calf, when he brushed against it, getting a large smear or gobbet of congealing gore on his sleeve. Most men would have looked for a way of cleaning themselves. Not Master Cornelius. He lowers his head like a heifer at a salt lick and laps the blood from his coat, as if it were finest nectar."

"Should've seen the expression on his face," Dean added. "Like a cat got itself the cream."

"Stooped and ran finger in pool on floor," Jak said. "Offered it to me."

Ryan pulled a face. "Sure get some odd barons around Deathlands," he said.

"He claims they aren't barons," Mildred said, "though you could've fooled me, the way he spoke. Not stupid. I felt he had a blazing intelligence operating beneath that Joe Cool mask."

"Let's get out of here," Forde said. "The stench of blood is turning my stomach."

OUTSIDE, RYAN TOOK a number of deep breaths, cleaning his lungs of the blood taint, shaking his head to try to clear the odd muzziness that he felt.

"Has that..." Krysty's fingers tightened like steel traps on his arm. Ryan scarcely missed a beat. "Has that snowbird flown back to his nest?" he asked, toning down what he'd been about to say about the albino.

"No, Mr. Cawdor, he has not. He has remained here to suggest to Mr. Johannes Forde that he might like to take a little film while he is here of my friends of the ville. Before they all scatter back to... to their 'nests,'" Cornelius said.

"No offense meant," Ryan said, breaking one of the Trader's cardinal rules that to apologize to anyone was to show a sign of weakness.

"And none taken. Mr. Forde?"

"Sure thing. Only take a few minutes to set up the camera. Out here?"

"In the street? Why not? I shall be the first member of the Family for many long years to be filmed."

"I can prepare it tonight, if I can bring the wag up to your house."

"But of course, Mr. Forde. I am sure some of the other members of the Family will be interested in what you do. We did not know that any such machinery still existed in Deathlands. It is of special concern to us, I assure you. Now, let us to this moviemaking."

"He's ready for his close-up, Mr. deMille," Doc said, getting a snigger of approval from Mildred. Nobody else understood the old Hollywood reference.

WINTHROP HAD SOME TROUBLE persuading his people to pose for Forde's German-made camera. The buckskin-clad man set it on an aluminum tripod, peering through his viewfinder, gesturing for the ville folk to close up.

"Want to get you all in," he called. "Don't worry about it. You all look scared to death. This won't be a frightening film. Be the same as the other ville films I showed you. Just get in an orderly couple of lines." He squinted at them again. "Would Mr. Cornelius want to be in it?"

Ryan heard the soft, insinuating voice, coming from much closer then he expected. The man had a definite talent for silent movement. "Yes, Mr. Cornelius would very much like to 'be in it,' as you put it. I shall place myself right in the middle, with Mr. Winthrop on my right hand, as befits the right-hand man. And Miss Simpkins on my left, as befits the oldest inhabitant of the ville of Bramton."

"Age ain't no benefit, as well you know," she spit. "To everything there's a season, Cornelius, and that means a time to be born *and* a time to die. Just wish you and the Family would recall that now and again."

Ryan waited to see if the white-haired man would respond, listening for the touch of barbed steel beneath the delicate silken glove.

He wasn't disappointed.

"My dear Zenobia . . . I may call you by that name, since we have known each other for all your life…for all of *my* life, I meant to say. It would be a sorry mistake to imagine that age alone was a reason for preserving life in that shrunken heart and those frail, withered lungs."

Ryan caught the fluttering note of panic in the old woman's voice. "Don't tell the other members of the Family that I spoke out of turn, Elric. Please?"

The man obviously had to have nodded some sort of agreement, as the subject was dropped.

And the filming took place.

Despite his objections, Ryan was placed in the front row, toward the left, at the center of his companions, his face turned to where he believed the camera to be.

"Even if I had my seeing, I wouldn't have wanted this," he muttered to Krysty.

"When your sight returns, you'll be pleased we made you do it," she replied. "Johannes'll keep a copy for us, and we can watch it in a few days."

"He getting paid by the ville for this?"

"Surely. One of his horses is lame and he'll get a fresh draft animal for nothing."

"Good deal," Ryan said.

Forde called out, "Quiet now. Here we go, ladies and gentlemen. No moving, but your best smiles. Now!"

Chapter Seventeen

"He put on a pair of rinky-dinky little sunglasses," Krysty said.

"Yeah. Square rims, just like Vincent Price wore in . . . What was it called? In *Tomb of Ligeia,* wasn't it?" Mildred said. "Saw it in a student film festival of movies by that director."

"Roger Corman, the unchallenged maestro of the cheapie-quickie," Johannes Forde stated. "I've read a great deal of all his wonderful works."

Mildred grunted her agreement. "Think that was it. Guess his eyes must suffer in sunlight. Elric, I mean. Yours do, too, don't they, Jak, sometimes?"

"Not on day like this. His worse than mine."

The weather had become humid and overcast again. Ryan could feel a trickle of sweat running down between his shoulder blades. Somehow, having lost his sight, everything seemed to be much more like hard work than before.

Though Bramton had a flowing river, it was still closed in by the mangrove swamps and bayous, with their oppressive warmth and insidious damp.

Ryan yawned and rubbed his eye, taking care not to press too hard as it was still tender and painful. He shook his head, trying to clear the slight feeling of sickness, closing his once-good eye tight, opening it to the momentary illusion that he could make out patches of light and dark.

He held his breath and repeated the experiment, but there was nothing.

Nobody spoke to him at that moment, so he guessed he hadn't been observed.

"How long before we need to make our move toward the house of the Family?"

J.B. answered him, having checked his chron. "About three hours."

"Want to take a walk, lover?"

Ryan turned to Krysty's voice. "Why not? Better than sitting around here getting sweaty for no reason. Anyone else fancy coming along?"

"I'd like to walk with—" Dean stopped so sharply that Ryan had the distinct feeling that the boy had been given an urgent signal from someone else, possibly from Krysty herself. "Oh, sorry, just remembered. Said I'd go out with Jak to see if we could scare up a gator."

"That's all right, son."

Krysty took Ryan's arm and led him away from the others, along the main street for about fifty yards, then turned to the left, toward the bank of the river.

"Watch it here. Steep down and the mud's slippery. Overhanging branch on your right. That's it."

The faint noises of the township had faded away behind them. Now there was only the noise of their boots sucking through the wet dirt and the buzzing of insects. Within six or seven minutes Ryan found himself becoming irritated by the slow pace caused by his own clumsiness.

"Mebbe you should leave me here to sit a spell and you go on ahead for a walk, Krysty."

"That what you want?"

"Best."

"Sure?"

He heard the hesitation in his own voice and hated it even more. "Fucking said so, didn't I?"

"What you say and what you mean aren't always the same, lover, are they?"

He bit his lip, feeling the familiar throbbing in the old scar that seamed his face. "I just... Fireblast!" He put his head in his hands and stood still.

Krysty didn't touch him, waiting a few seconds before she spoke. "Listen, Ryan, and listen good. I probably sound like a preacher at a river-crossing meeting, but it has to be said. If I put my arms around you now and give you a hug and tell you how I love you and it'll be all right, then I'll certainly start weeping right off."

"Guess I might, too."

"Sure thing. Anyhow, you know all that. Bad enough when you start feeling sorry for yourself. Worse all around if others start pitying you. That what you want? Pity?"

"You know it's not."

"Good," she said gently. "What's happened is rough. If it stays that way it'll be bad, but we can pull through it together and make the best we can."

"Guess so." He felt a tear brimming from the corner of his right eye. "Sure, that's right."

"And you know what Mildred said."

"Yeah."

"So... so let's get on with this walk."

KRYSTY KEPT UP a running commentary as they walked side by side along the narrow, winding path, going deeper into the heart of the bayous.

"Few houses around. All rotted down. Spanish moss thick on the tumbled roofs and vines twining in through where the windows used to be."

"No people?"

"Nobody. Looks like they might have been holiday homes. There's the remnants of a blacktop tilted sideways into the swamp on our left. Old church. Steeple collapsed into itself so it stands there among the angled white walls, like the mast of a weird ruined schooner."

"Wildlife?"

"Plenty of tracks. Big birds all around here. And those long slither marks you get from alligators. Deer. Could be wild pigs, as well."

He stopped and sniffed the air. "Wet and dark," he said. "Brackish water overlaying everything." He stared blankly up at the sky. "Overcast?"

"Patches of sun, but we're mostly in shade here. So you were right."

THEY STOPPED for a few minutes, recovering their breath in the warm, soupy air. They had come to what looked like an old tourist motel on the edge of a long-abandoned and clogged marina. Three or four small fiberglass-hulled boats were visible, sunk in the shallow water like the bodies of long-dead whales, held in the limbo of dream time.

"Smell of rotting meat," Ryan said.

"Can't catch that. Time was I could pick up a scent far better than you, Ryan. Clean living and never smoking helps. Now your sense of smell is sharper than mine."

He waited, sitting on a fallen mangrove, while Krysty went to explore. They had come across a narrow causeway that had almost vanished into the murky waters. At one point Krysty had told him that they were only a few inches clear of the scummy surface of the swamp.

The afternoon was drifting by.

After three minutes, or eight minutes—Ryan had lost the ability to judge the passing of time—he decided to try a little cautious exploration of his own.

He had left the Steyr rifle back with the others, but he still wore the SIG-Sauer on his hip, the long panga sheathed on the opposite side.

Krysty had picked a six-foot broken branch off a willow and trimmed the side shoots off with the panga, fashioning it into a serviceable staff for him to use.

Now he began to feel his way along the path, aware of tall weeds brushing against the sides of his combat boots. Krysty had told him that among the lush, rank plants there was a smattering of the ubiquitous

Deathlands daisy, its gold and white making a brave show among the leprous green and gray.

Ryan could imagine it.

He knew that the motel was about thirty yards ahead of him, slightly to his left, standing at the end of a ruined jetty that had fallen into the lagoon like a jumble of old bones, nearly a century past.

Ryan stepped with an assumed confidence, but in a half dozen paces he'd lost it. The stick probed at the air in front of him, tapping on the ground to protect him from tumbling straight into the water.

He stopped and listened for any sound of Krysty, but he could hear nothing. "Turned her back on me," he whispered, aware that his mouth was dry. It brought back a snatch of an old song that one of the cooks on War Wag One used to sing, about how a man who turned his back on his family wasn't any good.

The stick rapped on something solid. Wood or stone?

"Wood," he muttered, hearing an echo, which had to mean he had reached the motel. He considered whether it was a good idea to go a little farther.

The boards beneath his feet squished with water, and Ryan hesitated, wondering if he might go clean through them and plummet into the swamp below.

"Krysty?" he said halfheartedly. "Krysty! You there, lover?"

His voice rebounded sullenly, sounding muffled and deadened. Ryan had only the vaguest idea of what the building was like. Two-storied, Krysty had said, but looking decayed and totally uninhabitable.

He fumbled forward with his staff, feeling the sponginess of the floor, trying a couple of steps, but there was something lying in front of him that he didn't pick up on. Ryan tripped and fell clumsily, banging his elbow and losing hold of the long staff.

Panic sighed in his ears, flooding his mind with fear, overwhelming the honed combat reflexes that had kept him alive in Deathlands.

He scrabbled for the branch, fighting for control over his own blind terror, finally finding it with his right hand. He sat there for a moment, hanging on to the stick like a drowning man to a lifeline.

His breathing became steady and slow. "I am strong and I have no fear. I am strong and I have no fear. I am strong and I have no fear." It was one of the mantras that Krysty had taught him many months ago, as a way of reducing stress and bringing back calmness and peace to the core of his being.

He stopped a moment, straining his hearing, imagining he'd heard a faint rustling sound. Feet. Far away in the heart of the building? Or something different?

"I am strong and I have no fear."

Closer.

Something brushed against his ankle and he jumped, spooked by the almost silent approach of whatever it was.

"Krysty?" he whispered.

Another touch, on the back of his right thigh. He had the feeling that something was scenting him.

Ryan gripped his stick more firmly, trying to judge

where the creature was—or if there was more than one.

The attack was so sudden, taking him by surprise, that he yelled out. Something had jumped into his lap and bitten him on the inside of his left wrist. It felt about the size and weight of a small mongrel dog, and Ryan snatched desperately at it with his right hand.

Blindness hadn't slowed that part of his reflexes, and he caught the thing. Scrawny and hair, struggling like crazy, squeaking at him, its long tail lashing against his body.

Long tail?

"Fireblast!" he shrieked. "Krysty! Help me, I'm being attacked by—"

"Rats!" she shouted from some way off, her voice distorted by the distance, the walls and the broken doors and windows. "Stand up and swing the branch, Ryan. For your life! Now! There's dozens of the mutie bastards!"

He was up in a nanosecond, throwing the rat from him, hearing the dull thump as its body smashed into a wall. He flailed around with the long stick as the pack of vermin surged at him, feeling more helpless and hopeless than ever before.

Chapter Eighteen

He was bitten a half-dozen times in the first couple of seconds of the one-sided fight. Two of the rats were climbing up his body with a sickening nimbleness, light-footed as demons as they scampered toward his face and throat.

Ryan used the stick like a medieval quarterstaff, two-handed, swinging it in a tight whirring circle, catching several of his attackers, hearing the dry snap of brittle bones splintering. The squeaking had grown to a shrieking, and the animals were pressing around his legs, trying to bring him to the floor by weight of numbers.

His first impression had been right. The rats were huge, bigger than cats, gigantic creatures spawned in some postnuke inferno, fattened on the creatures that lived in and around the bayous. One tried to fasten its grip on his hand, and he shook it off, shuddering at the realization that the thing had a double row of murderous teeth. If he fell . . .

There was the sound of a shot, repeated twice more, the familiar waspish snapping of Krysty's Smith & Wesson 640. It wasn't a great blaster for any target much over forty feet away, but ideal as a stopper at closer quarters.

For a moment Ryan felt the rats hesitate.

Krysty fired twice more and the rodents retreated, leaving Ryan a clear space for a few moments. One of the mutie animals clung to the end of the staff and Ryan swung it to the floor with all his strength, crushing the creature to death.

"Let's go, lover!"

For a moment he was totally disoriented. Had it not been for Krysty seizing his arm, he could easily have blundered deeper into the rats' haunt or run out into the sluggish deeps of the swamp.

"This way."

His hands still held tight to the whittled stick, feeling on the one end the broken slivers where the rats had gnawed at the hard wood.

"Close call," he panted. "They after us?"

Ryan guessed they'd run about forty yards from the building, out onto the almost-submerged causeway that led eventually back to the ville of Bramton.

That much he knew.

Krysty slowed and twisted slightly as she looked behind her. "Nothing. The shots from the blaster did the trick, though you were more than holding your own with that chewed-up bit of stick you got there."

"Wasn't chewed up when I started, lover."

Now they stopped, recovering their breath.

Ryan considered telling Krysty to reload, knowing that she'd fired five from five. But her rescue of him had unsettled the balance of their relationship and he kept his mouth closed.

"Real pisser having to depend on someone else like that," he said finally.

"If I hadn't been there, then you'd probably have made it clear yourself," she replied. "You were holding them off all right, weren't you?"

"I guess so. But . . ." he let the words drift off into the silent afternoon, knowing without a shred of doubt that another minute or so among the mutie rats would have seen him down and done for, suffering a hideous passing.

"Anyway, we have to get back to the ville, ready to go and meet the Family."

Ryan nodded. "Sure."

He was holding Krysty by the hand when the water to their right erupted in an explosion of noise and violence, and something vast rushed up the shallow bank and snatched her away from him with awesome force.

Ryan heard the single scream and the sound of the hammer of the Smith & Wesson blaster falling on a spent cartridge. There was a hoglike grunt, then a tremendous splash to his left, the scream drowning instantly.

And Krysty was gone, torn away from him by what he knew instinctively had to be a monstrous alligator.

She was gone, and he stood there blind.

Chapter Nineteen

Ryan found that he'd drawn the powerful SIG-Sauer, holding it cocked and ready in his right hand. He'd automatically dropped the staff and drawn the blaster, without thinking for a moment what a futile gesture that was.

There was some kind of massive disturbance in the water, sounding about a dozen yards out from him, a noise that could only mean Krysty was fighting for her life against the saurian that had taken her. The fight would only have one ending as the great reptile rolled her under the frothing mud and rolled again and again, possibly tearing off an arm at the shoulder, or severing her trunk at the waist.

Ryan stood there in total darkness, knuckles white on the butt of the useless handblaster.

"I'm coming, lover!" he shouted at the top of his voice, hearing flatness and desolation all about him, aware of his isolation.

He holstered the blaster and drew the eighteen-inch steel panga, feeling the familiar weight and balance, which gave him a momentary sense of comfort.

He held his breath, closed his eye and hurled himself away to the left, half diving, half falling in a noisy belly flop into the blood-warm soup of the lagoon.

Some of it went up his nose and some into his half-open mouth, making him cough and splutter, while desperately trying to hang on to his sense of direction, working out that the noise was coming from ahead and a little to his right.

"No, Ryan, don't!" Krysty's voice was shrill with mortal terror, ringing out across the swamp, rising above the piggish grunting and snuffling of the gator.

"I'm coming, lover." Ryan's head was thrown back, his neck straining, the sinews in his throat as taut as bowstrings. He kicked hard with both legs, unable to feel any bottom under his boots, trying to steer himself toward Krysty's voice.

But it was uncommonly difficult.

"Keep away!" Krysty screamed. "You can't do—"

The words were drowned in an eruption of bubbling and thrashing water.

The blade held tight in his right hand, Ryan slipped into a fluid sidestroke that moved him more easily across the treacherous swamp.

The noise had sounded close, less than twenty feet. He should have reached the place by now.

He gasped, swallowing a couple of mouthfuls of the brackish mud, feeling something brush against his leg, something vast and immeasurably powerful.

Just for a moment Ryan had a mental picture of the great white shark that he'd once encountered. The dead black eyes had stared incuriously at him, as though they were weighing his immortal soul.

He kicked sideways, toward the movement, feeling the turbulent currents left behind by the monster's passing. Both of Ryan's hands were outstretched, and it was the left that made the first contact with the gator.

The thick scales scraped past him, giving him a clue of the creature's size and the direction it was taking. A short, muscular leg kicked out at Ryan as if the saurian sensed his presence close by.

Now that he'd finally made contact, all of Ryan's fears left him. The blindness no longer mattered. In the filthy, impenetrable deeps of the swamp, it was to be a battle decided only by touch, not by sight.

He wrapped his arms around the beast's powerful tail, acting like an anchor, slowing the mutie reptile, making it obvious that the creature had an enemy.

It was like a roller-coaster ride through hell.

One moment Ryan's head was out of the water and he was sucking in a frantic breath. The next second he was dragged deep in the midnight labyrinth, pulled through a knotted maze of mangrove roots, moving so fast he could hardly breathe.

He was knocked and bruised, but he still clung to the gator's tail, managing to wrap his legs around it, acting as a drogue anchor, slowing the beast a little.

Ryan knew that it could be only a matter of seconds before the reptile got tired of this annoying encumbrance and turned some of its small brain toward removing him. The hope was that the distraction would give Krysty a chance, however slight, of making her own escape from the scissoring jaws.

Suddenly he was above water, though there wasn't a flicker of change in his utter blackness. But he could breathe for a moment. And hear.

"For Gaia's sake, let go and swim left, lover. Land there. Fifty yards. Go, for me."

"Talk later," he managed to gasp. The words were cut off as the gator dived deep again, going so far down that Ryan felt his ears popping with the pressure and the consistency of the muddy water changed to watery mud.

Now he sensed that the creature was moving more slowly, as though it were trying to figure out the problem and find some way of dealing with it. With an enormous effort Ryan managed to haul himself a little higher up the tail, until his arms were around the belly of the beast, barely spanning its huge size.

Something brushed his shoulder, and he guessed that it was one of Krysty's feet, kicking out jerkily, at least telling him that she was still alive and fighting.

The gator jerked convulsively, wriggling its whole body from side to side, trying to flick off the irritating parasite that was checking its progress and get back to its underwater den, where it could examine its fine prey at its leisure.

From rapid movement it went to stillness, giving Ryan the half chance that he'd been hoping for during the battle.

He braced himself with his left arm, trying to get a purchase on the raised spine of the saurian, readying the panga in his right hand, probing with it to make sure the point was settled against the soft underbelly of the creature.

He lunged, feeling the liquid gush out over his hand and wrist.

Simultaneously the beast bucked against the stabbing pain in its guts, almost breaking Ryan's hold and throwing him helplessly off.

But he had been ready for its reaction, gripping again with both arms.

The gator started to roll, over and over, making Ryan feel sick and dizzy. But he clung on tight, wondering how Krysty was managing. Once or twice he sensed that he was out in the air again, and he fought for a small breath.

Unable to throw him off, the giant mutie creature changed its tactics.

Suddenly, racked with the pain in its belly, it decided to head for its den. It opened its jaws and spit out the troublesome prey that it had been looking forward to devouring, brushing the woman out of its way with a flick of the gigantic tail.

It powered its way across the swamp, knowing that it could deal with any enemy once it reached its comfortable hole, burrowed out beneath the bank of the bayou.

Ryan held his breath, face pressed to the flank of the gator as it raged through the soupy water. Once there was a painful blow on his right shoulder from a gnarled root of one of the ancient mangrove trees, and he nearly let the panga slip from paralyzed fingers. But he pinned it against himself until the feeling seeped back and he was able to hold it once more.

He was dragged through a narrow tunnel that squeezed in on both sides, while the gator's short, powerful legs scrabbled and kicked to get it through the slimy walls.

There was air, but not the fresh, humid air of the outer swamp. This was fetid and stale, stinking of rotting meat and fish. The odor of putrefaction was so strong that Ryan almost puked. He could feel soft, rotting branches brushing against him, creaking and cracking under the weight of the mighty saurian.

He had not a scintilla of doubt where he was.

This was the lair of the beast, the place where either he or the gator would die.

THREE HUNDRED YARDS AWAY, Krysty stood on the edge of the swamp, ankle deep in mud. She was soaking wet, clothes torn, streaked with the dark slime of the bayou. In her right hand was the empty Smith & Wesson 640, pointing to the dirt. Her fiery hair was dull, matted to her skull, like a cap of spun copper. Her vivid emerald eyes were wide with shock, her face as pale as Sierra snow. A vivid patch of bright blood was smeared across her forehead.

Her lips were moving slowly as she talked to herself. But you would have needed to be very close to catch a single whispered word.

"Great Gaia and all the Earth powers, help Ryan. Spare him for his courage. Mother Sonja, wherever you are, aid him to survive against the monster. Don't let him die to let me live. Couldn't bear that. Rather die myself if he's really gone. Please, oh please, oh please..."

Standing alone in the fading light, Krysty began to cry helplessly.

RYAN LET GO of the gator's body, easing himself away, reaching up with his left hand to try to gauge something of the proportions of the den. He was standing waist deep in the water. The roof of mud was less than four feet above him, and one end seemed to be filled with a nest of branches and rotting bones.

He could hear the reptile breathing, heavy and harsh, close by, making the piggish snuffling that he'd heard as it had grabbed Krysty.

"You there, lover?" he said cautiously.

His voice was flat and dead.

"Lover?"

There was no answer.

Krysty had either escaped before they plunged deep into the bayou, or she was lying within reach of him.

Unconscious? Dead?

It crossed his mind to risk using the SIG-Sauer. The immersion in water shouldn't have affected the sturdy mechanism. It wasn't like one of the fragile cap-and-ball pistols that were still found around Deathlands.

But there was an overwhelming risk that he would only wound the creature, driving it into a maddened rage. Standing there, blind, Ryan knew he would have absolutely no chance at all.

No. It had to be the panga and it had to be the closest of contact.

The thrust with the needle-sharp point of the eighteen-inch blade had been shrewdly struck. He knew that, had felt it drive deep, grating between ribs, into the intestines. For all Ryan knew, it could have been a mortal wound and the gator would be lying there, life ebbing.

"Come on," he breathed, bracing himself for a flurry of movement from the mutie saurian. But it was still. The water lapped around Ryan.

He took a careful half step forward, feeling with his combat boots for as solid a footing as he could find. Both hands were stretched out in front of him as he inched toward the noise of breathing, a noise that grew markedly faster and louder as the man moved across the subterranean den.

"Where the fuck are you, bastard?"

The water was growing a little more shallow. Ryan felt something brush the top of his head and winced, reaching up to find that the ceiling was becoming lower, as well.

The attack came without warning.

The power and size of the creature was unbelievable, throwing Ryan back off his feet, nearly knocking the panga from his hand. The jaws, fully six feet long, snapped at him, gripping across his upper chest, crushing his lungs so that breathing became instantly impossible.

But it was the murderous accuracy of the gator that gave Ryan his chance. Now he knew precisely where it was, and his blindness was no longer a handicap.

He had the free use of his right arm, and he brought the panga around and forced it between the jaws, feeling teeth splinter and snap. He turned his wrist, so that the keen edge of the steel sliced at the inside of the monster's jaws and tongue.

The grip relaxed for a moment and there was a loud exhalation of breath, almost like a shriek. The gator backed off, hurt by the panga, but Ryan wasn't going to let the creature get away.

He followed it through the foaming water, churned up by the gator's rage and pain.

As he advanced, Ryan swung the panga, twice feeling the satisfying jar run up his arm as it struck solidly home on flesh and gristle.

His left hand touched the gator on the foreleg, enabling him to work out precisely where the beast was lying. He threw himself on it, one arm clamping around the murderous jaws, holding them shut. Despite the straining efforts of the reptile to open its jaws and savage him, Ryan held fast.

It was a piece of lore that he'd learned from Trader. Even the biggest of saurians was helpless once you closed its jaws and held them shut. They were incredibly powerful when it came to their snapping shut on anyone, but surprisingly feeble when it came to trying to open them.

Trader had told Ryan that at least a dozen years ago, and he'd remembered it.

And it was true.

Pinning the beast down, Ryan was free to use the panga against its throat and underbelly, where the scales were much thinner. He used all of his strength, gasping out with the effort of each stabbing blow.

"Die...fucker...die...fuckin' die."

The gator wriggled harder, its legs kicking out great chunks of the muddy walls of its lair. It bounced Ryan against the ceiling, almost crushing him. But he held his grip and continued to hack at the creature. It felt like it was going to try to dive out under the water to the open bayou, but seemed to change its mind at the last moment.

The mutie's movements seemed to be getting slower and less violent.

Ryan continued to stab, thrust and hack away with the razored panga, digging deeper and deeper at the gator's innards, up beyond the wrist with each savage blow, feeling the soft twists and loops of intestines spilling into the water and coiling around him, aware of the most vile smell, deafened by the muffled roaring of the beast.

He became aware that he was using the blade on a corpse. The gator had become still, its muscles relaxed, fouling the water in its passing, floating at his side like a great sodden tree trunk.

Ryan leaned away from it, fighting for breath in the noxious air, struggling to hold off the sudden onset of panic at being trapped in this cramped underwater den with the body of the mutie saurian for company.

He fumbled for the sheath at his hip and put away the panga, avoiding cutting his fingers on it, feeling automatically to check that the SIG-Sauer P-226 was still safely holstered on the opposite side.

As he leaned back against the sloping wall of the den, as far away from the swaying corpse of the gator as he could get, Ryan felt a growing wave of claustrophobia sweeping over his mind. He had an awareness that he was buried somewhere deep beneath the earth, in a pit that was three parts filled with the brackish swamp water, with no way of knowing how to get out—and no way at all of letting Krysty—if she was still alive—know where he was. As far as she knew, the gator had taken him and he was gone forever, to be trapped, blind and alone.

"Fireblast," Ryan whispered, voice gentle and controlled. "Fucking fireblast." He could hardly hear himself. The only sound, apart from the soft whispering of the water, was the pounding blood in his skull.

He rubbed mud from his head, fingers inches from his eye. "Can't even see the hand in front of my face," he said, almost managing something like a laugh.

Almost.

It was totally black and silent.

Silent as the grave.

Chapter Twenty

Krysty had finally stopped the futile crying. Tears streaked her cheeks, and deep marks marred her palms where she'd dug in her nails.

Her shoulders slumped, and she stared vacantly out across the gray-brown expanse of the bayou. She ached all over from the violent battering she'd endured from the powerful jaws of the giant mutie gator, and her chest hurt when she took in a deep breath. But Krysty figured that there was nothing too serious done to her. No broken ribs.

She'd actually watched Ryan readying himself for his blind dive to the rescue, and had done what she could to stop him. But she might as well have tried to stop a maddened charging buffalo with a spitball.

A part of her brimmed with pride at the way her lover had come to her aid, though he had to have been aware how bitterly the dice were loaded against him.

And a larger part of her was filled with a hopeless bleakness at the certainty that he had offered his life in exchange for hers, and that she would never see him again.

"Never."

"ACTION WITHOUT THOUGHT can be time totally wasted. If you got the time to think, then do it."

The saying came into Ryan's mind as he leaned against the pile of wet twigs and gnawed bones, trying to regain full control of his body and his nerves.

"Yeah, thanks a lot, Trader," he said. "Ace on the line, as usual."

There had been a way into the creature's hidden lair, which meant that there was also a way out of it.

Ryan could remember the mad race along the narrow twisting tunnel, between the roots of the mangroves, hauled by the wounded gator. Then they'd exploded into the underground nest, hollowed from the living mud.

There was an exit from the hole, somewhere below the level of the swamp water. All he had to do was take a good deep breath and dive down to find it, then swim along until he was able to break free to the surface.

It couldn't be more than forty or fifty feet to swim under water.

Maybe eight feet?

"Hundred," Ryan offered. "Any advance on a hundred? Do I hear one-fifty?" The movement of the water had ceased and it was utterly silent. "No advance? Hey, are you speaking to me? Guess you must be. I'm the only one here."

He smiled.

If there had been light down there and anyone to see, they would have been appalled at the rictus of shock and horror on Ryan's face.

"Waiting won't make it any easier. Time to go exploring, Ryan. Find the way out is all. Deep breath and let's have a feel around under the water." He laughed, a harsh, abrupt sound. "Least being blind doesn't make much difference to this one."

He drew what he could of the foul air into his lungs and dived down out of sight.

KRYSTY HAD TWO CHOICES.

She could go back into Bramton and enlist help to try to find Ryan—or his body—though she wasn't sure if she could ever locate the place again. Trees, drooping with the white fronds of Spanish moss, were all around the edges of the dark, scummy water. One lagoon and causeway looked much like another.

The starting point of the old tourist motel and the time-frozen marina was a couple hundred yards away. Krysty knew that much. But she wasn't sure how far the gator had dragged her. Or in what direction.

The alternative was to try to follow the way the beast had taken Ryan. She'd been able to crawl out of the swamp in time to see the foaming turbulence that had man and reptile at its bubbling center. But that had disappeared behind a large group of drooping mangroves, a good hundred paces to the east.

Krysty glanced at the sky.

Light was already beginning to fade, the dull shadows lengthening, making the place even more dark and gloomy. There was certainly no hope of returning with rescuers from the ville before full dark, which meant the two options were really only one.

She began to pick her way cautiously around the edge of the bayou, stopping suddenly and carefully reloading her blaster, her fingers only trembling a little.

THE FIRST TWO DIVES were fruitless. All he found were hollows and pockets in the mud, none of which went more than a few feet in any direction before closing off in dead ends, which meant a difficult retreat, wriggling backward, fighting all the time to overcome the rising waves of terror at being helplessly trapped in the filthy hole.

"Third time lucky," Ryan panted.

As he filled his lungs, it seemed that the pocket of air in the den was much diminished in quality.

Maybe he wouldn't drown after all.

Just suffocate.

Ryan dived once more under the dark surface, hands reaching for the tunnel out.

IT WAS HOPELESS. Krysty knew that the big carnivores had their nests, dens or lairs some way beneath the surface of the water, hollowed out from mud, where they would take their prey. They often used the dark holes as larders, sometimes allowing their victims to stay alive for several days.

But there was no way of identifying them from outside, on the banks above.

No clue.

"Ryan!" she called again, croaking with the strain on her voice, listening to the way the swamp seemed to swallow up the sound, preventing it from traveling more than a few yards. "Ryan, you there?"

The background noise of insects faded at her yell, then came surging back again immediately.

She stood and listened, waiting.

RYAN HAD GONE TOO FAR. He was already more than halfway out of breath, his lungs straining with the effort of swimming underwater, twisting and turning as he battled his way between the slick roots. He'd swum too far to make it back again, even if he was able to turn around in the cramped space.

If he didn't manage to reach the outside within the next fifteen or twenty seconds, then he would suffer a bleak and miserable ending.

He could only go on.

KRYSTY KNELT, trying to draw on all of her own mutie special powers, the power to "feel" whether there was any life-form within the immediate vicinity.

Closing her eyes, she squeezed her hands together, scenting the region close by.

There was something, but it was very faint, faint and oddly muffled.

It wasn't like anything Krysty could remember ever having felt before.

"Ryan," she said doubtfully.

The feeling seemed to be getting gradually closer, gaining in strength—unless she was imagining it, willing it to happen, making it happen.

LIFE WAS EBBING. The oxygen in Ryan's lungs was gone, and he was swimming through the slippery tunnel on automatic pilot. His survival reflexes carried him through the stinking mud, his legs kicking more and more slowly, his hands pulling desperately at the elusive roots of the trees that threatened to entrap him and hold him in the slime for all eternity.

A part of Ryan's brain was actually aware that he had begun the inexorable process of dying, and it was beginning to close itself down.

The urgency had faded and he was barely moving at all, in any direction, his body still held in the grip of the narrow tunnel entrance.

It was nearly over.

From some deep, dark well of reserves, Ryan made a final despairing effort, giving a last kick with his legs and a last pull with both his hands, before the endless night finally swallowed him.

KRYSTY STOOD, shading her eyes against the dying of the light that speared between the trees, turning the clumps of Spanish moss into frail balls of living fire. There was something across the lagoon, to her left, only a scant twenty yards or so away.

It could be a floating log, almost totally submerged in the brown water. Or it might, more likely be an alligator, hunting silently and still.

Or it was Ryan.

She ran a few steps before launching herself, arrow straight, into the water in a classic racing dive, fast and shallow, so that she was already into her swimming strokes the moment she touched the swamp's muddy surface, heading toward the object that hardly showed above the placid surface.

Reaching it, she paused to shake her wet hair away from her eyes.

It was Ryan, facedown, inert, arms and legs spread like a huge starfish, his curly black hair floating motionless around his skull like a wraith.

Krysty didn't hesitate.

Reaching her arms around him, she tipped him over, then clutched him to her and started to kick her way backward, dragging him after her, cupping her hand under Ryan's chin to keep his mouth and nose clear of the water.

The few yards were endless.

Something long and sinuous brushed against Krysty's feet, but she pushed it away and carried on. Ryan was a deadweight, arms and legs trailing, his right eye open and staring up at the darkening sky.

"Hang on, lover," she panted. "For Gaia's sake... For my sake, hang on!"

Krysty glanced over her shoulder, seeing that the bank of the swamp was now only a dozen feet behind her.

She felt soft mud sliding under her feet and struggled clumsily to drag Ryan's body up out of the filthy water, onto relatively dry land.

Krysty immediately rolled him on his back, probing into his slack mouth to make sure he hadn't swallowed his tongue along with the gobbets of mud and watery phlegm, clearing his airway. She knelt by his side, took a deep breath and started the process of the kiss of life.

At first it seemed hopeless.

He was dead. His skin was sallow and cold. There was no reflexive movement when she touched his staring blue eye. She lifted a hand and it dropped like putty to the ground.

No respiration.

No pulse.

Nothing.

Alone in the dank wilderness, Krysty worked on, breathing in, pressing down on Ryan's chest, repeating the process again and again.

The light was almost gone, and she could barely see the white face below her. But she worked on.

Uncle Tyas McCann, back in the ville of Harmony, had once told her about a near-drowning in a ville that he'd lived in as a teenager, up in the cold north of old New England. A child had slipped through the thick ice of a fishing hole and had been thought lost despite all the efforts of the men of the settlement. They had smashed the ice for many yards around, eventually discovering the little body floating on the dark lake.

He'd been there for at least fifteen minutes, said Uncle Tyas, frozen and still. But the lad's mother had been the daughter of one of the last of the surviving predark doctors in Deathlands, and she had refused to give up all hope, working away until death had reluctantly loosened its hold on the small child and he had begun to breathe again.

"A miracle!" Krysty exclaimed when her uncle had finished the story.

"Not so happy as might be," he'd replied. "The boy was sorely brain damaged and died two weeks later."

But he had been drawn back from beyond the brink of the grave. That was a fact. And if it could work for a little boy, it could work for Ryan.

Krysty kept trying, ignoring the advance of night.

As she worked, she prayed, to Gaia and to her own mother, Sonja, prayed for another chance for Ryan. For both of them.

All her senses were on the alert for some flicker of life from the unconscious man.

"Yes?" she whispered.

There *was* something, a tiny spark in the darkness, a whisper in the night.

She reached for the artery at the side of his throat, below the ear, and felt a tiny, hesitant tremor of life.

There was still Tyas McCann's cautionary tale at the back of her mind, but Krysty was almost overcome with relief.

Ryan was going to make it.

Chapter Twenty-One

"Thought you'd all like to have what they used to call a sneaky preview of the latest epic movie." Johannes Forde grinned at the group of friends standing around his wag. "Before we go and take up the Family's offer of supper and accommodation for the night. What do you say?"

Ryan nodded. Once Krysty had revived that frail glimmer of life, he had recovered amazingly fast, his strong constitution helping to pull him through. It had taken another hour, into full dark, before he'd come around enough to pick a cautious path back to Bramton, where the others had been waiting anxiously. J.B. had already organized the search party, enlisting John Winthrop and some of the men of the ville.

They'd disbanded with undisguised relief once they saw Ryan and Krysty stumbling out of the darkness of the surrounding bayou.

Now, after a bowl of rich vegetable soup, so thick it was more of a stew, Ryan was almost completely recovered from the near-drowning, though he was still totally blind.

"I've got it all processed and we can take a look. Not what you'd call a finished cut, as there's a few bits and bobs that need trimming." Forde's neat white beard and mustache seemed to float in the gloom, with a life of their own. He was still wearing his fringed buckskins, and his ponytail was now tied back with a ribbon of brightest gold.

"When will you show it to the people?" Mildred asked. "That's when they settle up with some jack."

"Indeed, yes. Straight and true as an ebony rule, that is. But, friends first."

"Someone coming," Jak said, turning to peer into the darkness beyond the Clanton Corral and the livery stable. His nocturnal vision was the best in the group.

"Cornelius?" J.B. asked.

"Come to see why we're late for the meal?"

"No. The Mayor."

It was John Winthrop, scurrying along, keeping close to the shadows of the buildings that lined the main street. He wore a long duster coat, dark brown, with its collar turned up high. When he arrived he sounded out of breath and was visibly nervous in case anyone saw him there.

"I have a little time, outlanders," he panted.

"What is it?" Ryan asked.

"You seem decent, honest folk."

"Get on with it."

"Right, Mr. Cawdor. Indeed. Straightest point between two places is the shortest line." He scratched his head. "I don't think I have that quite right."

"We get the picture," Krysty said.

"Yeah," Mildred agreed. "We see."

"You go as guests with the Family."

Ryan nodded. "No secret, Mr. Winthrop. What of it? That what you came for?"

His head bobbed quickly, like a drinking bird. "That's the reason."

Everyone waited, but Winthrop seemed as though he didn't want to elaborate.

"Danger?" Jak said finally.

"Deep and dark," replied the mayor of Bramton. "The Family has reigned here for longer than anyone can remember. Word is that they never change. No, that's wrong. Because they change. Yes, they surely do that."

"You aren't making any sense," Forde said. "They never change, but they always change."

The clouds had drifted away and a bright moon hung over the bluffs to the east, toward the cliff-top house of the Family.

"Old people here, like Zenobia Simpkins, swear that Elric and the others have hardly aged a day in the last twenty years or more."

Doc snorted. "Old wives' nonsense! Stuff and damned taradiddle!"

"You may think so, Doctor, and you can surely not look to me for comment on that." Winthrop, despite his quaking fear, was a strangely dignified figure.

"Get on with it, man," Ryan growled, aware of time sliding by them.

"Just a word to the wise, outlanders. Bramton has been owned by the Family since just after skydark. Some say for centuries before that."

"You continue to spout the most arrant rubbish, Winthrop." Doc rapped sharply on the highway with the ferrule of his swordstick. "Before skydark there was no question of barons and the owning of land and of people. It was not the American way. Do you have any cogent proof for us of your preposterous conceits? No, of course you do not."

Winthrop turned to face the old man. "There have been young men and young women missing. Only one body, torn and raggled by the millstream. The others..." He snapped his fingers. "Never seen again."

Ryan shook his head. "Every frontier pesthole has the same story, Winthrop. Young folks get tired and up their roots and move away."

"There is the sickness and the way..." He stopped and looked up.

From far above them they all heard a strange, chilling cry, an unearthly shriek as something passed its shadow between the moon and the watchers, a creature that seemed to have a huge wingspan, oddly shaped. It swooped once more, turning at speed so that none of them could see it properly.

Then it vanished.

"What fuck was that?" Jak said.

"If you couldn't make it out, then none of us could." Ryan stamped his feet. "Sounded like a kind of mix between a gator and an eagle."

J.B. turned to the mayor. "Anyway, you were telling us about the Family, Winthrop. Go on."

The man was quivering like an aspen in a hurricane. "No. No more. They can see and hear everything. Why not just leave Bramton now? Leave this whole blighted area. Don't go to the dark house on the cliff.''

He turned and started to walk quickly away, neck hunched, head buried in the folds of his coat, stopping a few yards away. "I *never* spoke to you. Understand? Never! If you must go to the house, then guard yourselves. I can say no more, outlanders. Just guard yourselves!''

He bustled off, swallowed up by the night.

Krysty sighed. "Think we should take his advice and leave the place?''

Forde responded instantly. "Nay, nay. There can be rich pickings for us all around Bramton. I've sold one film and there seems a likely chance of another to this freakish Family. Move on because of some nervous old dotard? I should say not. If you outlanders want to run whimpering and shitting yourselves into the bushes, then I won't stop you.''

"We go to the house," Ryan said firmly.

"He was terrified, lover. You couldn't see how frightened Winthrop was.''

"Don't need to see fear. Smell it a country mile off. I say we go.''

BUT FIRST FORDE INSISTED on showing them what he called a rough cut of the 16 mm movie he'd made of the good folk of Bramton.

Krysty stood close to Ryan, her hand resting gently on his right arm, giving him a whispered commentary of the short film.

"Hey, it's brilliant! Sort of general view of the ville, from near to that weird store. Moving in closer. How do you do that, Johannes?"

"What?"

"Well, I can see you weren't moving, but your camera is. Kind of remote control."

"Called a zoom lens."

"How's it work?" Dean asked.

"Bit too complicated for you, son," Forde replied. "Watch now and you might see someone you recognize in—"

"It's me!" the boy whooped. "Hey, that's me. I never saw myself 'cept in a mirror or a glass door or a pool of still water. That's me, Dad."

"Believe you, son."

"Hey, don't I look like myself? There's Doc!"

"Calm down, Dean," Ryan said, barely managing to control his own bitter frustration at not being able to see this miraculous movie.

Doc was smirking. Ryan could hear it in his voice. "Didn't realize what a handsome fellow I was, what a dashing and roving blade!"

"There's Mildred standing close to J.B., talking. Now she's just looked over her shoulder and seen she's being filmed. Now she looks all shy and nervous."

"Didn't know I was on 'Candid Camera,'" the woman said to Krysty.

"Is it color or black-and-white?" Ryan asked. "I've seen old predark vids that were black-and-white."

"This is in rich true-to-life color," Forde replied. "Nothing but the best."

"Hair's whiter than thought," Jak said quietly. "Snowier than snow."

"Camera doesn't lie." Forde adjusted something on the projector that made it run a little more slowly. Ryan caught the change of pitch.

"Now it's me," Krysty whispered. "The things moving sideways to give a wide view."

"Called panning," Forde said, unable to keep the pride out of his voice at their admiration and delight.

"It's me again, lover. Walking with you, Ryan. Can't tell from the film that..."

"That I'm blind?"

She wasn't thrown by his spurt of anger. "Yeah, just that, lover. If I didn't know, I'd swear there was nothing at all wrong with you."

"Reminds me," Mildred said over the clicking whir of the projector.

"What?" Ryan snapped.

"Haven't checked your eye today."

"Nothing to check."

"Still best let me have a look. Maybe first thing in the morning."

"Waste of time, Mildred."

"Might be. Might not be. I'm the doctor, Ryan, not you. Let me decide."

"I'm looking at the projector. I can feel the heat of the light on my face. Must be a real powerful light to do that. It is, isn't it, Krysty?"

"Yes, it's very bright," she admitted reluctantly, knowing what he was about to say.

"Well, as far as I'm concerned it could be a hundred miles underground."

"Here's the townfolk," Krysty said, changing the prickly subject.

"There's Winthrop and the old woman." Dean was still bubbling with excitement at seeing something he'd only heard rumors about. "They look just like they do. I'd recognize them anyplace from this film. How much more is there, Johannes?"

"Not much. Just a little bit I took of the main street and a couple of shots of that Cornelius guy."

"There's the Banbury Hotel." Doc laughed. "I must confess, it looks a little more prepossessing on the film than in real life. You can't smell the damp or taste the persistent odor of burning onions."

"This is where Elric first appears," Krysty said quietly. "I can remember the moment he came. Just here . . . Oh."

"What?" Ryan said.

There was a general chattering from everyone that made it difficult for him to pick out any details of what had happened, what was happening.

"Fireblast!" he roared at the top of his voice. "Will one of you squawking jays tell me what's going on? Krysty! What's gone wrong with the film?"

"Nothing, really," she replied, though failing to hide the puzzlement in her voice. "Just that Elric Cornelius doesn't seem to show up on the film."

"How can that be?"

Forde had stopped the projector, speeding the film back, sending it rattling on fast rewind through the gate. "I never seen anything like it before," he said, running it forward again.

"What the...? Will someone please just tell me what the film shows if it doesn't show Cornelius? Is the film faulty or damaged, or what?"

"Sort of smudgy light," J.B. replied. "But everything around where he stands is sharp as a crystal. Everyone else is there. We're all there. Just Elric Cornelius."

"Damnedest thing I ever saw." Doc laughed. "If I wasn't a man of science who resolutely places arcane ephemera and inexplicable happenings into the 'X-Files,' then I'd say that Master Cornelius might be..."

"Be what?" Ryan pressed.

Mildred spoke. "I know what Doc is getting at. We're closer to sharing experiences than any of you." Her voice faded a little and Ryan figured she had to have turned away to address the old man directly. "No such things, Doc. You got a lot of faults, but superstitious gullibility isn't among them." She paused for a beat. "Or is it?"

"I share the beliefs of the master of mystery, Sherlock Holmes, my dear Dr. Wyeth. If you have carefully checked off all the possibilities, then what remains, however unlikely, must of necessity be the truth."

Nobody else in the group had the least idea what Doc and Mildred were arguing about.

Ryan tried for an explanation. "Just what the dark night are you two saying is the reason for this Family member not appearing in the film?"

"Something he was wearing," Forde said abruptly. "The totally dark black clothes in sunshine. Some trick of the light, I guess. Just didn't register on the stock. After all, it's way past its expiry date. Like a hundred years past it. Got to be that. Or something like that."

Ryan felt the unease, and he raged inwardly at his own helplessness, unable to see what they had all seen and judge for himself.

"Well," he said finally, "if we're all content with that explanation for this odd…happening, I guess we can all get going for supper at this big house on the bluff. We must be way late already."

"Better to be a few minutes late in this world than fifty years too soon in the next," Doc said.

Nobody could think of anything to top that, so they all set off for the Cornelius mansion.

Chapter Twenty-Two

"Incredible house, lover."

"Tell me."

"Victorian Gothic by the look of it. Real big place. All towers, turrets, spikes and spires. Stained glass at some of the windows. Perched on the top of a high scarp that drops down sheer to the river. Must be five hundred feet if it's an inch. And there can't be more than a few yards between the house and the edge of the cliff."

"Like the House of Usher just waiting for the word to fall," Doc added.

"More like the Bates Motel in that old horror film," Mildred said.

"Defended?"

Through her hand on his arm, Ryan felt Krysty shake her head. "Can't tell from this far off. Not by moonlight. There's a steep snake-back trail leading up to it."

"Looks ghostly, Dad."

"No such things as ghosts, son. People mix them up with memories."

KRYSTY FINGERED the fire-opal pendant as they waited for the huge oak front door to open, noticing out of the corner of her eye that Mildred was doing the same with her small golden crucifix.

Close up, the building was even more impressive than it had been from below in the river valley. Krysty guessed that the cliff had been the result of one of the violent earth movements that had followed the bombardment of the country by thousands of nuke missiles. All over Deathlands, gorges had become mountains, lakes turned into deserts and towering mountains flattened and moved many miles.

Now, in the heart of the level lowlands of the Louisiana bayous, there was this razor-edged escarpment. She wondered whether the house had been built later in such a perilous position or whether it had always been there.

It looked so solid that it could have been there two or three hundred years.

Doc rapped on the door with the silver lion's-head hilt of his ebony swordstick, the echoes fading away. "Some hosts!" he snorted. "They invite us to bed and board...bawdy beds and bawds that bore you... Boarding schools and bedding plants. Ready beds and..." He realized that his mind had done its familiar trick of slipping a few notches sideways. "My apologies, gentles all, for my addled pate."

"Don't worry, Doc," Ryan said. "Any sign of lights anywhere in the place?"

Jak answered. "Plenty. Most windows got light. Lamps in porch overhead. Oil, not electric."

"Feel anything, lover?" he asked.

Krysty was silent for a few moments. "Yeah. There's some people around, all right. Quite a few. But there's also... No, I don't get it."

"Get what?" Forde asked. Behind him the two horses were restless in the shafts of the wag, shuffling and whickering uncomfortably.

"Just there's a kind of feeling that I've never known before. Can't spell it out."

"Why're your animals spooked, Forde?" Ryan asked. "Cougar close by?"

"Could be anything. Wolves, mebbe. Mebbe bein' out so late at night. Normally bedded down long before now."

"What's the time, J.B.? Feels to me something like nine or ten o'clock."

"Close," the Armorer replied. "Twenty after ten. Hey, sounds like someone's coming."

Krysty, still holding Ryan by the arm, looked up, struck once more by the peculiar size of the door. It was solid oak, with bars of iron running across it and dozens of heavy iron studs dotting its surface. It looked strong enough to resist a direct attack by anything short of a nuke gren.

Now Krysty looked at the rest of the building, noticing that all the windows were covered with thick bars of cold gray iron, some with oaken shutters.

"This place is like a fortress, lover," she said quietly, giving him quick whispered details.

Meanwhile, there was the heavy, sonorous sound of massive bolts being drawn and the tumblers of sec locks being turned. But the door still remained firmly closed.

"Come on," Dean moaned. "I can feel my backbone rubbing on my belly."

"Probably all the food's gone," Mildred teased. "They'll have gotten tired of waiting."

"Oh, no."

The door began to move, very slowly, soundlessly, on oiled hinges.

"Shouldn't we be on red?" J.B. whispered to Ryan.

"Bit late for that."

The voice was light and feminine. "You are the outlanders from Bramton. We have been expecting you for some time. We heard of the accident to you, Ryan and Krysty, so we knew that you would be somewhat tardy."

Krysty leaned close to Ryan so that he could feel her sweet breath in his ear. "Little guy in rich velvets and faded brocades with a frizzed up mane of white hair. Looks to be around eighty. Very delicate, and I'd guess that he pitches and bats, as well, if you know what I mean, lover."

"Guessed that from the voice."

"Come in, come in. My name is Norman and I am butler to the Family."

"How about the rig and the horses?" Forde asked. "You got stabling?"

"You are the man with the magic lantern, are you? Delighted, Mr. Forde. Just leave everything as it is. It will all be taken care of. Now, follow me."

Ryan stumbled on the raised step as Krysty led him forward, but kept his balance. The door closed softly behind them, and he was aware of a strange stillness in the air.

Almost like that inside a tomb.

"Dinner will be served in the main dining room, which is halfway along the hall to your right. You will find your names printed upon cards."

"Where's Elric and the rest of the Family?" Mildred asked. "They eating with us?"

Norman's answer came as smooth as cream. "I regret that most of the Family have medical conditions that necessitate their having special diets. Vegetarian and that sort of thing. I'm sure you understand. They prefer to dine alone so that their 'special' needs don't spoil the pleasure of dining for others. But I believe that Master Elric may join you later."

Ryan's auditory senses were confused. He could tell that they were in a high, vaulted hallway, yet there was none of the echo that you might expect.

"Are there heavy drapes around the ceiling?" he asked Krysty. "Something's muffling the noise."

"No, nothing, lover."

The butler had caught the whispered exchange. "Is there a question?"

Krysty laughed. "No. Just telling Ryan what a chore housework must be in a place this size."

The man gave a lilting giggle. "Oh, dear, madame. I must tell you what I tell all of the ladies. The good news about housework. The gospel according to Norman. Don't bother dusting, and after three years the dust stops getting any thicker."

THE FOOD WAS ONLY a little better than adequate. The vegetables were considerably overcooked, leaving them limp and soggy.

"Bit like Norman," had been Dean's bad-taste joke on the subject.

By contrast, the meat was served almost raw, the chill of the abattoir barely removed.

"This bloody?" Ryan asked, struggling to cut through a piece of what Krysty assured him was lamb. It came with bullet-hard roast potatoes, watery cabbage and mushy peas. And a delicious and delicate mint jelly.

"Red as Jak's eyes," J.B. replied.

Ryan leaned to be closer to Krysty, pitching his voice low. "What's the sec side of the ville look like?"

"Not many servants, and not one of them carrying any kind of weapon. Most of them are bringing in the food and stuff like that, looking as if they've been at the loco weed. Or been doped up on jolt for the last two years."

"Weapons?"

Krysty was cutting up some of the meat for him. "Apart from some blunt knives and forks, not a lot. Haven't seen a blaster in the place. Yet. Actually the cutlery is kind of ornate." She paused. "Yeah, it's silver. Patterned with an acanthus pattern on the handles and engraved on the blades."

"Rather old and rather fine, if I'm any judge," Doc offered. "Possibly an English design. And the plates are certainly from England. Wonderful predark quality, Royal Doulton. Look at the detail on the flower paintings."

"Wish that I could, Doc," Ryan said, unable to stop his bitterness.

"My dear fellow, I do apologize. Thoughtless of me, *in extremis*. Yes, mea culpa, Ryan, old friend."

Ryan shrugged, one hand knocking into Krysty, sending the forkful of lamb clattering onto the floor.

"Forward!" Norman clicked his fingers, calling out to the servants in his fluting voice.

The meal dragged slowly on.

"Got some fruit juice smeared on your chin, lover. Let me wipe it." She leaned closer to him, her face close to his, dropping her voice. "Being watched. Gallery around the hall at second-floor level. Think it's what they called a minstrels' balcony. Very shadowy up there."

"Danger?" His hand dropped to find the comforting butt of the SIG-Sauer.

"Can't tell. I think..." She leaned across the table. "Jak, you got good vision in dark places. Take a look up in the black spaces between..."

"Elric Cornelius. Been watching eight minutes. Hasn't moved once."

"Anyone else?" J.B. asked, his glasses glinting in the light of the polished brass oil lamps.

The albino teenager glanced up again, looking all around the vaulted gallery. "Nobody. Haven't seen sign anyone looked like sec man."

Ryan sat in his own darkness, absently chewing a gristly piece of meat, pondering what he'd been told about the fortified mansion of the Family: servants that seemed like they were drugged, all except for the little butler, Norman; surprisingly poor food for a baron's home; no members of the baronial family coming to greet their guests, except for the snow-headed Elric, who was lurking in the balcony. And no sec men.

That was strangest of all.

Over the years of his life in Deathlands, Ryan had to have visited hundreds of villes, and met most of the barons who ruled them. Though he scratched hard at his memory, he couldn't recall a single case where a baron managed without any members of a security force.

Some barons ruled with terror. Some with brutal power. Some were comparatively kind and decent toward the people of their domain.

But not one could have slept easy in his bed at night without the sure and certain knowledge of the blasters that defended him.

It was a common fact that few barons in Death-lands lived out a natural span close to the biblical three score and ten. It was also well enough known that most were murdered by wives or mistresses. Next came sons or daughters, then brothers or sisters. You went way down the butchery tables to find barons who'd been deposed and slaughtered by their own sec chiefs or men.

He wondered how the Cornelius Family kept its grip on the people of Bramton and the surrounding lands if they had no sec men. It didn't make sense.

"Sec men must be out of sight, out of the way," he whispered to Krysty.

"They do not exist, Ryan Cawdor. We do not need them." The answering voice came from high above his head, making him jump, confirming his suspicion that Elric Cornelius had to have preternaturally keen hearing to have caught his muttered words from way up in the gallery—unless there was some cunning trick of the acoustics that carried sound around a building. Ryan had heard of such things.

Ryan stared blankly up. "Friend of mine used to say that a man who said he never needed help was already way beyond any help," he called.

A light laugh hung in the air.

There was the faintest whisper of feet on stone steps, then Elric was among them.

"I see that the food we prepared was not much to your liking," he said, glancing around at the plates, most of which carried the piled detritus of the disappointing meal.

"Long on quantity and perhaps a little short on quality," Doc replied.

"If you stay awhile with us, then you must instruct us on how to improve. Guests from the outlands are rare here. And food such as this—" he swept out a long arm, ending in pale, bloodless fingers "—is not what we choose for our own pleasures. Not at all."

Ryan hesitated, wanting to ask the man what they ate for their own pleasure. But there was something about being blind that held him back. Cornelius had already shown himself capable of anger, and without being able to see the man's face, Ryan felt himself unable to judge what his reaction might be.

"Have you done with the food?" Elric was moving around the room and had come to a halt directly behind Ryan, increasing his discomfort.

"We have," Krysty replied. "It's been a heavy day, especially for Ryan and me. I think we'd all like to get ourselves some rest now. If that's all right with you."

"But, of course. Norman will show you to the rooms that have been set aside for you. They all have running water and all facilities. It will not be *necessary* for anyone to leave his, or her, room during the night."

The threatening stress on "necessary" was unmistakable, and J.B. responded to it first.

"You saying harm might come if we don't stay in our rooms? What kind of harm would that be?"

Ryan heard the smile from Cornelius. "You make it sound as though you worry that your lives might be threatened, John Dix. This is a large and rambling house, and we would not wish any of you to come to harm. That is all. Norman, you may take over, and I wish all a good night."

Chapter Twenty-Three

Ryan slept fitfully. The passing of the hours had become an enigma to him, and when he woke for the fifth or sixth time he'd completely lost touch with how late or early it was.

There had been a dream where he was in the ruins of a great metropolis—perhaps Newyork. It seemed a center for travel, and there were dozens of commercial transport wags, filling with passengers. Ryan had known that he wanted to get to a ville in the Shens, but he couldn't remember the name of it. And the destination boards on the fronts and sides of the wags were all blank.

He had asked bustling men and women which was the right vehicle to catch for the Shens, but they'd all pushed by him, faces averted, intent on their own business.

Finally he'd taken the nearest wag, but it had been empty, with shuttered doors and windows and no way of communicating with the driver.

He had awakened from that jolting darkness to the blackness of the bedroom that Norman had showed him and Krysty late the previous night.

"Krysty?" he whispered, reaching to his left side, where he knew she'd been sleeping.

But the space was empty, the sheets cold.

Ryan drew the SIG-Sauer, cocking it automatically, the click sounding unusually loud.

A door creaked open to the right of the big, high bed. "Why the blaster, lover?"

He eased the hammer down and replaced the heavy automatic under the pillow. "Woke and you weren't there."

"Went for a pee. Found it hard to sleep. Something about this place makes me uneasy, Ryan."

"Yeah, I felt it, too. Got locked into a classic anxiety dream about getting lost on a journey."

"I was walking across a heather-covered land and it got evening and something was coming after me. Pretty ghosty. Goes with the look of this house."

Ryan had been sitting up and he lay down again. "When you get a chance, pass the word to the others to stay on orange. Something I don't like about the Family."

"Only met one member, so far."

"Yeah, well, that's enough to go on. Just tell the others to be careful and not to go around on their own."

"Sure." She slipped back into bed and made him jump by putting her cold bare feet on his thigh.

But she quickly grew warmer.

BREAKFAST WAS little better than the supper had been.

Servants knocked on every door at seven-thirty, just after dawn, waking everyone with the news that the food would be served in the dining hall in thirty minutes.

The house was so large that there had been a room for each person, on the second and third floors, opening off long, shadowy corridors.

There was also a fourth floor, but J.B.'s hasty recce the previous evening hadn't found a way up there.

"Think there's also a cellar," he said as he helped himself from the buffet on the ornate mahogany sideboard, picking from a wide and generous selection of magnificent silver chafing dishes, each set over a small spirit burner to keep the food piping hot.

"Open the wrong door in a cellar here and you'd probably fall straight into the gorge," Mildred commented.

"Where is the Family?" Doc asked. "Are we never to meet our hosts?"

"Time enough and time in plenty," replied Norman, who, Krysty told Ryan, appeared to be wearing precisely the same clothes he'd worn the night before. Indeed, the little man looked as though he'd never been to bed.

Not even Elric Cornelius appeared to join them.

The breakfast was a miserable experience. The room seemed even colder than the night before, and most of the shutters across the ornate stained-glass windows were still closed, giving it a gloomy atmosphere.

Runny eggs managed somehow to be blackened around the edges. Thick slices of fatback bacon had seen so little of the frying pan that sharp bristles were untouched. The bread was acceptable, but several of the pots of preserves had layers of green-white mold sitting comfortably on top of them. And the butter was rancid.

Every one of the seven companions knew that a basic rule of survival in Deathlands was always to eat whatever you could, whenever you could. But it was a struggle.

Johannes Forde seemed oblivious to the poor quality of the cooking and ate as if he'd eaten nothing for a month, tucking into a triple helping of a thick chowder. The others had avoided it, put off by the greasy, phosphorescent scum that floated on top and the leprous look of the chunks of meat that squatted here and there, like small, starving toads.

"Good, Norman," he called to the diminutive butler. "Chicken or pork?"

"Neither, Johannes."

"Then it's gator."

"No."

"Cottonmouth? I always hankered after a good rattler stew to break my fast."

"Coffin worm," Norman squeaked, clapping his hands delightedly. "Delicious, I'm told. Not that a team of the wildest stallions would drag me within a spoon's breadth of it."

Forde put a brave face on it. "Well, if that's coffin worm, then it's damned *good* coffin worm."

"What's a coughling worm, Dad?" Dean asked, his eyes wide with fascination.

"Coffin worm, son."

"Well, what is it?"

Norman answered the boy. By the time he'd gotten about three parts of the way through his explanation, Forde had turned a delicate shade of yellowish green and run from the room, hand clapped over his mouth.

"A piece of rotting fish is placed in a wooden box, about a foot square. Maggots are introduced. They come from the trout farm of the ville. Once they are busy, the box is sealed. As soon as the fish is gone, the maggots begin to devour one another. Survival of the nastiest. They reduce in a mathematical progression. Do you know what that is, young Dean? No? It means that there might be 256 maggots at their busiest. One eats another and there's 128. Same thing happens and there's 64. You get the idea?"

Dean nodded, turning his head to watch the rapid exit of the movie maker.

"Eventually there's two real big coffin worms alive in the box. Biggest eats the weakest and we cook the winner."

Mildred closed her eyes and swallowed hard. It had crossed her mind that the waspish little butler might have been playing an unpleasant practical joke on Johannes, but she guessed that he wasn't.

To distract herself she stared at the big arched windows, with a watery sun breaking past the shutters.

They were of superb quality, and she knew that they had to have dated from before skydark, perhaps close to the end of the twentieth century.

None of them were the traditional Christian design, with a suffering Jesus and mourning apostles.

These showed more modern scenes, finely detailed, in rich scarlets, purples and greens. Mildred's forehead wrinkled as she realized that many of the windows showed laboratories of all kinds of scientific experiments, bearded men with gentle, grave smiles and radiant women in shining white coats, measuring silver and golden liquids into beakers and test tubes.

Above several of them was inscribed the number 47 in ornamental Gothic script. Mildred knew that the number rang a bell somewhere in her memory, but she couldn't quite set her mind to locate it.

To her greater surprise, she recognized some of the cryonic and cryogenic equipment that she had so often used herself in what laymen called "freezing" experiments.

And there was one more detail that fascinated her more than all the rest put together.

Largely concealed by internal shutters, one of which had come unbolted, was the last of the stained-glass windows. There appeared to be another of the godlike scientists, or whitecoats, as Doc so bitterly called them, holding his arms spread wide as if bidding farewell to an angelic host of figures who were streaming away from him, bathed in what Mildred guessed was supposed to be a celestial glow.

The odd thing that she couldn't see too clearly, because of the half-open shutter, was that all of the heavenly throng appeared to have gleaming white hair

THE EARLY-MORNING SUN and its promise of a fine day faded quickly away under a belt of low cloud that moved in from the west. It seemed to fill the valley and hang over the bayou, making Bramton itself invisible.

With the cloud came the rain, starting with a light drizzle that strengthened and settled into sheets of remorseless gray rain that fell vertically and was obviously set in for the whole day.

It made any kind of expedition beyond the walls of the mansion out of the question.

NORMAN WAS MORE than solicitous, gathering them together in a big lounge, filled with silk-covered sofas and deep chairs, covered in a magnificently rich material, though Krysty managed to whisper to Ryan that they all looked rather ragged and faded.

"We have all manner of entertainment for guests." He sighed, placing his fingertips together in an exaggerated steeple effect. "Though some have not been used for many months. Nay, for many years."

A spinet sat in one corner of the room, and Mildred wandered over to it. She ran her fingers across the keys, getting a mix of discords and missing notes.

"Dear me!" Norman exclaimed. "I must arrange for the tuner to call when next he passes by."

There were a number of paintings hung on the walls, and Doc strolled around to examine them, finding the works mostly poor reproductions of minor-league pictures, with muddy colors and flat detail.

"Now, we have all manner of card games," the butler said. "Sets of Scrabble and Monopoly. Both very popular in predark days. They come with instructions."

"Books?" Krysty asked.

"A library is in the next room along. Through those doors there, my dear flame-headed goddess. Oh, forgive me, but flattery gets you everywhere."

"No vids or games or stuff?" Dean asked, sitting with shoulders slumped in the traditionally sulky position of the bored eleven-year-old.

"I fear not." Norman brightened. "But we do have some fine jigsaw puzzles. 'Showing His Paces' and 'The Landlord's Birthday' are two of my favorites. Along with 'The Monarch of the Glen' and 'Rounding the Horn.' You might like those, young fellow."

"Sure. Real hot pipe. Hope my brain doesn't boil with the excitement."

"Can we tour the house?" Ryan asked.

Norman sounded flustered for a few seconds. "Oh, dear me, I think that... Perhaps you can visit any part of this floor and the two above it. But not the top floor and attics or the cellars. They are all a tad dangerous and are kept locked."

"Outside?"

The little man considered Jak's question for several seconds, head on one side, ringed index finger poised against his chin. "I don't see..."

"Can't you ask one of the Family?" Ryan said tetchily. "It's not that hard a question to answer, is it?"

"Oh, no, it's not. But you must realize that the lives that are lived here are not what some people might consider ordinary lives."

"Noticed that," Krysty commented. "Where are they this morning?" Her eyes narrowed. "In fact, Norman, just how many members are there of the Family?"

He simpered prettily. "I fear that I've somewhat lost touch. They come and go. Perhaps more than four and less than ten would not be far off."

"Thanks for nothing," the woman muttered.

"Outside?" Jak repeated calmly. "We go outside?"

"I can see no harm in that. But I urge you to keep clear of the ville. There have been foolish tales over the years and we are not the best of friends."

"So, we can walk in the grounds, if we want to?" J.B. pressed, turning to stare out of the mullioned windows. "If the rain lays off."

"Doesn't look like will," Jak said.

"I am sure we could rustle up some oilskins. Oh, listen to me! Rustling oilskins. I love that silky sound, don't you? So sensual, I think."

Ryan turned away, steadying himself against the back of what he imagined was one of the large chairs. "Do we ever get to meet anyone except for Elric?"

"Of course. The members of the Cornelius Family have always been night birds, preferring the hours of darkness to the glaring light of the midday sun."

"Only 'mad dogs and Englishmen go out in the midday sun,' " Doc said, puzzlingly.

Norman gave a faint smile and half bow, then carried on as if the old man hadn't spoken.

"So, they are all resting in their...in their own beds. It is more than my job's worth to go and wake any of them. Perhaps at supper time...?"

With that he turned on his heel and clicked quickly away across the dusty hardwood floor, slowly pulling the heavy door shut behind himself.

Ryan fumbled his way around the padded chair and sat. Despite the thick glass, draperies and shutters, he could still hear the steady hissing of the rain.

"Going to be one exciting day," he said.

"I could get a book out of the library and read to you," Krysty offered.

"Yeah."

"Or you can sit there all day and be bastard illtempered and miserable, lover," she snapped.

Ryan sighed. "Sorry. Go get a book."

Chapter Twenty-Four

" 'Behind him, the sun was sinking far beyond the snow-tipped Sierras.

" 'The sky was flame-red, offering the promise of a fine, new day.' There.'' Krysty closed the book.

"Not bad,'' Ryan said grudgingly. "Guy who wrote that knew something about staying alive and about killing. Trader used to say that it's a craft like any other.''

Krysty had begun reading it shortly after Norman had left them to their own devices. The library was disappointing, with whole shelves of ancient volumes dissolving into dust as soon as they were touched.

"Bookworms!'' Doc had thundered. "There are rarities of all sorts here, particularly on the scientific side of literature. And all neglected so sadly. In many ways it is as great a tragedy as the destruction of the great library of Alexandria. I would wager good money that many of these books that have been irreparably allowed to slide into ruin are the sole examples of their kind in the whole of Deathlands.''

"Did everyone read books in predark times?'' Dean asked. "Thought they all glimmed vids.''

"Oh, indeed they did, young man,'' Doc said. "They 'glimmed' vids until their brains turned to warm oatmeal. And they sprawled on couches like bloated potatoes, stuffing their bodies with popcorn and their brains with pap. They had the attention span of a rabid goldfish. But there were still a few bearded prophets and suspicious eccentrics.... Were they or had they ever been members of...? Forgive me, as my mind wanders again down dark back roads. Books are sacred, young Dean. Mayhap your pending scholastic peregrinations..." He stopped, seeing the bewildered expression. "When you go eventually to school. Then they may teach you some love and respect for the underpaid and unacknowledged arcane skills of the author. But this—" he swept his ebony swordstick around the ranks of shelves "—this is a blasphemy against culture."

But there were still a few books left that had escaped the ravages of time. Doc turned up his nose at the tattered collection, mainly of cheap paperbacks, finally coming across a collection of the poetry of someone called Auden in which he immersed himself.

Dean wandered around looking angry at the world, until his attention was caught by a two-thousand-piece jigsaw puzzle that J.B. and Mildred had taken from a cupboard and begun, spreading all the hand-cut pieces over a stained and scratched refectory table.

"What're you doin' there? Just fitting the bits together to make a picture? Easy-peasy. Here, this bit of sky goes... Oh, it doesn't. Well, how about looking for that bit of tankard by the old man's hand?"

And he was hooked.

Jak was the most ill at ease.

There was nothing in the library that caught his attention, and the puzzles weren't worthy of his time. He kept lying down on one of the sofas, closing his ruby red eyes and dozing, waking to walk, catlike, to the windows that opened over the gorge, peering through them at the sheeting rain.

"Something sick here," he said finally, his face pressed to the cold glass.

"How do you mean, Jak?" Krysty asked.

"Books and state house. No norm baron would let all go like this."

Ryan turned his face toward the albino teenager. "You got any guesses to make?"

"No, Ryan. Because can't say exactly what's wrong, doesn't mean everything's ace on line."

"Agreed."

"I get feelings here like I've never had any other place," Krysty added.

Ryan shook his head. "What's the use of that? You think we should leave, say so. You think we should stay, then stop going on about odd feelings!"

It had been that kind of day.

LUNCH HAD BEEN BROUGHT into them by Norman and three of the serving women. It was decent new-baked bread with some surprisingly good cheeses and an assortment of fresh vegetables and fiery spiced dips.

After the food had been left, Krysty commented on the appearance of the servants. "Their eyes are kind of lifeless."

"And they all seem to me to be suffering from per-nicious anemia," Mildred said. "If I was their doc-tor, I'd be prescribing a course of iron and vitamins and I'd want them to have their blood tested. They look pale as parchment and they walk in such a list-less manner."

"What's the uniform here?" Ryan asked as he munched a buttered roll filled to the brim with thin-sliced peppered tomatoes and bean sprouts.

"Norman is a poem in tattered pastels," Krysty re-plied. "But the men and women we've seen all have a kind of medieval look to them. All wear either very dark blue or very dark gray blouses and pants. High-collared tunics. No hats. Soft shoes so you can hardly hear them moving. Men are clean-shaven. Women all have neat hair cut short."

"What are you doing?" Ryan asked curiously. "I can hear your fingers fiddling with something."

"Well, pardon me for living, lover," she said with a smile. "Just that fire-opal pendant from the store."

"And I was fiddling with my little crucifix," Mildred said from the table where the large jigsaw puzzle was slowly coming closer to completion. Only a large section of oak paneling at the rear of the land-lord's parlor still needed filling in.

"And I fiddled while Rome burned," Doc added, laughing in his fine, rounded, deep voice. "All right, friends. Not one of my mind warps. A reference to…" His voice faded away. "But I forget what."

THE RAIN NEVER STOPPED all day.

Jak, driven near mad by cabin fever, went searching for Norman and found him alone and asleep in the deserted kitchen of the big house, asking him for the loan of a coat.

"Told me couldn't find one after all. Servants must've took them," Jak reported to his friends as he returned disconsolately from his futile mission.

"It's odd," J.B. commented, trying a jigsaw piece shaped like a demented dragon and finding it didn't fit. "Dark night! Funny that they invite us here and seem to want us to stay here, yet they hardly treat us like welcomed guests."

"Give it another day," Ryan said, yawning and stretching. "Then we can move on. Fireblast! I never realized that doing nothing all day could make you as tired as this."

Forde had also been affected by the boredom of the long, drizzling day. He walked through to the library section and picked one of the undamaged books, flinging himself into an armchair and flicking through the dry, fragile pages for a few minutes. Then he tossed the book aside and hovered over the jigsaw puzzle, trying a couple of pieces and then wandering off again, staring blankly at the array of pictures. He ended up by one of the tall windows, looking out at the rain, shading his eyes to peer down into the deep valley below them.

"I reckon I'll go all the way around the bend and back again," he snarled, turning to the others, the fringes of his buckskins swinging with him. "Think I'm going to take one of my cameras and go and do some filming."

"The light good enough?" Doc asked. "I would have thought it a little too dismal for successful photography. But, what do I know?" He shrugged his shoulders. "The answer to my own question is that I know precious little about the process of taking moving pictures. Though my father knew the redoubtable Mathew Brady, of whom I'm sure you will have heard, Master Forde, as one of the immortals."

"Never heard of him, Doc," Forde snarled.

Despite Doc's warning, Forde had left the suite of rooms and not returned until close to supper time, when evening had fallen and the rain had finally ceased.

He was grinning broadly, wiping moisture from his forehead, brushing a few spots from his shoulders. The twin pearl-handled Colts gleamed in the soft golden glow of the oil lamps that Norman had lit an hour or so earlier.

"Any success with your filming?" Ryan asked, turning his head toward where he thought the man was standing.

"Think so. Just you all wait and see. Might have some surprises for you."

"What?" Dean asked. "Tell us."

"The best surprise is no surprise," Mildred said. "Why not wait and see?"

The boy's face fell. "Oh, come on, Johannes. Tell us what you done."

"What you've done. Or what you've been doing," Krysty corrected. "Not what you done."

"Sorry."

Forde sat on the sofa and stretched out his long legs, peering at his mud-splattered boots. "Sure is foul out there," he said. "Just blowing over when I came back in. Promises to be a fine, clear night. Found me a back way in through an overgrown herb garden. Sort of wicket gate, unlocked." His eyes were wide with excitement, and Mildred noticed that his fingers were trembling as if he'd been through a shock.

"What part of the mansion did that lead to?" Ryan asked. "Kitchen?"

"Through there. But you'll see on my film. I can't tell you. Too amazing. Most bizarre thing. The cellars are real old, with a low roof, and damp and smelling of salt and decay and iron." He was grinning more broadly, wolfishly, almost hugging himself with what Krysty saw as a mix of excitement and fear. "I'll process the film tonight after we've eaten and show it to you tomorrow night. And I swear it'll blow your eyes out of your head."

He turned to Ryan. "Sorry, friend. Bit thoughtless. But you'll hear about it."

"Will you show film to Family?" Jak asked.

"Will I not?"

"Will they like it?"

"Will they like it, Mildred? Well, now, I'm not quite so sure that I can answer that. Have to wait awhile and see for ourselves, won't we?"

Everyone except Ryan, sitting still on the sofa, had gathered around Forde. None of them noticed the small side door to the room, almost hidden in the shadows, open and close.

"Have you seen some of the Family?" J.B. asked. "Apart from Elric?"

Ryan wondered why the man didn't answer, unable to see Forde rubbing his fingers against the side of his nose, smirking at the others.

"What? Will someone just tell me what the man's fuckin' saying?"

Krysty answered, her words overlapping his anger. "Sorry, lover. Johannes has taken some film today that he thinks is special. *Double* special. Something to do with finding his way into the cellars of the house. And with the Family. Says he'll show them to us tomorrow night after supper."

"When I've processed them," Forde said. "I doubt I'll ever take any better film for the rest of my life."

Norman's voice from the gloomy corner of the large room made them all start, not knowing when he'd come in, or how much he'd heard.

"Ladies and gentlemen. Dinner is served." His voice was completely flat and toneless.

Chapter Twenty-Five

They found that there was a new figure at the head of the long table, sitting with Elric at his right hand and an empty chair to his left.

There was no doubting his kinship with Elric, though Krysty thought, as she helped Ryan to a seat, that either of them could have been related to Jak.

The only real difference in their appearance from that of the teenager was in height. The two members of the Family were much taller than Jak. Elric was around six feet three inches tall, and the new member of the clan close to six and a half feet.

But both men were almost skeletally thin, with red-tinted eyes and hair as white as Sierra snow. Both had the same strange skin, pale as wind-washed ivory, with an odd delicacy to it, like the finest lace.

As the outlanders were shepherded in by the ever-attentive Norman, the two members of the Family both stood, the older one more slowly, as if his joints pained him. Krysty guessed that he was in his forties, but he seemed much more frail than Elric. He was staring at his guests with such intensity it worried her. She chose not to mention that to Ryan.

"Do sit down, outlanders. I am Thomas Cornelius. Welcome to Bramton and our home."

"You the father of Elric?" Dean asked.

"Yes, I am," Thomas replied.

Simultaneously Elric Cornelius said, "No, he isn't."

They looked at each other with a flash of what Krysty thought was anger. Then both of them offered brilliant smiles, revealing amazingly white and perfect teeth, one of the rarest sights in Deathlands, where most people had lost most of their teeth by the age of thirty.

"Yes, he is," Elric said.

Simultaneously Thomas Cornelius shook his head. "No, I am not his father."

"Want to try a third time?" Ryan asked sarcastically. "Mebbe both give us the same answer this time around?"

By now everyone was seated and the older Cornelius had gestured to Norman to begin serving the food.

He spoke to the company, gesturing with his hands. Mildred looked away, feeling that the long, bony fingers with the carefully manicured, sharp-tipped nails were almost hypnotizing with their fine elegance.

"Perhaps I should explain straightaway, to remove any ambiguity or confusion, just who we all are and how we come to be here."

"Be nice," Ryan said laconically, wincing as Krysty kicked him under the table.

"I understand your unhappiness, Ryan Cawdor. We have been poor hosts. Indeed, you will probably not meet all of the Family until tomorrow. Some are away and some busy flying about their own business."

Doc was watching the fragile-looking man speak. There was a nagging suspicion about what was going on in Bramton and in the mansion on the cliff top, but Doc knew better than to engage his mouth before his brain had functioned. From where he sat, Elric was clear in his direct line of sight, and he could have sworn that he detected a thin-lipped smile at Thomas's words.

It was there, and then it was gone, like a late frost under the rising sun.

Perhaps it had never been there.

Doc kept his silence.

Thomas was still speaking. "I hope that Norman has looked after you. The weather has been inclement today, I'm afraid. We never saw the sun at all." It was said with heavy regret.

Doc thought he saw the same fleeting grin from the younger albino.

Why? he thought.

"I gather the food has been less than adequate. This is because our tastes as a family are not as other people, and the kitchen gets little practice of cooking for norms. Neither Elric nor I will dine with you here."

The first course was a mix of what looked like local trout, with bread-fried catfish, served on a bed of boiled rice with snow peas on the side.

Krysty quietly told Ryan what it was, and how good it looked. "Best we've seen since we got to this place," she said, biting off a slice of the baked trout. "Mmm, that is so good."

"There is wine," Norman said, bringing around a dark green bottle, frosted with the cold. "This is from the oldest part of the cellars." He poured out a glass for everyone, hesitating at Dean, waiting for a nod of approval from Krysty.

Doc snatched up the long-stemmed crystal goblet and swilled the pale gold liquid around, dipping his beaky nose into it, inhaling deeply and sighing.

"It's a Sancerre. And a very good one unless I totally miss my guess."

Norman giggled. "You're the first visitor in the past fifty years to know that. Wait until you try the Lafitte with the roast beef."

Doc smiled, sipping appreciatively at the French wine, glowering at Dean, who'd gulped his half glass down in what seemed a single mouthful.

Thomas waited for a few moments before resuming his little speech.

"I take it from your reaction that we have got it right. The people in the kitchen will be told. "Now—" he spread his hands expansively "—you came here through the mat-trans system in the old Redoubt 47, did you not?"

It was a bombshell.

Ryan paused, a forkful of food halfway to his mouth. He heard his son gasp with shock, and someone else dropped a fork. Doc was his guess.

He actually smiled at the foolish way his mind was operating, wasting a fraction of a moment on wondering who'd dropped a fork, when they were sitting at a table with someone who'd guessed their most secret secret.

Or, he quickly figured, someone who actually *knew* their biggest secret.

For twenty beats of the heart, nobody in the room spoke a word. The only sound was a high-pitched giggle from Elric Cornelius, which was echoed by Norman.

Finally it was Thomas who spoke again. "I have no need to ask you if this is true. Even if I wasn't already certain, your reactions would have screamed it out as plainly as if it were daubed on that wall in letters ten feet high."

Elric suddenly began to clap his hands, very slowly. "Excellent, Thomas. I told you that the outlanders would sit there with...what was the old expression? Ah, yes, with egg on their faces."

Ryan's mind was racing now, in full combat mode, examining and rejecting dozens of hypotheses and possible scenarios, trying to see how dangerous the information was, and how seriously compromised it might make them.

But he couldn't see a major threat: two men and a butler and a few zombielike servants, no sec men and no sign of any blasters against them.

"You are calculating whether we present any threat to you, Ryan," Thomas said, smiling. "I can almost hear the wheels spinning inside your brain."

"You backtracked us?"

The papery face creased into something of a smile. "An intelligent guess. Partly true. I see no reason to tell you more than that." The smile vanished. "What greatly interests all of us is the extent to which you have mastered the controls. Where did you learn the secrets of Project Cerberus?"

"Upon my soul!" Doc exclaimed, pushing back his chair. "How did—"

Ryan interrupted him. "Enough, Doc. Let me do the talking here."

"Of course, my dear fellow. Of course. But scarcely anyone now living can have knowledge of Cerberus."

"Or Chronos," Elric teased.

"Or Overproject Whisper," Thomas stated.

"Or Enterprise Eternity," Elric added.

"No!" Thomas shouted. "I told you before that we do not mention that. Not to anyone."

"It can't hurt."

Both of them stood, glowering at each other, their eyes seeming to glow like burning rubies.

Thomas threw back his head and hissed at the younger man like an enraged panther. "No more!" He pointed a long-nailed finger. "Leave us, now."

"You don't have the authority without the rest of the kindred."

Thomas dropped his voice to a whisper, sitting and sipping from a goblet of a red wine, so dark that it was almost purple, staining his lips. "Do it," he said quietly.

Elric stalked to the door without a word, jostling Norman out of his way, pausing in the entrance to the dining hall and spinning to face the company. He bowed low from the shadows, his black clothes making him almost invisible.

"I was foolish," he said calmly, seeming completely in control. "Thomas was correct. My mention of Enterprise Eternity was unwise."

The door opened and closed, and he was gone.

Ryan knew that Doc wouldn't be able to resist asking the question. And here it came, reliable as the sun in a summer wheatfield.

"Might I ask you about Enterprise Eternity?" he said. "I am not familiar with it. Was it something that was being researched in the redoubt nearby?"

"It was. You failed to penetrate into the main part of the complex, did you not?"

Ryan nodded, assuming the question was being addressed to him. "We did. You found the open door." He made it a statement. "That was the first time any of us had ever encountered the mat-trans unit. That was what the signs said it was called."

"Indeed?" Ryan could almost see the raised snowy eyebrows, hearing the undisguised note of disbelief riding in the calm, gentle voice.

"Indeed, Thomas."

"Where did you make the jump from?"

"Jump?" Ryan gave himself a mental pat on the back for hurdling that one.

"What they called utilizing the gateways. How did you find yourself in the system?"

"Accident. Mind if we leave it at that? Just slammed the door in a hidden fortress and that sort of triggered something. We all passed out and when we came around we were someplace else. You know how it works? Or how many there are of them? Be good to control something like that. Give a man real power."

"It would, Ryan. We know much, but that is a secret that has escaped us."

While the conversation had been going on, the first course had been finished, and plates piled high with roast beef were brought in. Norman had served the Lafitte, getting a nod of delighted approbation from Doc.

Thomas had eaten nothing, contenting himself with sipping at his own wineglass.

After the discussion about the gateways he appeared to lose interest in the whole gathering, sitting with his snowy head slumped down on his chest, tapping at his goblet with the end of his forefinger.

Like Elric, Thomas was dressed completely in black, with a shirt of satin and pants of velvet tucked into polished black knee boots.

A slender golden chain encircled his neck, holding a medallion that looked to Krysty like a silver ankh. Every now and again Thomas would lift a hand to it, as though to reassure himself that it was still there.

The last course was a choice between a steaming cherry cobbler and a pecan pie, with or without cream. Most of them chose helpings of both.

With cream.

Thomas ate nothing.

Mildred noticed that the hooded eyes kept turning to Jak, as though Thomas were trying to work something out about the albino teenager.

Finally he leaned forward and spoke to the young man. "Jak Lauren?"

"Yeah," the youth said, wiping a dribble of cream from his chin with the sleeve of his coat.

"Your age?"

"Sixteen, going on seventeen."

"You have always had that hair and those eyes?"

"Sure."

"And you have lived only sixteen years. And every year you grow older, do you, Jak?"

"Course. Everyone does."

Thomas nodded, smiling gently at Jak. "Everyone does, lad. Indeed. My own words to myself, a hundred times a day. Everyone does."

He stood and walked slowly around the long table, patting Jak on the shoulder, whispering something to Norman as he reached the door.

"Tomorrow you will meet everyone. And I look forward to seeing your film, Johannes Forde."

The door shut behind him.

"How did he know about the film?" Forde said.

Chapter Twenty-Six

Ryan didn't know what had awakened him.

After the meal, Norman had brought around tiny glasses with a choice of sweet, sticky liqueurs, bright rainbow colors, deep green and cerulean blue and violet and a sickly gold. All of them tasted of sugar and fire.

Krysty had described them to Ryan, who'd shaken his head at the idea. He'd eaten well rather than wisely and was feeling liverish. But she'd pressed him and picked one for him that she said was the color of ripe oranges.

Norman had poured him a glassful and it hadn't tasted bad, orangy with a hint of chocolate and a slightly bitter aftertaste that Ryan couldn't identify. But on principle he'd left most of it, and Krysty had finished it for him, without, she said, letting the butler see.

They'd all gone up to their rooms. Both Ryan and Krysty were exhausted and promptly fell asleep.

Now, something had awakened him.

"What was that?" he whispered to Krysty.

But she didn't stir. He could tell from the sound of her heavy breathing that she was deeply asleep, lying on her back. Ryan nudged her in the ribs, but she muttered and half raised an arm to vaguely push him away.

"Guess I'll just have to go and take a look-see myself. Or a listen-hear. Never heard of that. Mebbe I just invented it."

His head ached and felt muzzy.

Sitting up and swinging his legs out of the bed brought a passing wave of nausea, but it didn't last. Ryan slept with most of his clothes on, from force of habit. But he was barefooted as he padded carefully across the room, tucking the SIG-Sauer into its holster as he moved, both hands outstretched to try to avoid bumping into the furniture.

Behind him, the sound of Krysty's snoring grew deeper and louder.

Ryan was pleased that he made the walk to the door without even touching anything, his right hand dropping onto the cold metal of the ornate brass handle at the first attempt.

The door opened without a sound. Ryan hesitated. The Cornelius mansion was generally in poor condition. But every door hinge and lock had been recently greased. It was an interesting fact to store away and examine later.

Behind him, he heard Krysty muttering something about a milch cow.

He still had no idea what had awakened him, but the short hairs at his nape were prickling, and he knew better than to ignore such a warning.

The house seemed silent, except for the inevitable faint creakings and settling sounds.

Ryan had managed, during their time with the Family, to build up an accurate plan in his mind. Both Krysty and Dean had helped him, taking him on a repeated tour of the first three floors, telling him where all the doors and barred windows and sets of stairs were, who was in each room.

He eased himself into the corridor, head turning, alert for any noise.

A full set of armor was just to his left, and he reached out to touch the cold metal of the breastplate. To his right hung a large portrait of a stern-faced man. Doc had described it to him, saying he thought it was by an inferior Dutch artist called Van Helsing.

He recalled that Norman had shown them all up to this floor, and had repeated his warning about wandering in the night. J.B. had asked him where the threat might be, and the little man had skipped sideways to avoid the question.

"Who knows where danger might be? Who knows what evil lurks in the hearts of men?"

Mildred had given him some sort of answer to that. What had it been?

"Only the shadows know," Ryan breathed. Something like that, anyway.

He began to stalk along the passage, unconsciously closing his "good" eye, as if he were making himself blind and was, that way, kind of controlling his own destiny.

There was a long bench seat next, and he rounded it, barely brushing its surface with the tips of his fingers. The room where Mildred and the Armorer slept was on his right. Jak was opposite, and Dean immediately beyond that.

Ryan hesitated, fixing his position in his mind. A bathroom was to the right, its brass handle cool against his hand. Then there was a staircase that J.B. believed led up to the banned top floor of the rambling mansion.

But it was kept locked.

A floorboard squeaked under his bare feet and Ryan froze, putting out his arm to steady himself, feeling the carved wood of the heavy door, just as it had been described to him.

With one exception.

It moved at his touch, swinging away from Ryan, taking him so much by surprise that he stumbled and nearly fell. There was a breath of cold, dark wind. For a moment Ryan had an odd thought. He knew that he was near the attics and lofts of the building, yet the wave of air smelled as though it came from deep underground, scented by the buried roots of old trees.

He stood statue still, hand on the butt of the blaster, waiting.

The house was quiet.

Unless . . .

Was there a faint noise from somewhere ahead of him? Johannes Forde's room was last along there, filled with all his movie equipment, which he'd insisted on having carried from the stabled wag.

Beyond that was a heavily barred window covered with an ornamental tapestry. Dean had described that to his father.

"This gaudy slut, with hardly any clothes, though there's bits of bushes and tree over all her...you know, Dad. So you can't see nothing." Ryan had corrected the boy's grammar. "And there's this swan, with a long neck and yellow beak." Dean had sniggered with embarrassment. "And you just wouldn't believe, Dad, what the swan's doing to the slut."

Ryan wasn't sure whether he did believe his son, though Doc had confirmed the subject matter, making a comment that was triple obscure, though he seemed to think that it was amusing. He told Ryan that the picture on the tapestry was called *Take Me to Your Leader*.

Like most of the old man's so-called jokes, Ryan didn't understand it.

There was a draft from the opposite side of the passage, where Ryan remembered there was a fireplace that Krysty had said looked like it had been sealed off and hadn't had a fire in it for a hundred years.

That might have been right, but the chimney had to still be open. The cold night wind surging down it was very strong, ruffling at Ryan's dark curly hair.

There was a knocking noise ahead of Ryan, irregular and muffled, sounding like a shutter that hadn't been properly fastened and was banging in the rising breeze.

He hesitated once more, concentrating his attention on making sure where he was.

One more door. An empty room, locked. Then came the final bedroom, with Forde sleeping in it.

If there was any nocturnal danger in the house, it would be in either Forde's room, or in the supposedly empty chamber next door to it.

Ryan drew the SIG-Sauer. Though he was blind, he didn't need to worry about whether the automatic blaster was fully loaded. If a single one of the fifteen 9 mm rounds had been missing from the mag, he'd have known it immediately. It was like having a joint sliced off your little finger. No way you wouldn't notice that.

Now he was shuffling along, crablike, trying to keep his back to the wall of the passage, feeling behind himself with his left hand for the door of the room next to Johannes's, finding it.

Locked.

The sensation of danger was almost overpoweringly strong and he took several slow, deep breaths, steadying himself for whatever it was he might face.

His shoulder knocked against something that rocked and began to fall.

"Big pot on a stand filled with a bunch of dried-out dead flowers."

Now he remembered that Krysty had mentioned it to him earlier in the day.

Despite his loss of sight, Ryan's reflexes were still rattler fast, and he whipped round, reaching with his free hand, grabbing at the ceramic stand that held the pot and steadying it. He brought up his right hand, the muzzle of the blaster making a tiny chinking sound as it touched the heavy pot.

But it didn't fall.

Ryan edged around it, closer to Forde's room. Some kind of instinct told him that the door was open.

He breathed in again, trying to taste the air.

The brackish scent of a subterranean vault was there, and something else, something stale and bitter. And a third smell. Hot and salt. It was unmistakable, once smelled, never forgotten.

There was blood in the air.

Ryan considered turning and fumbling his way back to his own room to wake Krysty, get her to wake the others, make sure that everyone was armed and ready for the danger, whatever it might be.

While he would remain behind, sitting on the bed, blind and useless.

"No," he mouthed, convincing himself that the threat to Forde was so obvious and so immediate that it had to be confronted now. After all, he could pull the trigger on the SIG-Sauer and its angry bark would wake the whole house.

He moved closer to the doorway.

The hand that gripped his wrist was so powerful that Ryan gasped in pain and shock. His fingers opened and the blaster fell to the carpet. There was a rustling like the wind through the feathers of a huge condor, and the smell of dirt and decay became so intense that Ryan coughed and nearly puked.

He thought that he heard a voice, rasping the single word "Nooooo..." but he couldn't be certain.

Ryan reached for the hilt of the panga sheathed on his hip, before realizing that he'd left it behind in the bedroom.

The grip on his lower arm was numbing. No norm could have such strength, making Ryan aware that he'd been attacked by some sort of murderous mutie.

He tried to snatch at where the man's groin might be, but his hand became tangled in material, and it was easily parried.

A second hand reached for his throat, pincering off the breath.

Ryan felt himself actually lifted clear of the floor and pressed against the paneled wall so that he couldn't even kick out at his enemy. It was like being a rabbit gripped in the paws of a gigantic grizzly.

He was helpless, choking, blood pounding in his ears and behind his eyes, his tongue feeling like it had swollen, pushing out between engorged lips.

He couldn't make a sound. All of his friends were within a scant dozen yards of him, and not one of them would know of his passing.

Ryan felt all of the lines going down throughout his brain and body. There was little pain, except for the pressure on his throat. His eye seemed to be on the edge of exploding from its socket. There was blood on his face and neck, seeping from eye, ears, mouth and nose.

Though he was trying to flail with his fists at the man holding him, his blows seemed to be filled with cotton candy and had no effect at all.

There was a roaring in his ears, then there was silence.

SWIMMING ON A secret ocean, rising and falling on the slow, measureless swell. A gray shadow on the sea and gray clouds floating over his head. No hint of sunlight.

It was very quiet and peaceful, and Ryan found himself content to drift. The fact that he was slowly sinking into the cold water didn't matter. The sooner that happened, then the better it would be. No more pain.

"Ryan."

It would be good to lie still in the primordial ooze with the blind eels.

"Come on, man!"

Something had brushed against his shoulder, jerking him around in a most uncomfortable way. Ryan screwed up his face and tried to push the creature away.

"By the Three Kennedys, come back to me!"

The voice was familiar to Ryan, but it was a puzzle why Dr. Theophilus Algernon Tanner should be out on the rolling billows with him. And why would good old Doc be behaving like such a bastard, ruining Ryan's rest?

"I know that you can hear me, Ryan. Do make an effort, or your attacker might return and complete his murderous task at any moment. Wake up."

"Fuck off, Doc."

The voice was cracked and feeble, like a forgotten godling in an abandoned tomb.

Ryan could hear relief in Doc's voice. "Excellent, my dear fellow, excellent. Let the anger flow, Master Cawdor. Up to the surface."

It really was Doc and he was struggling to lift Ryan into a sitting position, babbling of a murderous attacker. There was a memory of being thrown against a wall, fingers like steel traps, circling his throat.

"Triple strong, Doc," he whispered.

"The man who did this to you?"

Ryan nodded. "Yeah. Shoot first. Wake others."

"Wouldn't care to leave you here. In case..."

Ryan had opened his eye and for a moment he thought he detected a flicker of golden light above him, like the bright flames of a torch on the wall.

But when he closed his eye and opened it again, the light was gone into the dark.

And he had slipped back into unconsciousness.

Chapter Twenty-Seven

When he came around again he was lying on a bed, sensing a number of people surrounding him.

"Krysty?" he breathed, just able to hear his own voice dropping into stillness.

"Here, lover. Don't try and talk. Your throat's been badly bruised. Mildred thinks the voice box could've been damaged. If Doc hadn't come along..."

"Thanks, Doc."

"Think nothing of it, dear friend. I only wish I had come a little earlier, when my trusty Le Mat could have chilled your lethal enemy."

"You see him?"

"No. When I ventured into the corridor my door stuck and I had to push it hard for several seconds. I don't know what woke me. You were lying down at the far end, in the darkness beneath a wall lamp. I thought you dead." The old man's voice broke with emotion.

"Not yet. Critical but not desperate."

J.B.'s voice cut through. "You got any idea what hit you, Ryan? The attic door was locked, and the shutters and bars in place. Could only have come in from the lower floors. From outside the house."

Ryan shook his head. "No. Attic door was open."

"Locked when Doc fetched us to you."

"Is everyone safe? Dean there?"

"Sure, Dad." A hand rested on his arm.

"Forde not here." Jak's voice came from somewhere over near the window.

Ryan remembered. "Anyone see him?"

A moment of silence. He could imagine everyone looking at everyone else.

The Armorer answered Ryan. "Doesn't look like anyone saw him. Too worried for you. Guess he must still be in his room. Probably slept right through the trouble."

Ryan swung his legs over the side of the bed. A hand reached and steadied him. "Noise I heard was right by his room, and I was outside it when I was attacked."

"I'll go look," Jak stated.

Ryan shook his head. "No. Not on your own. J.B., go with him. Take the Uzi with you. Whatever got me isn't going to be stopped by a single bullet. I never felt such strength and raw power in my whole life."

"Should we all go?" Mildred asked. "Safety in numbers and all that stuff."

Ryan shook his head again. "No. We were told not to wander at night. We can find out in the morning what might have happened. Less disturbance now, the better."

"Might be a clue on the movie that Johannes took," Dean suggested.

Ryan reached and rubbed at his sore neck, wincing at the pain. "That's . . . I'd forgotten the film. He was pleased, wasn't he? Said he'd discovered something that would amaze us. And that he'd done some secret filming.''

''Thomas Cornelius knew about the film, didn't he?'' Mildred said slowly, thinking back. ''And Johannes wondered how he knew. Remember?''

''Sure,'' Ryan answered. ''And something woke me. Something down that end.''

''Didn't wake the rest of us,'' Krysty said. ''I slept much more deeply than usual. And I got a headache behind the eyes. You think we might've been—''

''Drugged!'' Mildred exclaimed. ''Those pretty, sweet liqueurs Norman offered.''

''But we all had some of that,'' Dean said. ''How come Dad woke up when he did?''

''Because I never finished my drink. Gave it to you, lover, didn't I?''

''Yes, you did. Gaia! Don't like the smell of all this, friends.''

J.B. stood and worked the action on the Uzi. ''You ready, Jak?''

''Sure.''

''Then, let's go recce.''

Ryan sat again, waiting quietly for the two friends to return. The attack had left him close to the edge of clinical shock, and he wished that he could have something hot and sweet to drink. It struck him that he didn't even know how much of the night had gone by.

''What's the time?'' he asked.

"Close on five," Doc replied. "The light through yonder window is beginning to break and it is the dawn."

"Want to lie down, Ryan?"

"No, thanks, Mildred. Throat's feeling a bit better." He decided not to mention the illusion that he'd had out in the passage after the near throttling, the moment when he'd thought that he could see the light of the torch. Since it hadn't lasted long enough for him to even hope, there seemed no point in mentioning it to the others.

There was no conversation while they waited for Jak and J.B. to return. Mildred walked quietly over to the door and peered along the gloomy corridor.

"Nothing," she whispered. "Looks like they must've gone into Forde's bedroom."

Ryan lay down, straining his hearing to try to catch any sound from outside.

But both the Armorer and Jak were masters at silent movement, and they were back in the room with the door closed behind them before he heard any clue to their return.

"He all right?" The question came from Dean. "Is Johannes all right?"

Ryan knew.

As soon as he heard the long hesitation from Jak and J.B., he knew.

It was the Armorer who finally broke the silence. "He's chilled."

"Master Forde is dead?" Doc said disbelievingly. "How can he be dead?"

"Easy," Jak replied. "Murdered."

"Should I go look at him?" Mildred asked. "Anything I could do for him?"

J.B. answered her. "Nothing. We tried to close his eyes, but they were so wide the lids wouldn't clamp down. He'd been butchered. Seems likely it was the same man or men that Ryan encountered in the passage."

"Signs of great strength?" Ryan felt himself beginning to sweat again with the instant memory of the immense power of the thing that had gripped him and held him so tight.

"Yeah." Jak coughed and cleared his throat. "Head turned clear around to look over back. Spine snapped like dry twig. Beaten. Ribs so broke the jagged ends stuck out through skin."

"Arms broken," J.B. added. "Thighbone protruding through the pants he'd been wearing. Face as bruised and black as a high-plains thundercloud. Doubt that you'd have recognized him if you hadn't known."

"Drying blood all over bed. Came from eyes and nose and ears and mouth, well as places where bones snapped out of skin. Bad sight."

Jak went to the corner of the room and poured himself a cup of water from the blue-and-white bowl, dashing some of it onto his face.

The Armorer sat on the bed beside Ryan, touching him on the shoulder. "One other thing."

"His films and stuff."

"Yeah. That a guess?"

"Sort of. I wondered why the killer would go for Johannes Forde, rather than any of us. And why he'd been put right away from the rest of us with an empty room between him and us. Like they wanted him isolated."

"You think it was the Family?" Krysty asked.

Ryan moved his head from side to side, feeling the tightness in his throat. "Johannes took films. Last time, Elric didn't appear on them. Some technical problem. Could be they really don't like being put on movies."

"Why?" the Armorer asked.

"Could be lots of reasons," Ryan replied. "I'm starting to wonder if this place is a fraud. Their history. Barons for so long. Could be they're all well-known chillers and they just don't want their faces flashed around on film in case they get recognized.

He could sense that his idea hadn't gone down all that well among the friends.

"They've smashed all his equipment," J.B. said. "All the film's been pulled out and mangled and torn. Doesn't look like any could be saved."

"Projector broken, as well?" Doc probed. "Guess they'd want that spoiled, too."

"You got a theory about them, Doc?" Ryan asked. "Let's all share it."

The old man shook his head. "I am only too aware of the reputation that I have with all of you. A foolish, time-trawled dotard whose brain and imagination carry him too often into dark woods and pastures peculiar. No, don't contradict me." He laughed. "Not

that any of you were about to do so. No, I have an idea
that falls into the land of faerie and should not yet be
exposed to the ridicule of others." He hesitated a moment. "But, whatever my guess, I can only urge the
greatest caution while in this place and with these
people. The greatest caution."

NORMAN BROUGHT THEM the tragic news of the mur-
der. It was just a little after six and the building was
stirring, the smell of fresh baking bread drifting up
from the first floor.

Ryan had insisted that they should be ignorant of
the death of Johannes Forde, to avoid any suspicion
falling on them. So they were all suitably shocked at
the announcement.

"We believe that someone from the ville, who bore
a grudge against us, broke in. A door had been forced
around the back by the garden. Master Thomas has
suggested that the films taken by Johannes might have
upset the villagers. Poor, sentimental and superstitious folks. They could have believed that Johannes
was, somehow, robbing them of their spirits."

"Their immortal souls," Doc said. "Is that not a
better way of putting it?"

"Perhaps. Yes, perhaps."

Ryan had pressed the butler over the precise manner of Forde's passing.

"He had been badly beaten, as though by a strong
man in a rage, with all of his possessions scattered and
torn apart. We shall ask questions in Bramton. Oh,
yes, indeed, we shall."

"Nobody saw or heard anything?" Ryan asked. "Must've made some noise, way you tell it?"

Norman shifted uncomfortably from foot to foot. He wore rings on most of his fingers and they were clicking nervously, one against another.

"The house has thick walls and floors and ceilings," he said finally.

"And there was nothing at all left of his films?" Mildred asked.

"Sadly, not. It would have been interesting to view the material he shot here."

"But how...?" began Dean, who was sitting on the bed beside his father, who reached across and rested his hand gently on the boy's shoulder, his fingers gripping him tightly, cutting off the words.

"My son was about to ask how long it would be before breakfast. Not the most tactful thing for him to say after such sad news of a friend."

"I... Yeah, I guess it was. Sorry, Dad. Stupe of me not to think."

"That's all right."

Norman giggled, the high heels of his shoes rapping out a positive fandango of nerves. "Well, I can give the lad the answer. For those who feel like eating, there will be a light breakfast served in ten minutes' time."

"We'll be there," Ryan said, standing, his hand still on Dean's shoulder.

"What about burial of Forde?" Jak asked. "You look after that for us?"

"Of course we can. He shall have as good a burial as any chrisom child."

Ryan nodded. "Thanks."

NORMAN HAD GONE ON AHEAD, leaving them to make their own way along the passage and down the wide stairs. Dean insisted on helping his father.

"Wouldn't mind a look at Johannes's body," Mildred said. "Be just a minute."

She was gone for about three minutes, while they waited for her near the top of the staircase.

"Not just beaten to hell and back," she said. "Someone also drained most of the blood from his carcass."

Ryan picked his careful way down the stairs, his mind trying to unravel this latest macabre twist.

"Really bright sun," said Krysty at his side. "Spearing through the shutters here."

Ryan could feel the warmth and he turned his head in that direction, hesitating as he thought that he actually saw a glint of molten golden light from his right eye.

But, like before, he couldn't be sure, and the moment quickly passed.

Chapter Twenty-Eight

A woman sat at the head of the table when they reached the dining hall.

Krysty saw instantly that she was from the same genetic stock as Elric and Thomas, looking as though she might lie between them in terms of age. Possibly in her middle to late thirties, was Krysty's guess.

Her hair was as fine as spun silk, so white it glittered like polished silver. She was close to six feet, wearing a black dress of embroidered satin, with a high collar. Her skin was like Elric's and Thomas's, tight and white, like parchment, stretched over sharp cheekbones like straight razors.

Like Jak's, her eyes were a deep smoldering crimson, set in deep sockets. The heavy silver ring on the third finger of her left hand was shaped like a human skull, with a blood opal in its forehead.

"My name is Mary Cornelius. I was so sorry to hear of the tragic, untimely death of your companion." Her voice was soft and warm.

"Most death is untimely," Ryan replied. "But we thank you for your thoughts."

"Sit next to me, Ryan Cawdor. I can help you with your food and you can tell me something of yourself."

"I help him with the food," Krysty stated, not bothering to conceal the coldness in her voice.

"Can you help him to see again, Krysty Wroth?"

"What?"

"I think that you heard me. You don't suffer from deafness, Krysty. Or poor sight. Indeed, we believe that you can see, if that's the proper word for your unusual skill, better and further than most norms can."

"Are you implying that you can help Ryan to see again? That it?"

The woman gestured for Krysty to help Ryan to the seat at her side. "I do not imply. You and Dr. Wyeth have admitted defeat over the problem of seeing. I believe that we might be able to do a little better."

"Impossible," Mildred snapped. "Right now Ryan is blind. The damage to his eye could heal itself in the next three or four days. Or it might not heal at all."

"You have your beliefs, Dr. Wyeth. We believe in other powers."

"You can make me see again?" Ryan said, hating that he stood there like a spare prick at a gaudy wedding while others talked about and around him.

Mary Cornelius looked at him. Despite his lack of sight, he could almost feel her eyes burning into him, seeming to penetrate through the core of his brain.

"I think so. After we have finished eating, you must come to my room and we shall see." A new note of sudden anger entered her voice. "Norman, there is light piercing through a gap between the draperies and the shutters. Close it."

"Dark as a dungeon down here in the mine," Doc said. "Get any darker and I'll bump into myself coming back. See mice elf in a glass very damned darkly indeed. Why not throw back the draperies? It's a lovely morning. Bit of bright sunlight never hurt anybody, did it?"

The woman leaned forward in her seat, staring intently at the old-timer. "There are things about many of you that puzzle us. The white hair and ruby eyes of Jak. The medical skills of the black woman. The seeing of the redhead. And you, Dr. Tanner, you puzzle us a great deal. If you stay here long enough, I think we would all be eager to ask you some searching questions. You interest us."

Doc took a half step back, as though a whip had been raised to his face. "You don't..." he began. "But I disremember what you don't do."

Ryan found himself sitting down next to Mary Cornelius. She had doused herself in a light but potent perfume. His guess was lily of the valley. But beneath it there was an unpleasant smell, the same dank, subterranean odor that seemed to fill every room of the mansion.

"What do you want to eat, Ryan? Trout or chicken or veal or prawns? Soup or croissants? Eggs Benedict or a plate of *huevos rancheros?* When you came to us, the skills of the kitchen had been—how shall we say?—had been mislaid. Now they have been found again."

"Plain omelet would do just fine," he replied, knowing that it was something that he could eat without making himself look stupid.

"We have some cuts of beef that might prove a tad underdone for your palate."

"No. Just omelet."

AS HE ATE, picking at the cool, leathery omelet, Ryan struggled to get events into some kind of perspective, trying to make sense from what had happened.

What was happening.

But he was bewildered. They had entered an isolated ville, not far from a well-preserved redoubt that seemed to have been used for high-tech, top-secret military research, research that was somehow linked to the strange members of the Cornelius Family.

The people in Bramton were, so he'd been told, more like zombies than norms.

The Family had pressed them to visit their mansion on the cliff top, but they hardly ever saw their hosts. Either late in the evening or early in the morning, with all of the draperies tugged tight shut.

Now there was the hideous slaughter of Johannes Forde, shortly after he had boasted of taking secret films of the Family, films that had been destroyed along with the man himself.

Last of all, this woman, Mary Cornelius, had delivered unveiled hints that she could heal his damaged sight, could make him see again.

He felt around the plate with the tines of his fork, checking that there was no more food left on it. He set down the cutlery and picked up his coffee mug.

Krysty's words were quiet in his ear. "You feeling all right, lover?"

Before he could reply he heard the paper-thin voice of Mary Cornelius, showing once again the uncanny hearing that the Family seemed to have. "He's as well as can be expected, Krysty. But with my help he can be so much better."

"If you can make him see again, then you've got my support, every step of the way."

The albino woman's voice was dismissive and patronizing. "Thank you, my dear, but I believe that we can manage perfectly well without your support."

Krysty instantly pushed back her chair, the legs grating on the floor. "Why don't you go take a flying fuck at a rolling pretzel, lady?" she said, storming away from the refectory table, the sound of her heels diminishing until they ceased altogether.

"Dad?" Dean's voice sounded worried.

"It's all right, son."

"What a sadly disappointing reaction," Mary said. "I had thought better of her. Still..." Ryan could hear her crumpling a napkin and dropping it by her plate. "Let me lead you to my room, Ryan. There is so much that we can do for each other. Unless..."

"Unless what?"

"Unless you are frightened of me."

"Course not." He turned to J.B. and the others. "Get together for a talk in our room, around noon."

"Sure," the Armorer replied. "Take care now."

Mary's hand was on his right arm, her grip surprisingly powerful for a woman, as she led him across the galleried room, up the main stairs.

They walked along a carpeted corridor, stopping in front of what Ryan guessed was the entrance to the topmost story of the mansion. He heard a jingle of keys and a door swinging open, releasing another wave of the stinking air.

"Up here," she said, helping him through, then locking the door behind them. "Nearly there."

NORMAN HAD WAITED until his mistress had taken Ryan out of the dining hall before he tugged back the heavy velvet draperies, releasing clouds of pale dust, the motes floating in the rectangles of bright sunlight.

"There," he said. "Let there be light and there was light. Makes one feel quite like a little god, doesn't it?"

"The lady somewhat dislikes sunshine, does she not?" Doc asked.

Norman picked his way around the room, stopping in front of the old man. "Did you hear the fable of the heron whose beak was so long that he had it trapped in a jar of gold, and thus he perished? It's a parable of inquisitiveness, Dr. Tanner. A moral for us all."

"The moral being to keep your beak out of other people's affairs," Mildred said.

The butler nodded, the smile vanishing from his face like that of a rich man encountering a beggar. "Precisely. I have lived as long as I have in the employ of the Cornelius Family only by studiously closing my eyes and ears ... and my mouth, when I felt it proper to do so."

"Proper? That another word for cowardly?" Jak asked sarcastically.

"Cowardly is another word for keeping your head when all about are losing theirs, Master Lauren."

THE ROOM WAS large and cold. That was Ryan's immediate reaction as Mary closed the door. His keen hearing caught the faint click of a key turning in a lock, and he dropped his hand to the reassuring butt of the big SIG-Sauer.

"Here we are, Ryan. Can I help you to a chair? Does the chamber feel at all chill?"

"Yeah. Cold and damp. Like the Banbury Hotel back in the ville."

He felt her shudder, transmitted along his arm. "There is a fire laid. I can light it."

"Be good."

He eased himself into a deep armchair, feeling the worn brocade that covered it, sitting still while she bustled around. He heard the hiss of the material of her dress, the striking of a self-light and then the crackling of tinder and dried twigs. There came the faint smell of green wood smoking.

Mary coughed, waving her hands in front of her face. "Dear me, such a smell."

That was the moment that Ryan realized they weren't alone in the room. Someone else was fighting to control his or her breathing, finding the cloud of billowing smoke intrusive, trying hard not to cough.

Two others.

At least two others.

"There," the woman said finally. "The wood's caught at last. It was hard to see with only one guttering oil lamp to light the room."

"Why not draw the draperies?" Ryan asked. "Seems it's a good bright morning."

She totally ignored his question.

"Once it's warmed up a little, we can get on with our business."

THE SIX FRIENDS FOUND themselves back once more in the warren of high-ceilinged rooms with their jigsaw puzzles and antique rotting books.

"Least can get out," Jak said.

"Remember what happened to poor Johannes when he went outside. It was only yesterday." Mildred stood alone by the windows, looking across the silvery gray rocks, her eyes falling to the shadowed river far below.

"Dad be all right?" Dean asked, standing by Krysty, who was looking up at the rows of moldering volumes. "Can they make him see?"

Krysty shook her head, the fiery sentient hair clinging tightly to her nape, a sure sign of an atmosphere of threat and menace.

Mildred heard the question and turned from the casement. "Ryan's blindness is in God's hands, Dean. I can't pretend otherwise. Back in the predark times, folks expected doctors to have a total and absolute knowledge. Medicine isn't like that. Take a crude example. Put a .38 round through one man's brain and he dies instantly. Second man lives but is a vegetable. Third man recovers, untouched. Same with your father's loss of sight. In the next two or three days we'll know, one way or the other, whether Ryan has good luck, or no luck.''

FROM THE WEIGHT of the crystal goblet, Ryan knew that it was old and of top quality. He tapped the edge with his nail, hearing it ring like a fine bell.

Mary was at his side. He could smell her body. There was the odd staleness, overlaid with feral sweat. Despite the strangeness of his position, Ryan found himself reacting to her scent of sexual excitement. And he was still aware of the presence of at least one other person in the room.

Liquid gurgled into the glass, the flavor of peppermint filling the bedroom. Ryan recalled the suggestion that the liqueurs the previous evening had been drugged.

"Drink up, Ryan," Mary said, her hand feather light on his shoulder.

Chapter Twenty-Nine

Ryan had drunk the liqueur. Trader often said that in a situation where you were going to have to do something, then you might as well do it willingly, with a good grace.

And watch your chance for retaliation.

The peppermint flavor almost covered up the slightly bitter aftertaste of the drink. Almost, but not quite.

Ryan contrived to spill some of the fiery liquor, but he caught a whisper of warning from one of the other people in the room with himself and Mary.

"Take care," the woman said very quietly, her fingers tightening a little on his shoulder. "Don't want it to go to waste. It's so fine, so rare. One of the last vintages from before the days of skydark. Let me fill your glass once more. There. Now finish it."

Ryan drained it, feeling his head already beginning to swim a little from the combination of alcohol and the drug that he was certain it contained.

"Feeling dizzy, Ryan?"

"Yeah. Some. You put some kind of sleeper in the drink, didn't you?"

"Possibly."

Mary's voice was coming from a long way off, sounding as if it drifted into his mind from the back of an underground cavern filled with dark water.

"Anything happen . . . me, others'll see . . ."

"I'm sure they will," the voice said, echoing around and around his brain.

"Blasters good enough to . . ."

Then the darkness rose, boiling around him, and Ryan slipped away into it.

"DELIGHTFUL THOUGH these jigsaw puzzles are, recapturing the many happy hours that I spent with my darling Emily locked away in such activity, I feel a deep unease racking my aged bones. Do none of you others feel this? Am I quite alone in my suspicions? Krysty, my dear lady, do you not?"

The redheaded woman sat by the empty grate, her booted legs stretched out in front of her, head back on the antimacassar, green eyes closed.

She answered without stirring.

"Sure, Doc. We all feel it."

"But do none of you share the midnight terror that possesses me?"

"What talking about?" asked Jak, who had been wandering around the room like a caged snow panther.

Mildred looked up from the new jigsaw that she and J.B. had just begun, an infinitely complex design of birds and lizards in black and white.

"You got a theory about the Cornelius Family, Doc? Like to hear it. Find out if it matches one that I'm developing. What do you reckon?"

"I would prefer it if you were to tell me what your theory is first, Dr. Wyeth."

"No, Doc. I'm not going to risk looking triple stupe. You show me yours and I'll show you mine. That's fair, isn't it? What do you say, Doc?"

"I say that I am going to take a recreational stroll about the grounds. Perhaps I may even venture as far as the attractive little village of Bramton. Until I have found some facts to support my theory."

"Can I come, Doc?" Dean asked. "Going ape crazy hangin' around this old dump."

"I'll join too," Jak said, turning back from the window. "Get some good bayou air into lungs."

"Very well, my *compadres*. We three, we happy three, we band of brothers. One for all and all for one. My house is your house." He stopped, looking confused. "But I wander from the trail. Yes, let us go and then we can report back to Ryan. Let us hope we shall find him much recovered."

RYAN TRIED TO LIFT A HAND to check whether his right eye was open or closed, but an enormous weight seemed to have attached itself to his wrist. To both wrists.

To both ankles.

The drug still held him in its power, but he had recovered a sort of consciousness. It was a feeling a bit like making a jump, where your brain was swirling in free-fall inside the bony shelter of the skull.

"He's coming around."

Ryan partly recognized the voice, a man. Perhaps the one called Thomas.

"Keep quiet, Brother," Mary said.

Ryan tried to speak, but his tongue had turned to wet string and his voice came out as a mouselike squeak. He didn't bother to try again. Since he was helpless and tied to what he figured was a bed, there wasn't really all that much that he might want to say.

"Can you hear me, Ryan?" He didn't respond to her voice. A hand shook him by the shoulder, and he mumbled inaudibly under his breath. "I know you can hear me."

"Yeah . . ." he drawled.

"Good. I have brought you here for one reason only. I will explain it, though I doubt you are clear-headed enough to understand me."

He could feel that his eye was opening and closing, but could see nothing.

"Blind," he managed to mumble.

"Yes, you are blind, Ryan Cawdor. And we fear that you will always stay that way. There is nothing that we can do to help you. Our makers would have had the skills, but they lie long beneath the good earth."

Makers? Ryan thought, confused. What could the woman possibly mean by using that strange word? Perhaps he hadn't actually heard her properly.

"We were safe inside our capsules when the missiles fell, scattering their seeds of death, blighting the land and anything that walked or crawled upon it. Safe inside Redoubt 47, where we were created."

Again an odd usage. Created? The drug was so powerful that Ryan couldn't hang on to a single thought for more than a few seconds. Part of him wanted to pursue this mystery, but most of him knew it was impossible.

"Don't waste time with this idle talk." The voice was a man's, insistent. "Get on with the mixing."

Ryan closed his eye and slipped back into deep unconsciousness.

IT WAS A FINE ENOUGH DAY, though the sky had clouded over and it had become humid. Doc complained as he mopped sweat from his brow with his swallow's-eye kerchief. Dean didn't seem bothered by it, and Jak positively flourished in it.

"Like old times," he said. "When was young. Summers always like this."

"When I was a young stripling, the summers were longer and sunnier than now. Blue from coast to coast from morn unto night. The air smelled sweet and birds sang. Grass grew and the corn was as high as... I disremember how high. But it was not this blighted wen that is Deathlands."

Nobody stopped or questioned them as they left the mansion through the unbolted front door and began to stroll down the steep, crumbling path that led them above the river, toward the settlement. Smoke was already coming from the houses, and they could hear the hollow clunking of an ax somewhere deep among the trees. Down on the trout farm, they could make out the silvery flashing of the surging fish as a couple of Bramton women fed them from baskets.

"What you think of Family?" Jak asked, casually tossing one of his leaf-bladed throwing knives from hand to hand, occasionally launching it with a whipping, vicious underhand throw, striking the center of the trunk of one of the live oaks that lined the track.

"I think we flirt with deep and dangerous water. And I fear for our bodies and for our immortal souls. That's the truth, my dear friends."

There was a group of young children playing catch with some round pebbles, their backs to the approaching trio of companions.

They were so involved in their game that Doc, Jak and Dean were within a dozen feet of them before they noticed the crunching of boots on the highway.

Then one of them turned around, staring at Doc, his face without expression. He looked at Dean, with a similar lack of reaction. And, finally, the urchin touched on Jak.

His eyes narrowed as he took in the pale skin, the burning ruby eyes and the mane of snow-white hair.

"Family!" he screamed, rising to his feet and haring off down the main street of the ville. He was followed by all his friends, every one of them boggling at the albino teenager, ignoring Dean and Doc in their obvious terror of the youth.

"Perhaps you should be more careful of your personal freshness, dear boy," Doc joked.

"Because I look like Cornelius men," Jak said flatly. "What kind hold they got over ville?"

"That is precisely what fascinates me, Master Lauren. But I doubt that we shall find a satisfactory answer from any of these poor wretches."

"We still going into Bramton?" Dean asked.

Doc and Jak glanced at each other, the old man answering the boy. "Though I fear that it's a waste of time, we can but try. After all, we do not have anywhere better to go."

THE NEXT TIME RYAN recovered consciousness, he was surprised, to put it mildly, to realize that he was having sex with someone.

Not making love.

Certainly not that.

And it would be more accurate to say that someone was having sex with him.

He was still spread-eagled, tied to the corners of the bed, with thick cords that held him motionless. Someone was squatting astride him, gripping his thighs with heels, riding him like a stallion, rising and falling on a diamond-cutting erection, someone who had amazing control of her internal muscles and who was milking him dry, bringing him rapidly toward the brink of an astoundingly powerful orgasm.

"Yes, take him, Sister." It was the voice of one of the Cornelius men, thickened and hoarse with the sickly excitement of the voyeur. "Take him."

For a moment Ryan felt his erection begin to shrink and diminish. The woman felt it, as well, and she leaned forward over him, naked breasts brushing his chest, her powerful hands roaming over his body.

Despite her charnel-house breath, Ryan felt himself recover, despite himself, hating her with a bitter loathing for using him like a gaudy slut, detesting himself even more for becoming so painfully aroused.

He was very close to the edge.

Again she somehow sensed it, and her vagina began to tremble around him, fluttering like a butterfly. "Give me your essence, that we can all live," she whispered, her voice sounding drugged and ecstatic.

Ryan sensed the watchers drawing closer to the bed, tasting their sweat and their stinking breath, hanging over him like a foul miasma. But there was nothing he could do to hold himself back. The woman's power was awesome.

Ryan had never bothered to try to keep track of his sexual activity, but since his first experience in his early teens, there had to have been hundreds of partners.

Making love with Krysty was consistently the best that he'd ever known.

But there had never, ever been anything quite like Mary Cornelius.

It felt as though she were draining his heart, lungs and brain . . . and soul, out through his penis, sucking the life force from him.

Ryan's back arched as if he were in the grip of a fearsome poison, lifting him off the bed, head thrown back, the straining muscles in his neck like whipcord.

A tiny part of his mind wondered whether his spinal cord were going to snap with the burning intensity of his racing orgasm. His mouth was open and he could hear his own breathing, feel his heart pounding so hard that it felt like it could leap clear out of his chest.

There was a terrible pressure behind his eye.

Ryan could feel warmth across his hands, where his own nails had drawn blood.

"Yes, yes, now..." the woman said on a sigh, raising herself so that he almost slipped out from her, then dropping down onto him like a stone.

Ryan came.

KRYSTY HAD BEEN BACK to her room, using the bathroom, admiring the blue-flowered porcelain of the bowl and the dark oak seat. On her way to rejoin J.B. and Mildred she had paused to look through the stained-glass window that dominated the front landing.

It was a complex pattern, showing a frosty landscape. A hare limped trembling across it, and a band of hunters, dressed like medieval peasants, were trudging through the snow, carrying muskets and long bows. In the background was a house that bore an uncanny resemblance to the Cornelius mansion.

The main trail to the house was visible through the distorting panes of the colored, leaded glass. Krysty saw movement and realized that the three figures had to be Doc, Dean and Jak, returning from Bramton.

She hurried down the stairs, stopping in the hall as she noticed the slim figure of Norman standing still in the shadows beyond a huge seat with the word *Sapientia* carved above it in Gothic letters.

"Where's Ryan?" she asked.

Norman minced across to stand close to her. Krysty caught the musky scent of perfume.

"I think his treatment will soon be completed," he said in his high fluting voice. She noticed that his hair was dyed an odd mixture of ginger and lilac.

"Will he come back down here?"

"More likely they'll take him to the bedroom, Krysty," he replied, favoring her with a brilliant smile that showed a set of rotting teeth.

"I'll just see Doc and the others. Then I'll go up and wait for him."

"Of course. Whatever you wish. Liberty Hall here, my dear lady."

RYAN CAME AROUND TO FIND his wrists and ankles were free, though they felt chafed and sore. His mouth was dry, and it seemed as if his genitals had been sandblasted and then boiled in molasses. It was a bizarre sensation, burning and painful and exceedingly sweet.

"Why?" he said.

He could almost see heads turning toward him, and a muttered conversation ceased immediately.

"Why not?" Mary asked gently.

"Why me?"

"Because you are a man of unusual strength and character," a man's voice replied, not sounding quite like either Thomas or Elric.

"We are not as others," the woman stated.

"I figured that. What I don't get is just who you are and where you come from."

A hand brushed his cheeks, making him wince. The woman. "Don't worry. We don't mean to kill you. But we need you. Need you in ways you can't begin to understand."

The man spoke once more. "Within the day, you will know more. That I promise. Within the day."

Chapter Thirty

Mildred had become bored with the latest puzzle when it became clear that there were several pieces missing, including the head and arm of the tinker who leaned on the wall in the foreground of the picture, surrounded by mournful cattle with extraordinarily long horns and shaggy coats. J.B. had also given up and found a tattered paperback.

Mildred left him deep in the book while she wandered out and across the hall, passing an elderly woman in a mobcap lethargically polishing an elm bench.

She climbed to the second floor, where most of the rooms were locked and bolted, giving the impression that they hadn't been opened for a hundred years.

Mildred nearly passed a room without noticing it, as it was concealed by a long tapestry, so faded that it was impossible to tell what its subject had been. But it moved slightly as Mildred passed, giving the clue that it hid a doorway.

Glancing around to make sure that she wasn't being observed, the woman slipped behind the dusty hanging and tested the brass door handle, which moved with a certain reluctance, as though it were resisting the stranger.

The open door revealed a musty chamber, lined with books, its shutters bolted shut. Mildred saw a number of oil lamps standing ready, each with a supply of self-lights at its side. She closed the door behind her and fumbled to strike a light and illuminate the room.

The oil-soaked wick caught, and Mildred slid the glass chimney over it, quickly trimming it down so that it gave off a steady, golden glow.

The books seemed to be in far better condition than most of those on the first floor. Mildred walked around, holding the lamp raised in her hand, examining the titles as she went. The collection seemed to be split into two distinct halves, both equally well thumbed.

The more modern books were textbooks, by publishers familiar to Mildred. Most of them seemed to deal with the subject of genetic engineering. *Manipulation of DNA, Reversing the Helix* and *Molding the New* were just three typical titles from the collection.

But it was the older books that Mildred found more fascinating. Many had full morocco bindings, or were beautifully calf-bound with superb marbled endpapers. They smelled of age, and a significant number were dated before 1800, with deckle-edged paper and *f*'s for *s*'s.

A Perfon of Night had a frightening frontispiece of a gibbering demon with scaly wings, tearing the living heart from a human baby. *Almoft the Future* seemed to be about reading tarot cards.

Virtually every book in the large section covered some aspect of mysticism, every classic title that

Mildred had ever heard of, plus hundreds that were grotesquely arcane.

Of course there was a copy of the *Necronomicon,* by the mad Arab Abdul Alhazred, bound in human skin, bearing the imprimatur of the University of Miskatonic. Mildred opened it cautiously, breathing in the chill wind that blows between the worlds, the angular printing on the yellowed parchment seeming to blur and shift its nameless shape under her eyes.

There was the work of the renegade priest, Buebo of Ishmailia, some privately published and singularly vile poetry form H. P. Lovecraft, an unexpurgated copy of short tales by Monk Lewis and a long-banned novel from Cecilia Pewcell, a Victorian mystic who had been found dead in a locked room with her throat torn open by razor-sharp teeth.

Mildred shuddered, feeling cold, wiping her hands down her pants to try to remove the clinging damp stickiness. She picked up the lamp and walked back toward the door.

"There are some seriously sick people in this house, Millie," she whispered to herself.

Doc, Dean and Jak had just found their way back to the room with the puzzles as Mildred reentered. Krysty was already there, sitting on the edge of one of the long sofas, hands clasped around her knees.

J.B. had finished skim-reading the paperback and was standing by the empty fireplace. He looked up immediately as Mildred came into the room, standing and walking to her side, taking her hand. "You all right?" he asked.

"Been better. Found this library of some, well, strange books. Science at an advanced level from the very end of the last century, just before the final war. And some ancient volumes on witchcraft and devil worship and all kinds of obscene black magic. Nasty stuff."

He squeezed her hand tightly, then turned back toward Doc and the others. "Find anything down there in Bramton to prove your theory?"

Doc sat in a deep armchair, sighing. "Quite a hike, that trail from down by the river. I fear that I'm getting too old for all this tarry-hooting."

Dean sat on the floor, leaning his back against the sofa by Krysty. "Some kids nearly shit themselves when they saw Jak. Thought he was a member of the Family out hunting soft meat."

Doc nodded, his face grim. "Our young friend here may not know it, but I suspect that he might have put his finger on the heart of the matter."

"It's like what saw when down with Johannes," Jak said. "Real fear. Nobody'd talk proper about Family."

"And there is this strange zombielike slowness about them all." Doc rubbed at the stubble whitening his cheeks. "So pallid, all of them."

Mildred cleared her throat. "Everything points one way, doesn't it, Doc?"

"Yes, it does, Dr. Wyeth. I noticed that everyone wore high collars and long sleeves."

"What's that mean, Doc?" Dean asked.

"It might mean that they're trying to conceal something from us."

"Like what?"

"Bite marks."

Jak looked up, glancing at Dean. "Hey, remember when was sick?"

"Sure."

Mildred looked at the albino. "What're you talking about, Jak? I remember Dean being ill one morning. Real tired. I looked to see if anything had bitten him on the neck, but there was nothing there at all."

"Not neck," Jak said. "Elbow. Puncture mark there."

Doc coughed. "Then I think that we are being forced to a bizarre explanation, are we not?"

Mildred nodded. "Yeah, we are, Doc."

Krysty shook her head. "Can you two stop this triple-stupe game and tell the rest of us what you suspect. Gaia! It might affect Ryan."

Doc bit his lip. "Yes, I am very much afraid that it might, Krysty. It might."

RYAN WAS BEING CARRIED down a fight of stairs that he now guessed led from the attics above the corridor where he and his companions had been settled.

He was certain that the man carrying him was Thomas Cornelius, and that it had been Thomas who'd attacked him in the corridor the night that Johannes Forde had been butchered.

Though Ryan had made a token effort at struggling when he'd been picked up from the bed, he'd known immediately that he was wasting his time. The man had enormous, unearthly power, holding him tight to his chest, walking effortlessly along, whistling under his breath. Again, there was the faint sound of whispering material, like hissing silk or rustling feathers.

And the same revolting graveyard breath.

"Just who the fuck are you?" Ryan panted. "Or should that be *what* the fuck are you?"

"Don't waste your breath, Ryan."

"You'll tell us tomorrow all about yourselves?"

"Probably."

"If you hadn't drugged me before making me... making me fuck, then I'd have chilled all of you."

"Talk is cheap, Ryan. But as a man of your coinage knows, the price of action is colossal."

Despite the helpless absurdity of his position, Ryan couldn't stop himself from laughing. "I reckon that I've heard Doc say exactly the same thing."

Thomas stopped as if to let someone move past him. "There is something about every one of your friends that fascinates us. And we shall find uses for all of you."

"Uses?"

"Wait."

Ryan had a ferocious headache, and the rocking movement was making him feel sick.

They had gone through the door and were now, he was sure, on the landing. There was a sudden flash of silver-gold light that seemed to burn his retina, and he winced, wondering what it was that he'd seen.

Thomas had stopped, his grip tightening. "Close that bastardly drapery, Sister. It's blinding me."

"Sorry, Brother. I brushed it open as I walked by. Here's Ryan's room."

"First check that all of the draperies and shutters are closed inside."

Mary's voice came faintly from inside the room. "All right. It's safe and dark."

The man lowered Ryan onto another bed. "There," he said. "Home again, home again."

Ryan lay still, glad that the swaying had finally ceased. Though he was trying with all of his might to see out of his damaged eye, there didn't seem a trace of light or a hint of any movement near him.

The woman's hand was on his cheek. "It was amazing, Ryan. Of all the others, you were so much the best. I knew when I first saw you that night that it would be something very special for me and for all of us."

Anger pulsed in Ryan's mind, anger at the casual way they'd taken advantage of him, something that would never have happened if he'd had his sight.

And if, by a miracle, he ever recovered his sight, one of the first things he'd look forward to seeing was the face of Mary Cornelius and her depraved family staring at him over the sights of the SIG-Sauer.

"We'll leave you now," the man said in his hoarse whisper. "And we'll make sure that Norman tells your friends that you're back here again."

"Yeah." Ryan tried to make himself comfortable, still wondering about the amazing strength of the Family, how and when they became so bizarrely mutated.

Once again the woman touched his face, and he managed not to pull away, recognizing his own damned weakness and the importance of trying not to offend them.

The door closed and Ryan was left alone with his thoughts and his shame.

THE CONVERSATION in the library had been interrupted at a crucial stage by the appearance of Norman, carrying a chased silver tray with goblets of orange juice.

"Newly squeezed by my own fair hand," he said, giggling. "Fresh as tomorrow's sunrise."

"And the eggs you serve tomorrow are still inside the hens," Mildred added.

"Oh, you're so sharp you'll cut yourself. You must have been sleeping in the cutlery drawer."

"The drink drugged?" J.B. asked, sniffing suspiciously at one of the glasses.

"Of course not. The very idea of it! I can see that I might have to slap you on the wrist, John Dix."

"Try it and I'll whack you," the Armorer said. "Thanks for the drinks, now get out."

Norman pulled a pettish face and flounced out, closing the door firmly behind himself.

"Think safe?" Jak also picked up one of the drinks and touched it to his lips. "Tastes good."

"If there's drugs, you'll probably spot it in the aftertaste," Mildred said, sipping at the juice. "Seems all right to me."

Doc hadn't moved from where he stood staring out of the window at the frothing river, far below the house. Finally he turned to face the others. "So?"

Mildred nodded, solemn. "I guess we both suspect the same about the Family."

"I believe that we do."

To J.B., Dean and Jak, he said. "Dr. Wyeth and I believe that we are in a household of vampires."

Chapter Thirty-One

J.B. was particularly scathing about their vampire idea.

"Look, I've seen some bits of old vids and read predark comics and books. So I know what their ideas were on vampires. There was some writer who had big sellers about vampires, but it was just fiction. All of it was made up."

"I find your argument strangely unpersuasive, John Barrymore Dix. If you will forgive me for saying so, the idea that someone has written fiction about a subject means that the subject doesn't exist in reality is absurd."

"Course," Mildred agreed. "Man writes a novel about the Civil War. According to your theory, John, that means that the War between the States never happened. That what you're saying? It can't be, can it?"

The Armorer shrugged. "I've traveled the old battlefields, Millie—Antietam, Chancellorsville, Manassas, Shiloh. Load of them in our travels with Trader. Course they existed. But I never met anyone who saw a real ghost or a vampire. Reason is, they don't exist."

Jak had been standing by the fireplace. "Folks in bayous believe ghosts, J.B., and see them."

"Vampires?"

The albino shook his head. "Don't know vampires. Voodoo believes them. Walking dead like zombies. Suck blood. Kill with stake in heart. Or silver bullet. Or cut off head. Or expose in sun. Vampires don't like sun."

J.B. sniffed. "You're all crazed. Been browsing among the locoweed for too long."

"What do you think then, love?" Mildred asked. "You got a better explanation?"

"For the Family? I don't deny for a moment that they're mutie freaks. But vampires?"

Doc stood with legs slightly apart, thumbs hooked in the buttonholes of his vest, looking as though he were about to begin a lecture on The Place of Romantic Poets in a Schismatic Society.

"Their skin and reluctance to appear in light. That's one. The locked cellars and attics. Unusual strength. Rotten breath like moldy earth. That's two and three."

"And four," Dean said, grinning at having caught the old man out.

"Right. The fact that they don't appear on the film of poor Johannes. It was a well-known fact about vampires that they didn't leave a shadow or cast a reflection in a mirror. The blurring of the film stock is a modern version of that."

"And there was that strange research section, locked away up at the redoubt. Could be that has something to do with them," Mildred stated.

"The pallor and weakness of so many of the poor devils from Bramton." Doc pointed a gnarled finger at J.B. "Oh, ye of little belief! The evidence is so strong. What we should do is try and find where in this rambling pile the Family go for the rest from their evildoing."

"I saw a comic, Doc, where some vampires with pointy teeth lived in coffins filled with the dirt from a graveyard and drank blood from girls with big tits. Sorry, Mildred and Krysty. But they did have—"

Krysty held up a hand. "All right, all right. I think we get the picture."

It was at that moment that Norman had appeared from a door hidden behind rows of books to announce the news about Ryan being back in the room upstairs.

RYAN HAD BEEN DOZING, still under the influence of the drug, when they all burst into the room.

He woke with a start.

"Fireblast! What's...?"

"Hello, lover," Krysty said, sitting on the side of the bed, reaching and holding his hand. She noticed without comment that Ryan jumped nervously and started to pull his fingers away from her touch.

"Hi. Don't feel great. Head's like the inside of a lumberjack's ass."

Mildred perched on the other side of the bed, Ryan knowing it was her from the faint whispering of the beads in her plaited hair.

"How about the eye?" she asked casually. "They do anything for it?"

"No."

"They try anything while you were drugged?"

"No."

"How can you be sure?" J.B. asked, "if you were out colder than a snow bear's dick?"

"I'm sure, is all. Just what the fuck are you getting at, anyway?"

"Nothing. Settle down, Ryan. They said they could help you to see again. So it's not unreasonable to ask you a question about what they did and how you are."

"Yeah, I guess... Sorry." Ryan could hear J.B. take off his glasses and start to polish them, which he often did when something had embarrassed him.

"So, what did they do, Dad?"

Dean was leaning on the end of the bed, making it rock back and forth in a distinctly irritating way. But Ryan held his temper.

"Nothing. Like I said, they drugged me. But I was conscious all the time." He fumbled for a believable and convenient lie. "I think they did try to do something with my eye. They rubbed some kind of grease on it and stuff like that."

"But it hasn't helped, lover?"

"No." He decided not to mention the odd flashes of light and color that he thought he might have seen, not wanting to raise anyone's hopes, not wanting to raise his own hopes.

"Your pants are buttoned up wrong, Dad."

"What?"

The room was flooded with stillness.

Ryan could feel everyone stopping whatever it was they were doing, all looking at the front of his pants, where Dean was pointing.

"Boy's right, lover," Krysty said, her voice calm and cool. "Buttoned up crooked and one of them's not done up at all. Surprised you didn't feel the draft."

Ryan reached down, his fingers clumsily putting things to rights.

"Stupe," he said. "Must've happened when I went for a piss on the way back from the attic."

"Up the stairs on the top floor?" J.B. sounded excited. "They took you there? What was it like? What did you . . . ? Oh, dark night! Sorry."

"What did I see, old friend? That your question? Answer is, not a lot."

"Looks like they got some of that grease you mentioned on the front of your pants, Ryan." Krysty's voice moved remorselessly from cool to cold.

"Yeah. I can just feel it with my fingernail."

He hastily changed the subject. "What've you all been doing today? While I was out of it?"

It took some time to tell him everything, culminating in Doc and Mildred's theory.

"VAMPIRES."

Krysty patted him on the leg. "Nobody tried to suck your blood, did they, lover? I mean, like that Mary Cornelius didn't try to suck your . . . blood?"

The pause was slight enough, but Ryan heard it. Everyone except Dean heard it.

He tried to ignore it, clearing his throat. "No, she didn't, Krysty."

"Good. Glad to hear it, lover. So, what do you think of the theory?"

Ryan lay back. "Sorry. Felt a bit sick again." He closed his eye. "I reckon it's possible. Like Mildred says, they aren't old ghostly vampires. I believe they don't exist. I don't believe they ever existed."

He heard someone walk across the room and tug back the draperies. From the lightness of the feet, it had to be Jak. But there was a shaft of brightness that Ryan saw.

Really *saw.*

This time there was no mistake about it. But he still kept quiet.

They sat around the bed, talking animatedly about what they should do.

There was a general acceptance that the Family wasn't a force for good, therefore it made sense to get away from their house as soon as possible.

"Dawn," J.B. said.

"Agreed." Ryan looked blindly around the room. "Watch yourselves at supper and keep close. No wandering. I'm not sure that the Family is completely finished with us yet. No. Not by a long country mile."

EVERYONE WENT back downstairs, leaving Krysty and Ryan with some time alone.

He heard the door close with mixed feelings, hoping that the subject of precisely what he'd been doing with Mary Cornelius might not be raised.

"You fuck her, lover?"

So much for a vain hope.

A part of the cement that held Ryan and Krysty together was honesty. However unpalatable the truth might be, and however much it might harm their relationship, it never occurred to Ryan that, faced with a direct question, he should lie.

"She fucked me."

"While you were drugged and tied hand and foot to the bed? Was that it, Ryan?" The bitterness of betrayal rode at the front of her voice.

"It was just like that."

"Sure it was. And I just bet you hated every moment of it, didn't you?"

Again there was the temptation to shift sideways and sort of skirt around the truth.

"I hated the way they made me do it." He coughed to clear his throat. "I hate anytime that anyone makes me do anything beyond my control."

"But you didn't actually hate it when it was going on. That what you're saying?"

"Not really."

She copied his voice, mocking it. "Not really. Oh, no, Krysty. I hated being fucked. In fact it didn't work because I never even got an erection." She changed back to her own voice. "You get a hard-on, lover?"

Ryan turned on his side, away from her, but she grabbed at his arm and tugged him back. "Don't you fucking do that to me, Ryan! Not ever!"

"Sorry, I told you. They drugged me. There were three of them there. At least three. Thomas and Elric, as well as the woman. They've got strength that . . . And I was blind. Krysty, I swear I couldn't have stopped them. It was as close to rape as it can get for a man."

"All of a sudden, my heart bleeds," she said bitterly. "What happened to the blaster?"

He sat up, staring blankly at where he thought she was, wondering with a small part of his mind whether he was imagining seeing a spark of sunlight burning off her bright red hair.

"The blaster never left my holster. You can't imagine what it was like. If you'd been tied down and forced to have sex, I wouldn't behave like this. Blaming me. Hating me. Hurting me even more than I'm already hurting."

To his dismay, Ryan found that his voice was breaking and his right eye was brimming with unshed tears.

The silence stretched on and he felt Krysty stand up from the bed and walk across the room.

"Think running away'll change anything?" he shouted. "Because it fucking won't!"

The sound of boot heels on the carpet stopped. "I wasn't running away, Ryan."

"Well . . . well, I guess that's something. So, where were you going?"

"To look out the window. Sort of gather my thoughts together. Work out just how I was going to tell you that I was sorry for behaving like I did."

"Krysty." He stretched out his hand toward where he thought she was standing.

"What is it, lover?"

"Just wondering..."

"What about?" She moved back and sat again on the edge of the bed, her fingers clasping his hand.

"I was wondering."

"You just said that, lover."

"Wondering how you felt about taking off some of your clothes and climbing into the bed for a while?"

"I feel like that's the best offer I've had for... Well, the best offer today."

They made love three times before a gentle knock on the bolted door told them that supper was ready.

Chapter Thirty-Two

When Krysty led Ryan down the long sweep of stairs to the dining hall, through the large vaulted doors, he felt her start with surprise.

"All here," she whispered. "Thomas, Mary and Elric. And another one. Older. Looks real sick."

Norman was at their elbow, smelling of patchouli oil. He nudged Ryan in the ribs from the other side. "Honored, you should be. First time I've seen Melmoth Cornelius down here for a meal in...must be thirty or forty years."

Doc heard the muttered message. "Melmoth?" he said in his deep, booming voice. "Melmoth was the wanderer, was he not? Are you, too, a wanderer, sir?"

The voice was as dry and dusty as a windblown papyrus, so quiet it hardly seemed to stir the air. "I have not been more than fifty miles from this place all my life, Dr. Tanner. It is you who should be called the wanderer and not I."

"How so?"

Ryan could feel the crumbling health of the man. The room was brimming with the flavor of the tomb, a scent of the solitary damp of the graveyard.

"How so?" repeated the head of the Family. "We had access to all manner of data. And your name featured among it, Dr. Tanner."

"What data? You mean on disk up in the redoubt? What sort of stuff and nonsense would they have about me?"

"Born in Vermont in 1868 on the feast day of Saint Valentine."

His voice changed, got stronger. "Norman, that oil lamp, third along, is in need of trimming. You should know by now how our eyes are affected by any kind of... Where was I, Doctor?"

"Just told me my birthday, but I knew that, anyway. Anything I don't know?"

"Do you know the circumstances of your wife Emily's death? Or of what happened to Rachel and bonny little Jolyon? I suspect you do not."

Mildred was glancing at Doc when Melmoth dropped his bombshell, and she saw a blank and horrified shock on his features. He actually turned white and staggered a few steps, steadying himself on the high carved back of one of the dining chairs. Mildred began to move toward him, but he made a swift, fighting recovery.

"You suspect correctly, Master Melmoth. It was information that I tried for many a long day to drag from the files of the whitecoats. But they had sealed it and locked it away with great cunning. You have this information?"

"I can tell you that your son and daughter both died in the same year that you were trawled as a glimmer of light in the seething blackness that was Operation Chronos."

"And Emily?"

Mildred looked from Doc to Melmoth, seeing the cavernous cheeks and the palsied hands, the ruby eyes, set in caverns of wind-washed bone, and a trickle of what could only be blood dangling bright at the corner of the trembling lips.

"It had gone from the files, Dr. Tanner."

"You bastard! Raising my hopes and then plunging them into an even deeper abyss."

"No, no, that was not my intention. There was a massive comp failure in Redoubt 47, our birthplace, as it were, during the long winters. We realized too late, or we could have recalled information from it. Your tragedy, Dr. Tanner, is that you can remember virtually nothing. Ours is that we remember virtually everything."

"And you can't remember what happened to my family?" Doc's voice was quavering with tension and shock. "Forgive me, but I find that difficult to believe."

Ryan was sitting down, listening to the argument, trying to work out some puzzling arithmetic. The long winters that Melmoth mentioned had been around eighty years ago, and he was talking about it as if he, and the others, had been alive and active at that time. From everything that Ryan knew about the Family, it obviously wasn't possible.

"You know about the Totality Concept?" Ryan asked, eager to discover the parameters of their wisdom.

"Of course. But we were only a small part of it. As was Cerberus and Chronos. My brothers and sisters and I were formed as a result of what was known to the government whitecoats as the Genesis Project."

Doc was sitting, and he looked up at the name. "I heard about it. Casual words dropped when they should have been caught. Genesis. Gene manipulation. Some kind of triple-secret genetic engineering."

"The books."

Everyone turned to look at Mildred. Ryan squinted, becoming increasingly certain that the tiny spots of light he could see in his injured eye were really there and related to the number of dimmed oil lamps he could smell around the galleried room. He tried to concentrate on them, but they wriggled sideways like mercury under a thumb.

"You found our private library of scientific and mystical works, Dr. Wyeth," Mary said. "We knew that you'd been there. We saw your aura, which you left behind. There is nothing hidden from us here."

Ryan caught another glint as he stared toward the woman, and he remembered that Krysty had mentioned a polished silver ring in the shape of a skull worn on her hand.

"So, if you're all so bastard all-powerful, why did you want us here?" Ryan asked. "And why did you have to use me the way you did?"

Krysty answered in a loud, ringing voice. "I think I know, lover."

Elric interrupted her. "I said that she had the seeing power and would put us to the risk. I said she should have been terminated with extreme prejudice."

"Ah, the old, familiar security euphemisms," Doc said. "Yes, I remember them well."

"Quiet, brother." The order was layered with a silky menace, from Melmoth.

Krysty laughed bitterly. "We all thought you were some kind of vampires. Seemed triple stupe. Fantasy world. But it wasn't stupe, was it?"

Thomas said gently, "No, it wasn't. We thought you particularly, Krysty, would make that deduction. It was unfortunate that Johannes found we left no clear image on his film. We don't truly understand that ourselves. Something to do with our inverted electromagnetic field."

"You need human DNA samples to continue your rotten lives." Krysty was on her feet, at Ryan's side, almost shouting. She was leaning on the table, and he could feel the vibrations through the tips of his fingers from her shaking anger. He casually let his right hand drop out of sight, to rest on the butt of the SIG-Sauer, hoping that J.B., Jak and the others would see the gesture and realize that they were racing toward great danger. The Family wasn't like any ordinary quartet with ordinary weaknesses. But just what were the limits of their power?

Doc was also up on his feet again. "Blood! Just like real vampires. When you were . . . What was the weasel word you used about that?"

"They said 'formed,' Doc," Dean said.

"Indeed, sweet boy, indeed they did. Formed. Sent before your time, part made. Malformed is a better word for obscene mutated anomalies like you four. Four? Is that all there are? You must all be the same age, give or take a year or two. My, Melmoth, how sickly you look."

"I am near death," Melmoth replied. "What you short-timers call death. There were twelve of us formed in the laboratory of Redoubt 47. The apostles of tomorrow, we were called. One by one we have succumbed to sickness, transmitted from you norms. Now there are only four of us left to carry on."

"Can't you carry on milking the poor devils from Bramton of their precious body fluids?" J.B. asked. "That's what you've been doing all these years, isn't it?"

"They have become too weak and inbred for us," Melmoth replied. "We need fresh blood and fresh genetic sampling to enable us to live on for another hundred years."

"Why they let you?" Jak asked. "Why not chill years ago?"

"A good question, Jak." This time it was Thomas who spoke. "We had hoped when we were first aware of you that you might possibly be one of us. From another gene pool. Perhaps from another lab somewhere else in Deathlands. Then we saw that you were just a common albino freak.''

"Fuck you and your grandmother too," Jak replied. "And didn't answer question."

"Why have the cattle of the ville never risen against us, Jak? Oh, but they have, haven't they, Sister?''

"They have tried, let me see, at least a dozen times since skydark."

"And failed?" J.B. queried.

"Not every time," Melmoth replied. "We have had losses, despite our strengths.''

"Strongest man in the world can get chilled by a five-year-old with a .22 blaster," Ryan said. "There are so many of them and so few of you."

"They fear us." Mary was walking around the room, dimming the oil lamps one by one. "We can move against them, among them, silent and unseen. And we can make them pay the blood price any night."

"Or any day?"

"No, Dr. Tanner, any night."

"As our sister says," Melmoth stated, "the one weakness in our makeup, apart from the incessant draining of our DNA, is that our sight is sharp as an eagle's in the dark. Poor as a cave bat's in the noontime sun."

"You've kept the poor men and women of Bramton as your slaves for nearly a hundred years!" Mildred was unable or unwilling to hide her disgust.

"And the children," Mary added. "There are not many of those now. But they are the sweetest and most fresh and tender for our purposes."

Ryan pushed his hands down on the table. "I guess that they aren't our concern."

He stood. "They have to make their own luck, good or bad. And we have to move on."

"It will be dark before you can get to the redoubt," Melmoth said. "A dangerous time."

"That a threat, you sick, sickly bastard?"

"Threats are for the impotent."

"We have the firepower to take all of you out in a couple of seconds. Can't you see that, you stupe?"

"I see, Ryan." The old man's voice seemed to be getting stronger. "I see better than you do."

"Seeing won't turn aside a 9 mm full-metal-jacket round."

Ryan was taken by surprise at the reaction from all four members of the Family. They laughed, sounding as if they were genuinely amused.

It was Thomas, walking around the table, who replied. "Turning aside a bullet isn't necessary for us, Ryan Cawdor. You have felt the touch of our power. Bullets can't harm us."

The calm confidence was unsettling.

"You saying you're immortal?" J.B. sniffed. "Never saw a living soul didn't go down under a bullet."

"We are not like any other life-form on the planet," Thomas stated. He had stopped on the far side of the room. As near as Ryan could figure, the strongest of the Cornelius Family was now standing close to Dean. He felt a prickling of discomfort.

"Enough talk." Ryan said. "We leave at dawn."

"We don't think so," Elric said.

There was a flurry of movement, and Ryan heard his son cry out in pain and shock, the sound quickly muffled.

"No," Thomas stated. "We don't think so."

Chapter Thirty-Three

The dining room was filled with the clicking of blasters being cocked. Ryan had the SIG-Sauer in his right hand, pointing it at the ceiling, holding up his left hand. "Nothing sudden!" he shouted.

"He's got Dean," J.B. said calmly. "Arm around his neck in a choke hold."

"Let him go," Krysty called, "or you all get to be real dead real soon."

"That which has never been alive can never truly be dead," Elric replied.

Though Ryan was secretly convinced that his damaged sight was gradually returning, he could still see nothing but a faded blur of movement and color all around him. None of it made any sort of sense.

"Tell me," he shouted to his companions. "Tell me exactly what's going down."

"They got no weapons," the Armorer said. Ryan could almost taste the doubt in his old friend's voice. "Woman and the old man and Elric are close together, around Thomas. He's got Dean off the floor, holding the boy in front of him."

"Hurt?"

Krysty answered him. "No. Shaken up. Can't speak. Thomas has him real tight."

"But you've got clear shots at the other three?"

"Yeah."

Ryan felt the short hairs prickling at his nape. Something was very wrong. Unless the members of the Family were total crazies, they would all be dead in moments. At that range there was no possibility of any of the bullets missing their mark.

"Something's wrong," he said very quietly.

"I feel it too, lover." Krysty was right at his side. "This makes no sense."

"Let's just take them," Jak said. "Can't be easier. They want chilling, we give chilling."

"Yes, young man," Melmoth whispered. "Give us chilling. In some ways it might even be a mercy and a kindness. Try shooting at us and see what happens."

"They haven't got body armor on," J.B. observed. "So it's not that."

"Are we drugged?" Doc's voice betrayed his bewilderment. "Some sort of hallucinogenic? Are they playing with our minds, showing us some kind of virtual reality that they control?"

"None of those things," Thomas said. "And you must make your minds up quickly what you intend to do. Or the boy will suffer and that is not our wish."

"Then let him go." Ryan was turning his head from side to side, trying to make some sense out of the shapes that flickered and danced at the edges of his seeing.

"No. He is the key. You are all the lock. Now, if you have done with your empty talking, we shall take Dean with us to our rooms on the top floor. You will all come back here at breakfast tomorrow morning, and we will begin the new regime where you offer us your essence in return for keeping the lad alive. Simple, is it not? So simple."

"Want me to open fire, Ryan?" J.B. sounded as though his usual confidence had been eroded.

"Can you take out Thomas without hurting Dean?"

"Sure. Range is twenty feet. Thomas is well over six feet. Leave me plenty of target."

Ryan still hesitated. What was the factor that he didn't understand?

"One moment."

"What is it, Melmoth?"

"I guessed that we would need to make a small demonstration for you. You are far more insistent than those dumb wretches in the ville."

Mary spoke to Krysty. "You must describe carefully to Ryan what is happening. It's important that you all fully understand what is going on."

"Elric is taking up a knife, lover, from the table. Steel carver."

"He threatens Dean, then chill him."

"He's not. Holding the knife in his right hand and baring his left arm. Rolling up the sleeve to the elbow."

"Watch carefully," Thomas said. "So far you've seen nothing."

Krysty continued her running commentary. "Edge of the knife touches his skin. Now he's . . . Gaia!"

"Has he cut himself?" Ryan asked. "Sure it's not a trick knife?"

"Let young Jak come and make another cut, Elric," Thomas said. "So there shall be no doubters."

He paused. "But take care, outlanders. The neck of a boy like little Dean is so fragile and accidents happen so easily, don't they?"

"There's some blood, lover," Krysty whispered. "But very little. The cut was deep. I saw the lips, white as snow, then the crimson seeping from inside."

"Going cut now, Ryan," Jak said.

The tension in the room was so strong that you could breathe it in with the fumes of the guttering lamps.

"He's made a gash about a hand's breadth long, down the arm." Krysty's voice was tight with tension. "Same thing's happened. Some blood but not much. And... Gaia! The first cut's already healing itself."

"We are almost indestructible," Melmoth said. "A bullet will make a hole. We are not superheroes who can't be harmed. But it is only with grave difficulty that we are killed."

"There was tall Boaz who was crushed in a logjam, down in the river that winter's flood," Mary said. "His body was smashed to pulp."

"And dear Clementine in that fire." Melmoth's voice dropped. "Just charred sticks were left. Not even we can resolve ourselves from such a fate."

"Now both the wounds look healed," Krysty said.

Jak dropped the knife, letting it clatter on the table. "No trick, Ryan."

Mildred was closest to the door, and she had an irrational desire to turn and run out of the dining hall, out of the mansion on the cliff, to run into the surrounding bayou and run and run until she could run no more.

She fingered the tiny gold crucifix around her throat, hardly aware she was touching it, when an idea struck her.

"Vampires," she breathed to herself, so quietly that not even the sharp-eared Family heard her.

Mildred quickly took the cross on its narrow chain from her neck and gripped it firmly in her right hand, advancing toward Melmoth, closest of them, who turned as he saw the stocky woman walking doggedly toward him.

And he laughed at her.

"I curse you, Satan!" Mildred called, every eye in the room turning to her. "With this holy cross of blessed Jesus Christ I banish you back to the black shadows of the deepest pit in the purgatorio."

"She got her crucifix?" Ryan asked.

"Yeah," Krysty said. "Just like in those old horror vids and books. But..."

"But what?"

Melmoth answered his question. "But this is real life and fiction is fiction, Ryan Cawdor."

"And the cross is the cross, you blasphemous pile of shit!" Mildred shouted, holding the tiny gold cross before her, raising it toward Melmoth Cornelius like a laser weapon.

He began to slowly give ground across the room, before her anger, backing away toward the shadowy corner where there was a large glass display case filled with porcelain, crystal and items of jewelry.

"See how the force of evil falls before the force of light," Mildred said exultantly. "The old stories were true, friends, all true."

"I'm afraid, Mildred," Melmoth said, reaching the cabinet.

"I see that."

"No, let me finish. "I was going to say that I was *not* afraid of your totem, Dr. Wyeth. It holds no more terror for me and for my brothers and sister than any child's bauble."

"It is a crucifix."

"No." He took something from the case. "*This* is a crucifix, Doctor."

Mildred gasped. Even in the dim light of the darkened room, the crucifix that Melmoth had withdrawn from the cabinet glowed with its own brilliant light.

It looked to be very old, perhaps sixteenth century. The racked figure of Christ was gold, set on the cross of heavy lustrous silver. The whole thing was set with rubies and diamonds, emeralds and onyx, chalcedony and amethysts.

It was eighteen inches long and was one of the most beautiful things that Mildred had ever seen.

And Melmoth the vampire was holding it calmly in his long-nailed right hand.

"You see how little I fear your precious symbols of Aramaic superstition, Mildred."

Melmoth lifted it to his lips and kissed it. Then put out his long serpentine tongue, like a white worm, and licked the rough surface of the crucifix, touching the fetid tip to the thorny crown of Christ.

Mildred's right hand rested on the butt of the ZKR 551 target revolver, and at that moment she was as close as she had ever been to shooting a man down in cold blood and hot rage, though Melmoth Cornelius was not truly a man.

Melmoth held the cross between his cupped hands in a gesture of mock piety. "If only you could see the sporting tricks that sister Mary gets up to in her own private room with this pretty toy, Dr. Wyeth. I think even you would be convinced that it does not frighten us."

A long silence followed the disgusting demonstration of the Family's power, which was broken finally by Ryan. "You've made your point," he said. "We'll stay as long as you like. Just let the boy go. Let Dean alone."

Thomas, his smile shining through his words, said, "I think not. We have not lived close to a hundred years by being stupid, Ryan. And to let you have your son back would be the same as opening the main doors and giving you fast horses to ride away. No, the boy will live with us for a time."

He moved his hand from Dean's mouth, allowing him to speak. "I'll be all right, Dad. Be a hot pipe with them. Don't worry about me."

"Sure."

Thomas yawned, his mouth opening so wide they could all hear the sinews cracking in his jaws. "Well, this has all gone as we hoped it would. As we knew it would, outlanders. Remember that we have no wish to harm any of you. That would be against our own best ends, wouldn't it?"

Melmoth was already leaving the room, heading for the stairs that would eventually take them up to their attic rooms. "Tomorrow we will have worked out a detailed plan for when we will need each of you."

Mary followed him. "Once we have gone, Norman, you may raise the lights so that our guests can see

properly to enjoy their meals. I look forward to starting the osmotic process with you all. Especially with
you, again, Ryan. The idea of reconnection is thrill-
ing.''

Thomas and Elric left together. Ryan could hear the
sound of his son's feet dragging, reluctant, across the
echoing hall.

The door closed behind them.

"Well, now you know, people," Norman chirped
brightly. "Could be worse, believe me."

"How?" Ryan asked, the single syllable as cold as
Sierra meltwater.

"Well, the Family could have chilled you all. Last
night. You saw what they did to that silly-billy of a
filmmaker. They all have dreadful strength. Even
Melmoth, and he's weak as a kitten compared to his
usual old ways."

"Some of them have died," J.B. pointed out. "So
they *can* be chilled."

The butler shook his head slowly. "Even the
mightiest sequoias will fall eventually in the deeps of
the forest. But if there is nobody there to hear the
thunderous crash, is there any sound at all?''

"Don't play fucking Zen games with us, you
preening little shit!" Mildred walked toward him, her
beaded plaits swinging. "Don't come on with 'What's
the sound of one hand clapping?' and 'How when is
now?' and all that crap! You serve what must be one
of the most perverse and vile families in the whole of
Deathlands and doing your chirpy and amusing little

gay act with us doesn't... By God, it doesn't make you winsome, Norman."

Her shout echoed around and around the vaulted gallery at the second floor.

"Well, pardon me for living!" the butler exclaimed.

"Living and partly living," Doc stated. "Have you opened the door to the secret garden and taken the path least traveled? By the Three Kennedys, but what a pathetic whining bastard you are, Norman."

"Well, you can whistle down the pussy's well for food for all I care." Norman glowered at them. "You'll see, as well. See I'm right. It could be much worse."

Ryan heard the door open and close again. "Might be worth scavenging into the kitchens. J.B., mebbe you and Jak could go see what you can beg or borrow or steal."

"Sure thing," the Armorer said.

"After we've eaten, then all meet up in our room for some serious planning. Krysty, could you and Mildred and Doc turn the lamps back up?"

"Sure, lover. The sight of the Family in any kind of light's poor as anything."

Mildred came around the table and laid her hand on his arm. He could feel her tension and anger. She lowered her head so that her mouth was close to his ear.

"Anything you want to tell me, Ryan?"

"Like what?"

All around the huge room he could hear Doc and Krysty turning up the wicks. And he could definitely *see* the patches of shimmering, golden light.

"Like, whether you think your sight might possibly be creeping back, Ryan?"

Krysty heard her and whirled. "Ryan! That true?"

"Mebbe."

Chapter Thirty-Four

Because of the mutie hearing that the four surviving members of the Family seemed to possess, Ryan had whispered to Krysty, Mildred and Doc not to let on about his sight returning, to wait until they were alone in their room.

When J.B. and Jak returned, about fifteen minutes later, they were each taken aside by Mildred and told the exciting news, both of them warned not to show any reaction.

They had brought some bread and butter and several jars of preserves—strawberry, blueberry and lemon cheese—as well as a couple of bottles of pre-dark wine that Jak had found in a dusty corner of the cellar.

"A Sancerre and a very good claret," Doc pronounced. "I can tell you that those bottles will either be the nectar of the gods, or, if they have not been properly tended, then they will taste like rancid camel piss."

Sadly they had not been properly tended and were both bitter and deeply undrinkable.

"Still, there's the best of Adam's brewery, from a barrel out near the rear entrance to the house," J.B.

said. "Least the water's good and wholesome. Only thing in this rad-blasted place that is."

"Can we get out that way?" Ryan asked.

"Sure. But why bother, Ryan? Front door's bolted from the inside. Not locked. Guess it's done to stop any would-be assassin getting in and trying to wipe out the Family. Doesn't stop anyone from getting out."

"From what we've seen about their invulnerability they'd have a tough job," Mildred said.

"I don't know." Ryan allowed Krysty to spread his bread with the fruit jelly in case anyone watched from the slabs of deep shadow above them.

"Got a plan, lover?" she asked.

"Let's finish up down here and get to our room. Take my arm to guide me, Krysty ."

"I WAS WONDERING WHETHER a house like this might not have secret passages in it," Doc said, once they were all gathered safely together in Ryan and Krysty's bedroom. "Maybe a priest's bolt hole that could hide a rat or a ferret or a weasel or some other sneaking wildwooder?"

"Good thought, Doc," Ryan said, pitching his voice low. "Gather around close. Jak, open the window if you can. Windy night might also help to confuse any listeners."

Once that was done they all sat on the bed.

"First things first," Mildred stated. "I need to check your eye, Ryan."

"All right. But make it quick. Every moment that those sick bastards have Dean in their power is a triple-dangerous moment. I know they said they'd not harm him as long as we cooperated, but I don't trust them as far as I could throw them."

For several minutes Mildred carried out what tests she could, making Ryan move around the room, staring up at the oil lamps, spending some time with him in front of the opened windows, testing the extent of his vision.

"Definitely some return of sight, Ryan. Nothing much to write home about. Not yet. But a quantum leap forward from total blindness."

"Will it carry on improving?" Doc asked. "Remember a man I knew called John Stuart who had a horse—a real champion—called the Old Campaigner. John was losing his sight, but he decided he wanted to ride her one more time. And all the boys around the ring—"

"We heard that story before, Doc," Krysty interrupted. "Good story, but we heard it."

"You asked if it would carry on getting better, Doc," Mildred said. "Answer is, I had no way of knowing if Ryan would ever see again. Even the blurry lights with a hazy halo around each of them. Even the slightest movement. Since I didn't know that, then there's no way I can give you a continuing prognosis. I just hope it carries on improving."

"When did you first think you might be able to see?" Krysty asked.

Ryan hesitated. "Can't really say. Just sort of noticed that bright light seemed to be penetrating."

"Bright lights." J.B. said. "Now that's something we should talk about."

The discussion, argument and planning went on for several hours.

Ryan had never come across a situation where the enemy appeared to be literally indestructible.

That, combined with the fact that the Family held Dean as hostage against the good behavior and obedience of the others, meant that composing a combat strategy was uniquely difficult. Normally their powerful weaponry lay heavy on their side of the scales. Here it seemed almost valueless.

Much of the discussion centered on just how immortal the surviving Corneliuses were.

"One was crushed to death in a logjam on the river," Ryan said.

"And other burned. Means can be chilled. But have to completely whack them. Mebbe decapitate?" Jak was playing with one of his throwing knives, tossing it from hand to hand. Suddenly he lobbed it in the air and caught the needled tip between his teeth, smiling at the others' surprise. "Old Lakota hunting trick," he said. "But my blades not much use here against Family."

"Wish we had some grens. I reckon that a few implodes might get rid of them, for good and all." J.B. shook his head. "But we don't have grens."

"I still like the idea of taking Norman as our hostage and offering a deal for Dean," Mildred said. "Why is everyone so opposed to it, John?"

"Because none of us thinks there's the smallest hope of the Family being interested in a deal like that. They do want Dean, and they don't seem to care all that much for Norman. Just a kind of servant, anyway."

Mildred stood and stretched, then walked to the window and peered out. "Day's about done and we still don't have much of a plan."

"We got the makings of one," Ryan argued. "Just have to throw the dice and see what comes up. Then make our moves. Keep on triple red.

"The Family said that they'd have worked out a scheme for using us by tomorrow. They likely won't expect us to try anything until we've heard what their plan is. Might not expect any rebellion. They likely reckon we're cowed like those poor bastards in Bramton."

J.B. was pacing the floor, furiously polishing his glasses. "Like the old vampires, they seem to do most of their living from dusk to dawn. I still think we might do better to wait and try and hit them in daylight. When they might be locked away in their rooms, sleeping."

"I personally favor the idea of creeping into their vault, where they must sleep in coffins filled with graveyard dirt. And striking them through their evil hearts with a sharpened stake of good oak."

"Probably be about as successful as my attempt with the crucifix, Doc," Mildred said. "I figure they'd just laugh at a sharp stake."

Doc sighed. "I fear that you're right."

Ryan clapped his hands gently to attract everyone's attention. "Come on, people," he said quietly. "Trader used to say that the best ace-on-the-line plan was the one that the enemy expected least of all. J.B.'s right about them moving out and about during the time of darkness. So that's when we hit them. Around midnight. When they'll least expect us to go against them." He gazed around at the pale blurs that were the faces of his companions. "Pluck away Dean from their hold and head at top speed for Redoubt 47. And for the gateway and a jump out of here."

JAK HAD DISCOVERED on one of his earliest recces through the house that the servants' quarters were completely separate from the rest of the mansion, in a west wing with its own locked and barred entrance.

The Family only seemed to let them out when they needed them in the kitchen or to do any cleaning or washing.

But after eight o'clock at night the main section of the place was deserted. Except for the ubiquitous Norman.

Ryan's sight was improving all the time, and he decided to go out of their bedroom and hunt for food, along with Krysty and J.B.

There was an ancient clock in the tower at the east flank of the house. A discordant bell chimed the quarters. At the hour a creaking door at the top of the clock face snapped open and out came a pair of jerky mechanical figures, a knight in armor, about half life-size, the metal of its cuirass stained green with verdigris, followed by old Father Death, a grinning skeleton, wrapped in the folds of a carved linen cloak, clutching a long silver scythe that it swung every couple of seconds in the general direction of the knight.

Both figures revolved twice, then Death struck the bell with the blade of the scythe.

Ten times.

"Two hours to go," Ryan whispered, leading the way down the wide sweep of the staircase toward the dining room and the kitchen beyond it.

"Odd feeling," J.B. commented, "making our way through the heart of a deeply hostile ville without having to worry about sec men. Must be a first."

"How's the eye, lover?"

The lighting in the house was subdued, with many of the ornamental lamps turned right off, the rest giving out only dim pools of watery gold.

But Ryan still found that he could see fairly well. There was a kind of tunneling to his sight, with a sharp spot at the center of his eye and increasing blurring the farther he looked toward the side.

"Not bad," he replied. "When we get to the kitchen it might be worth taking something extra."

"Now, why would the guests of the Cornelius Family be wanting to take some extra food?" Norman asked from the side of a long, bedraggled wall hanging. "Wouldn't be they were thinking of leaving, would it? If they did, then the little lad's life would be measured in short, panting, throttling, choking, sobbing moments. It can't be that."

"We thought we might not come down to breakfast tomorrow," Krysty said quickly. "Show them that they haven't got us beaten. Eat in our rooms."

Norman put his head on one side, index finger touching the dimple on his right cheek. "Well, my advice would be to avoid any conflict. In the morning their tempers can be particularly bad. I recall Melmoth ripping an arm off a scullery maid because she spilled some rich blood-thick soup on his hand."

"Perhaps you know best," Ryan said. "All right if we just go and help ourselves to some food for tonight?"

"Of course, dear heart, of course." He moved closer, his eyes fixed on Ryan's face. "Did I see you making your unaided way down the stairs, lovie? Is your eye recovered? Because if it is, then I think the Family would be interested. Especially little Mary, who has such a special care for you, Ryan."

"Are you immortal, Norman?" Krysty asked, taking the few steps that brought her right up to the little man, towering over him by several inches.

"Not I, my fire-headed kestrel."

She placed the middle finger of her right hand on the center of his forehead, holding it there for a moment while she closed her own bright green eyes. Norman staggered suddenly and would have fallen if she hadn't supported him by the arm.

"If you're not immortal, then you could find how easy death can come calling," she whispered menacingly. "It can come in waking and in sleeping. Remember that, little man."

He pulled away pettishly, his face contorted with anger and hatred. "Think your pathetic power'll help against them, lady? I'll live to dance and smile on your grave."

He spun and stalked away, the sound of his clicking high heels fading gradually into the stillness.

"You sure enough put the fear of Gaia into him, lover," Ryan said.

"Didn't want him pressing you about how well you could see. We don't hold too many cards in this game, so we might as well keep what we've got close to our chests."

Ryan nodded. "Yeah. Let's just grab some bread and whatever and get back to our room."

"And make ready for the move," Krysty added.

"Two hours." Ryan peered at his wrist chron, able to read the tiny digital display for the first time in days. "One hour and fifty-four minutes."

Chapter Thirty-Five

Jak had the door slightly ajar, his head at the gap, straining his hearing. "There it is," he whispered. "Twelve strokes on clock. Time to go."

"Everyone checked blasters?" the Armorer said. "Don't look at me like that, Millie. Once you've heard the hammer come down on an empty chamber, you don't ever want to have that feeling again. It's always safe if you check. If you don't, then you might have a real terminally nasty shock."

"Sure. You're right, John. Sorry. Guess it's just a touch of nerves."

"Older I get, the more nervous I get," Ryan admitted. "When you're young, you just don't appreciate what real danger is. Or how permanent death can be."

They made their way slowly along the passage, toward the attic door where Ryan had been taken by the Family for his ordeal. There didn't seem any doubt that the maze of small interwoven rooms on the top floor of the house was where they would be holding Dean. So it was no surprise to find the door locked.

"Under, over, around or through?" Ryan whispered, quoting one of the Trader's most famous sayings.

"Around or through," J.B. replied. "Anyone any idea whether there's another way up to the top floor? Jak, you did most of the recce?"

The albino shook his head, his mane of snowy hair blazing like a magnesium flare in the dim light of the long corridor. "Probably back way up there. Could be if went down through kitchen. Risk run into Norman that way."

J.B. had dropped to his knees, peering at the ornate brass lock, head on one side. "Some of these old locks look like they could keep a baron's fortune safe. But they open up like a baby's smile to a pick. See what I can do."

Ryan knew well enough that this wasn't a job to be rushed. The tiny lock picks that the Armorer carried in one of his capacious pockets would need some delicate handling, probing past the range of tumblers in the heart of the lock, operating by touch alone, ears straining for the fragile sounds.

He sat and leaned back against the wall of the passage, careful not to bump into a tall porcelain jardiniere.

"This going to take long, lover?" Krysty asked, coiling herself with a feline grace beside him.

"Could take fifteen seconds. Could easily take a half hour. Could be that J.B. won't be able to pick it at all."

"Then?"

"Shoot the lock off and go in with all guns blazing. Or try Jak's idea and risk finding another entrance. Don't much care for the guns-blazing strategy."

"You think Mildred's theory about how they regenerate their wounds is right?"

Ryan rubbed at his chin, wondering in passing when he might have another shave, the stubble rasping against the back of his hand. "She's the doctor, love."

"It's somehow in the blood, and that's why the blood needs refreshing all the time. So the bones and ligaments and other parts that don't have a blood supply might be a lot more vulnerable to a bullet."

"Could be." He grinned. "Course, if it's right, they'd hardly tell us, would they?"

EVERYONE WAITED in silence, a silence broken only by the faintest metallic scratchings.

Ryan peered down at his chron. "Eight minutes," he whispered.

J.B. heard and turned toward him, his sallow face glistening with perspiration from the concentrated effort. "You going to time me, partner?"

"Sorry," Ryan muttered. "How's it going?"

"Getting there."

Eleven minutes and forty seconds later the Armorer hissed in triumph. "Yes! Got her."

"I'll go first," Ryan said, unholstering the SIG-Sauer, levering himself upright, aware, as he moved from the sitting position, that his genitals were still sore.

"Sure you can see well enough?"

"Sure, J.B., sure."

The Armorer folded up the neat pack of lock picks and stashed them in his coat. The door to the attics stood a little way open, and a cold wind filtered down, with the now-familiar stench of rotting earth.

"Ready," Ryan said. "Don't have to tell you that we're all on triple red. That's shooting first and not bothering to ask any questions. We know what we're up against and how we agreed to try and take them out. Let's go."

THE LOW-ROOFED ROOMS WERE all odd angles and blind corners, cobwebs trailing across the face and mouse-droppings that crunched underfoot.

The dust was so thick that it was possible to move in almost total silence. Ryan led them all up the steep uncarpeted stairs, pausing to try to get his bearings. An occasional oil lamp, the wick trimmed low, threw patches of yellow light among the lakes of dark shadows.

Some of the rooms were empty, while others were piled with heaps of old furniture, chairs covered with rotting brocade and tables with broken legs; tall electric lamps and shelfless cupboards; wind-up gramophone with a large horn, split down its center, and the scattered parts of a child's toy clockwork railway.

"I don't feel anyone living up here, lover," Krysty whispered, "unless the Family give off a different kind of aura to ordinary people."

"Think they've gone? Taken Dean with them on some sort of mission?"

Krysty shook her head, the brilliant red hair curled tight against her skull with the nerve-stretching tension. "Doubt it. Seems much more likely to me that they've got the boy hidden someplace else in the house.''

"Cellars?" Doc suggested.

"Could be. Fireblast, but it's dark as sin up here! Be much worse in the cellars. You got everything all prepared for the lights, J.B.?''

"Yeah. Ready-mixed in my pocket. Just hope that it works like you say, Ryan."

"I'm not saying it'll definitely work. Saying it *should* work, is all."

One of the biggest of the attic rooms had a large double bed in it, with a stained mattress and knotted cords fixed to the four corners of the heavy brass frame. But that was the only chamber on the whole of the top floor that seemed to show any sign of recent habitation.

"Down we go," Ryan said, turning quickly away from the sight, the memories of his time there too recent and much too painful. Krysty said nothing.

THE DOOR TO THE CELLARS was unlocked. Ryan took the handle and turned it, letting go immediately, wiping his fingers on his pants to try to remove the horrible chill dampness that felt disgustingly stuck to them.

The smell that filtered up seemed to come from the bowels of the land, stinking far worse than anything else around the house. It seemed to grip by the throat, with its overwhelming carrion odor of decay.

"Dark night!" J.B. exclaimed at Ryan's heels. "Something's died there, long ago."

"Bad," Ryan added, gagging, closing his eye and swallowing hard, breathing through his mouth to try to avoid puking all over the top of the flight of stairs that led into the cellars.

"Maybe I'll wait here," Mildred said. "Sorry, but I just don't think I can face that stench without passing out. It could actually be poisonous, you know."

Ryan turned to her. "Why don't you wait here with Krysty and Doc? We need a rear guard. If something goes wrong down there in the pit, then we have to have backup."

"There's something down there," Krysty said, her face as pale as parchment, eyes glittering with an unnatural emerald brightness. "I can feel them."

"Then we'll go. Just me, J.B. and Jak. Rest of you stay and chill anything that comes out of here."

Krysty licked her dry lips. "This is real bad, lover," she said, voice trembling. "I mean, seriously evil. I've never felt anything so potent and wicked as what's down there, below the good earth."

"Could we not possibly all wait here? Ambush them as they come out into the hall." Doc wiped perspiration from his high forehead. "I vow that I feel a greater fear at this moment than I ever did before."

"Me too, Doc," Ryan admitted. "But our plan only has a real chance if we can split them. We come up against all four of the Family together, and I reckon we could find ourselves neck deep in big muddy."

He gave Krysty a quick kiss on the cheek, not wanting to prolong the parting. He glanced at the others, nodded and smiled. Checking that the Ar-

morer and Jak were at his heels, he began to pick his
way down into the basement blackness.

There was even less light here than up in the attics.
At least there had been a sort of breeze, sliding under
the eaves, giving some refreshment from the smell.
Down in the cellars of the mansion, the miasmic, clo-
acal air was quite still.

Ryan took a step at a time, slowly lowering each
foot in turn, testing to make sure there was no creaking. The blaster was in his right hand, quizzing the
darkness like the flickering tongue of a diamondback.

His eye was becoming used to the poor light, and he
could make out a faint glow somewhere almost directly ahead, at the bottom of the stairs.

And hear the low mutter of voices.

If the members of the Cornelius Family were talking among themselves, then it had to mean they had
no idea of the closeness of the ambush.

Jak ghosted to Ryan's shoulder, tugging at his arm
to make him lower his head.

"I see best. Go first?"

Ryan nodded. What the teenager said made very
good sense. His pink eyes saw better in poor light than
anyone Ryan had ever known. The only catch to the
whole plan was the likelihood that the Family could
probably see even better than Jak, as well as having
their other unnatural, genetically engineered strengths
and powers.

Despite the array of ace-on-the-line blasters, the
odds weren't with Ryan and his companions.

Jak's hair blazed a path for the others to follow as he picked his way through the cellars, taking blind turn after blind turn, moving all the closer to the light and the sound.

Three voices—one a woman, Mary; a younger, stronger voice that had to be Elric; and the other, weaker tone had to be either Thomas or Melmoth, which might mean that only three of the four were within yards of them. Or it might mean, which was worse, that one of the four wasn't even in the basement region of the big house.

But was somewhere outside, somewhere else.

Going back was the worst alternative. Having come this far, they had to go on.

"... first is only fair," Mary said.

The response from the voice that was either Thomas or Melmoth was inaudible.

The woman spoke again. "I could do the same with the little one. So like his father."

"Why not?" Elric said. "But not just you, Sister. All of us for all of us. Melmoth first. His need is much the greatest."

"But he hunts tonight. The outlanders have given him new hope so he seeks fresh power in Bramton."

At least that answered part of the equation. Three of them were just ahead, now so close that Ryan could see their shadows moving on the wall a few yards in front of him.

Jak had stopped, showing that to go any farther would be to emerge from hiding.

The moment of attack was very close.

Ryan inched past the teenager until he could squint with his good eye around the angle of the underground passage into a circular chamber, around thirty feet across, with a stone seat most of the way around it. There were niches for lamps, but only a couple of them held lights. At the center of the room, surrounded by the three members of the family, was a rectangular table of multicolored marble.

On it lay Dean, fully clothed, eyes closed, hands folded across his breast. For a single heart-stopping moment, Ryan thought his son was dead, and his index finger tightened on the trigger of the handblaster. Then he detected the slow rise and fall of the boy's chest and guessed he lay in a drugged sleep.

On a smaller table, by a second entrance to the chamber, Ryan spotted an array of syringes and clear tubing, looped and curled over a chromed stand. The sight made him wince in horror and disgust at the thought of how the apparatus of transfusion might be used on his child.

Mary was touching Dean, stroking his cheek with her fingers, the long hornlike nails brushing at the soft skin. She smiled, and Ryan saw the needle-sharp incisors between her full, red lips.

"In the morning it will be a new dawn for us all," she said to her freakish brothers.

Ryan looked to each side, seeing that J.B. and Jak were both ready.

"Now!" he yelled.

Chapter Thirty-Six

Thomas was perceived as the most powerful of the Family, and he was the prime target for their attack. Ryan leveled the SIG-Sauer and fired five rounds, each bullet striking home at the center of the black-clad chest, as a head shot was chancy in such poor light. A ripple of sound erupted from the Uzi, and the vampire staggered back under the punching force of the 9 mm rounds.

Jak shot three times at the woman, two of his bullets hitting her in the upper arm and shoulder, spinning her. But none of them struck in vital parts.

Elric swung his cloak, extinguishing one of the lights, and darted for the farthest entrance. Ryan hesitated for a moment, then the lithe figure was gone.

Thomas was steadying himself against the wall, blood streaming down his arm over his hand.

"Bastards," he hissed, pointing at them with his unbloodied hand. "You'll all—"

Ryan shot him twice more, aiming at the knees, sending the giant figure toppling to the dusty floor. As he fell he staggered in front of Mary, who snatched at her moment. She picked up Dean's unconscious body and ran at the three invaders, knocking Jak out of her way with a backhanded blow that sent him falling to his right, his Colt Python exploding uselessly, the round sparking off a distant wall.

Ryan tried to grab at her, but she was too fast and too strong, seeming hardly affected by her wounds, leaving him gripping a handful of torn black cloth. She elbowed J.B. aside and rushed away along the passage toward the stairs.

"Let her go. Others can take her. Get Thomas. Quick!" Ryan holstered his warm SIG-Sauer and beckoned to J.B. to hurry and help him.

They'd rehearsed the next few seconds in the bedroom.

J.B. took out the small thermite bomb that was shrouded in a plastic tube. He'd carefully prepared the mixture of one part magnesium to four parts of the powdered barium, all that they had left of the ingredients after their adventures in the jungle. Now he handed it to Ryan, simultaneously reaching for a self-light from another pocket.

He'd primed the bomb by carefully opening a half dozen spare rounds of ammo, and it was ready to fire.

If it worked.

But Thomas Cornelius wasn't prepared to go gently into the good night. He was already trying to sit up, and the cascading flow of blood from his shattered chest was already easing. His eyes were pits of crimson in the dim glow from the last of the lamps, and he hissed furiously at them, groping unsteadily toward Ryan's face with his long right arm.

"Done for now," he crowed. "The boy and all of you are bastard done for."

He threw his head back to laugh, and Ryan seized the moment, jamming the homemade bomb in between the gaping jaws. Thomas reacted by trying to bite off Ryan's fingers, but the one-eyed man was too quick this time.

"Light it," he gasped.

The tiny red-orange flame flickered into life, and J.B. lowered it toward the pinched end of the tube.

For three or four breath-snatching moments, nothing at all happened.

Thomas punched out at Ryan, catching him a glancing blow on the shoulder. The pain was considerable, and the force of it knocked the one-eyed man on his back, the SIG-Sauer jolting from his hand into a shadowed corner of the chamber.

With a maniac roar of triumph the white-skinned vampire reached into his sharp-toothed mouth, ready to pull out whatever it was jammed in there.

And the thermite ignited.

Ryan and J.B. tried to shield their eyes from the dazzling incandescent glow that began to burn, deep between Thomas Cornelius's iron jaws.

"Out!" Ryan yelled, his voice cracking.

The huge man began to thrash around on the floor, arms and legs flailing in the white agony from the thermite. A fearsome bubbling scream surged from his tortured lungs.

The mutie vampire had no chance of removing the bomb from his mouth, his breath sucking the flames and the fumes into his chest.

At the angle of the corridor, right on the heels of J.B. and Jak, Ryan glanced behind him.

It was a scene from the worst imaginings of Hades.

Thomas was rolling around, his back arched in a spine-cracking curve. The thermite had burned its way through his throat, up past the soft palate, attacking the base of the brain and the spinal column. His eyes were melted, and his whole face had fallen into the silver-bright flames. Despite the appalling injury, the man still clung to a fragment of life.

But, even as Ryan stared with horrified fascination at the last throes, the body jerked twice, then lay still, while molten brains and skull dribbled over the floor and the bomb continued its work of totally destroying the man's head.

"Come on, Ryan!" J.B. yelled from the top of the cellar stairs.

"He's done!" Ryan called as he made his way through the basement of the house. "Nobody could rise again from that. I mean nobody."

Despite the promising start to their plan, everything else had gone sorely wrong.

Doc was sitting up, rubbing at a bump on his cheek that was weeping crimson. And Mildred was swaying from side to side, doubled over, clutching her stomach.

"What?" Ryan said.

"Woman was like a fury uncontained, a Valkyrie in strength and glory."

"Where? And where's Krysty?"

Mildred straightened, a thread of vomit trickling down her chin. "Went after Mary. She had Dean in her arms. Went toward the stairs. Go, Ryan!"

"Thomas is dead. Permanent. Elric fled up another passage. Could be loose anywhere in the house. Remember our plan and watch yourselves. Jak, stay with them. J.B., come with me. All take greatest care."

He had used the pause to reload the SIG-Sauer, noticing the Armorer doing the same to the Uzi.

Now they ran together, up the stairs, pausing on the second-floor landing to listen for any sound. But the Cornelius mansion was oddly silent.

"Higher?" J.B. said, panting from the exertion.

"Must be. In the attics. Just hope that we aren't going to be too late."

KRYSTY HAD MANAGED a shot at Mary as the white-haired woman burst up the stairs and out of the cellar door, Dean's unconscious body clasped to her breast. But the genetic mutie had been too quick, blood-filled eyes glaring wildly at her enemies, knocking Doc and Mildred out of the way with a kick and a punch, spitting at Krysty, then running away at inhuman speed toward the big central staircase.

Krysty had her Smith & Wesson 640 drawn, snapping off two bullets at the fleeing figure's legs, missing both times. She didn't dare to risk a body or head shot in case she hit Dean, lolling helplessly in Mary's grip.

"Stop and let him go!"

"Fuck a dead hog, norm slut! Nothing can stop us. Nothing! We're made to live forever!"

Mary paused at the door to the top floor, fumbling with the handle, screaming in sudden anger and ripping the brass lock out of the frame, throwing it behind her, making Krysty duck as it sliced by her.

"Stand and fight, you cowardly, murderous, raping bitch!" Krysty screamed.

For a moment Mary seemed to hesitate, then she vanished up the last flight of stairs.

Krysty was right at her heels, gripping the short-barreled pistol, knowing she had only two bullets left.

She raced up the stairs, stopping dead when she saw that Mary had turned and laid the boy behind her, standing and waiting for Krysty, beckoning to her.

"I heard you, norm," she said, smiling gently. "Murderous and raping..." She laughed. "Won't argue there, Krysty. But not cowardly. Oh, no, not cowardly. You want the male child, then come and fight me for him. Beat me and he's yours. Lose and you die with him."

Krysty picked her way carefully until she was less than three yards from Mary, noting that she was topped by a couple of inches. And she knew the supernormal power and strength of the whole family.

"Gaia, help me," she whispered, closing her eyes for a moment. "Grant me again the power of the Earth Mother to fight for good against evil. Give me the power."

Krysty knew from previous experience that, on rare occasions, she could draw on the secret mutie powers inherited from her mother, Sonja, though to use it always took a terrible toll on her own health.

"Prayers are futile, slut," Mary hissed. "Pagan superstition. Fight me or die." She laughed again. "Fight me and die."

Ryan and J.B. were standing on the second-floor landing when they heard that manic laugh, echoing from room to room throughout the house.

"Up," Ryan said, leading the way.

Krysty could never tell how the power entered her body, but she could feel it, flooding like liquid fire through the arteries, the veins, along every tiny capillary.

She opened and closed her fingers, rejoicing in the surge of strength.

"Die, bitch," she said, closing with the vampire.

Mary hadn't a shred of doubt what the outcome would be. During her unnaturally long life she'd killed, with her bare hands, dozens of times. There was no difference to her in breaking the neck of a full-grown man or a newborn baby. And the redhead would just be another corpse on the road.

Despite the Earth power, Krysty knew that this wasn't going to be easy. She had to use speed, intelligence and cunning, as well as strength, and the faster and sooner, the better.

As Mary reached for her, ready to drag Krysty into a lethal embrace, she ducked and kicked out as hard as she could with her left leg, remaining perfectly balanced, striking the vampire in the center of her right knee. The chiseled silver point of the elegant boot smashed the delicate joint into shards of splintered bone and torn cartilage.

Mary cried out in pain, thin and high, like a stallion under a thin-bladed gelding knife. She toppled sideways, tripping over the unconscious boy, falling full length on the wooden floor, raising a choking cloud of dust.

She rolled over, sprawling by the legs of a squat, immensely heavy marble-topped table.

Ryan and J.B. were on the top landing when they heard the piercing scream and the thunderous crash.

They stopped for a moment, checking their bearings. "Didn't sound like Krysty," J.B. said.

"No," Ryan agreed.

Krysty took in a long, deep breath, looking at her fallen enemy, feeling no shred of pity. "This is for all the nameless, faceless dead," she said quietly.

She saw a movement out of the corner of her eye in the filthy attic, but she guessed it was only a rat and ignored it, focusing all her power on the helpless vampire.

Mary was rolling from side to side, clutching her ruined knee, blood seeping from her mouth where she'd bitten through the tip of her tongue.

Krysty finished the job with calm efficiency, picking the spot and kicking out again. The boot cracked into the small of the woman's back, snapping her spine, cutting the nerve highways to arms and legs. She flopped back helpless on her back, staring up at her slayer.

The red-haired beauty reached for the massive table with her left hand, pulling at it, tilting it effortlessly onto two legs so that it hung over the doomed vampire like a great stone.

"Goodbye," Krysty said.

Ryan and J.B. arrived at the top of the final flight of stairs, blasters drawn, just in time to see the last act of the murderous drama.

The table tipped over, and the great slab of marble that was its top landed flush on Mary Cornelius's skull, crushing it to a grue of blood, brains and powdery bone. The noise in the attic was almost indescribable, like a mighty apple being squashed by a giant's boot heel.

"You used the power, lover," Ryan said. "Quick, come down before you pass out."

Krysty shook her head, the fiery hair tumbling loose and free across her shoulders. She smiled at Ryan. "No need. Don't know why, love, but this time the power came and now it's gone, and it hasn't harmed me. I feel terrific."

"Where's Dean?" J.B. asked, staring around the dark caverns of the attic.

"Just over there by—" Krysty stopped, pointing into a black space. "He was, just before."

"Well, he's not now," Ryan said grimly.

Chapter Thirty-Seven

"Norman," Ryan stated.

The friends were together again, Doc and Mildred recovered from the attack by the woman. With the one-eyed man leading them, they'd gone back through the dining hall, past the kitchen, toward the main front door to the mansion.

"Norman!" Ryan repeated. "Let the boy go and you don't get hurt."

The diminutive figure was wearing a flowing dressing gown of lilac silk, belted in tightly at the waist. He was half carrying Dean, who seemed to be coming around from his drugged sleep, and holding a long carving knife to the side of the boy's throat. The front door was partly open and he stood in the gap, almost completely covered by Dean.

"Steady," Ryan warned. "Don't go doing anything foolish that we could all regret."

"You've murdered Mary and Thomas. But Melmoth, out hunting, has escaped you. He'll take his revenge for his brother and sister."

Suddenly the funny little man wasn't funny anymore. There was a lethal glint in his eye and steel in his voice.

Out of the corner of his good eye, Ryan noticed that Jak was no longer with them.

"And Melmoth'll make me master of the village. So that I can pick and choose anyone that takes my fancy. Power to rule. All power."

Doc nodded, leaning on his swordstick. "All power corrupts, Master Norman."

Mildred finished the quote for him. "And absolute power corrupts absolutely."

Norman giggled. "Then I'm ready to be corrupted. Ready as I'll ever— What was...?"

Ryan had spotted something that whirred across the hall, like a venomous dragonfly, something that reflected for a nanosecond the gold light of the oil lamps. It struck Norman on the side of his neck, just below the ear, hissing within inches of Dean's tousled head.

For anyone else it would have been an absurdly hazardous throw. For Jak Lauren it was easy as hitting a barn door at fifteen paces.

The heavy-bladed knife had hit Norman precisely where it had been aimed, so speedy and silent that the butler still had no idea that he'd been mortally wounded.

"Something swine of... stung me... Hear raining. Outside the door?"

Blood pattered on the stone flags, smoking in the cool night air. Norman's grip on Dean had gone, and the boy had slipped away, taking a few faltering steps to Mildred, who had moved quickly to support him.

"Warned you," Ryan said.

Norman was down on his knees, still with the same almost comical look of surprise on his pinched face. His hand finally touched the taped hilt of the throwing knife that jutted from the severed artery.

"Ah, a knife," he said slowly. "That was clever...clever of..."

And he slid forward gently onto his face, like a swimmer entering deeper water.

"How's Dean?" Ryan asked, while Jak quickly retrieved his knife, wiping it on the pretty dressing gown.

"Fine Dad." The voice sounded slurred. "Tired and been sleeping and had double-strange dreams of... Can't remember."

"I'll look after him," Mildred said. "If Granddaddy Melmoth's out hunting, we'd best shake the dust of this place off our feet and get moving toward the redoubt."

"What's the time?" Ryan asked, trying to angle his wrist chron to catch the faded yellow glow of the lamps.

"Still well before half past twelve," J.B. replied.

"Doesn't time just race on by when one is having positively loads of gingery fun?" Doc whispered, carefully avoiding dabbling his cracked knee boots in the spreading puddle of Norman's blood.

"Which is the best way?" Krysty asked.

Jak pointed out of the door to the right. "Go all way around, by cliff top. Pick up trail."

"Where do you think Elric's gone?" J.B. queried.

"Probably trying to track down his big brother, Melmoth," Ryan said. "Mildred's right. Sooner we make the next jump out of here, the better." He paused a moment. "I'll go first." Ryan looked at the others. "Skirmish line. J.B. as rear guard. Mildred and Dean in the middle. Keep on triple red."

The night was cold and damp, with a fresh breeze from the north that sent tattered clouds scudding across the face of a hunter's moon.

The cool air speeded Dean's recovery. "Dad, I have learning to do, to stop being a stupe? Learning about drinking drugged drinks and stuff."

Ryan grinned at his son. "Yeah, and you had a lesson today. But there are others to learn, right, Doc?"

"Yes," Doc said. "Life's curriculum for all occasions, you could say, my young friend. And other bits of book learning could be useful...some day perhaps...."

The gravel scattered thick on the path that marked off the flank of the big Gothic house crunched under their feet as they hurried along. The cliff fell away sharply, dropping to the foaming river, way below. Ryan had noticed that the old iron-spiked fence that marked the edge of the fall had rusted and broken down in several places.

"Keep away from the brink," he warned, looking behind him to make sure everyone had heard him.

When he turned back, Elric Cornelius was standing a few paces in front of him.

Superficially the youngest of the vampire brood, his skinny height was still dressed in the beautiful black suit, covered by the black satin cloak with the scarlet silk lining, though his clothes were smeared with gobbets of mud and trailing cobwebs.

But he appeared to be unharmed.

In the moonlight his stark white face seemed to shine with a supernatural phosphorescence, the eyes glowing at Ryan like fire embers.

"Mary dead, and poor Thomas destroyed. Both gone beyond any hope of rebuilding. You've been clever. Nobody in a hundred years has been as clever. But you are not clever enough for myself and Melmoth."

"Where is Melmoth?" Ryan asked.

"Oh, he'll be here. I sent him word."

"Thought transmission? That it?" Mildred said. She'd let go of Dean's hand and now stood facing Elric in a shootist's pose, slightly sideways, hand hovering over the butt of her target revolver.

"It would take too long, Doctor. Even for a relatively sophisticated brain like yours. There are concepts in genetic communication that you would never understand. The language of it would leave you struggling. But if you wish..."

"Stalling for time," Jak said.

Krysty backed him up. "Right. I feel that, too. He knows Melmoth is on his way."

"With most of Bramton," Elric stated boastfully. "It's not who wins the skirmish. It's who wins the war."

"We're doing fine," Ryan told him. "And we're about to blast you to eternity."

"You know how pointless your leaden missiles are against us. No, I think not."

Mildred had drawn the ZKR 551, using the short-fall thumb-cocking hammer, extending her right hand with the .38-caliber revolver aimed at Elric.

"Fire away," he said, spreading his arms.

Mildred shot twice, the explosions riding on top of one another, echoing across the gorge.

The range was about ten paces, in poor light, but her targets glowed like ice rubies, drawing her aim like twin lasers.

The first round hit Elric through the center of his left eye, pulping it in the socket, the full-metal-jacket round driving through the back into the brain.

The second bullet was just as perfectly aimed, hitting Elric in the right eye, completing the blinding.

"Heal that, sicko," she yelled at him as he staggered back, howling like a rabid wolf at the moon. His hands were pressed to the wounds, and he was backing away toward the rickety iron fence at the edge of the cliff.

"Going," Ryan said.

The wind seemed to catch the full cloak, tugging at it like a billowing sail. Elric fought for his balance, stumbling into the fence, spiking himself on a jagged stump of rusting iron that drove into the center of his chest.

He fell against it, and there was a loud metallic crack as the predark fence collapsed under his weight and he tumbled, shrieking, into the void.

"Gone," Ryan said.

THEY'D WALKED ONLY a little way down the rough track from the Cornelius mansion when they saw the pinpoints of light, winding toward them like a fiery snake, from the outskirts of the ville of Bramton. And they could just hear, borne on the wind, the sound of yelling and jeering.

"Melmoth's rent-a-mob," J.B. said. "Got them all charged up to come get us."

"Think he's leading them himself?" Ryan asked. "Can you see anything of him, Jak?"

The teenager stepped to the edge of the trail, shading his eyes against the fitful moon, staring intently down into the gloom, at the advancing crowd.

"No. Light's about right for seeing good. No Melmoth. About thirty or forty coming."

"We have the firepower to take the whole lot out, don't we, Dad?"

"Sure we do, Dean. But I kind of draw the line at butchering three dozen fairly innocent people. Not their fault that the Family had them as victims for so long."

"I fear that I can't perceive any reasonable way around them," Doc said. "Am I not correct in my assumption that this is the only road out of here?"

"You're not wrong, Doc." Ryan joined Jak at the edge of the graveled highway and peered down the sheer face of the cliff. He could still make out the pallid corpse that lay smashed to pieces beneath the broken fence. "I reckon there might be a way down here."

"No, absolutely not," Mildred said angrily. "Rather do the slaughter of the innocents, if you don't mind too much, Ryan Cawdor."

He grinned at her. "It'll be fine, Mildred. Take us a little time, but we'll keep quiet and pressed in while the folk of Bramton go rampaging past us. By the time they find we're gone and the house is empty, we'll be at least a couple of miles away from Bramton."

"When they discover the two permanently dead vampires up there, they might all decide not to come after us, anyway," Krysty suggested.

"Possibility. But with Melmoth still around some-place, the fear might be too bone deep for them to rebel." Ryan looked down the trail again. "If we're going to do this, then we should be moving. Don't want anyone down there to spot us going over the side. Be like shooting fish in a barrel if we're spotted."

"True." J.B. had his scattergun slung over his shoulder, the Uzi in his hand.

Ryan hefted the Steyr rifle in the same way and led his companions off the track, down onto the face of the cliff.

IN DAYLIGHT it would have been a relatively simple climb, as there were plenty of hand- and footholds and the rock itself was in good condition with very little crumbling.

At night, in the fitful light of the cloud-racked moon, it was immensely hazardous.

Dean still hadn't recovered properly from the effects of being drugged, and Krysty and Jak tried to keep the doped boy safely between them, watching him every perilous step of the way down.

Ryan tried to find a route that would parallel the trail, so that he would have some clue when the villagers were close by, listening for them above the rumbling water.

They came quicker than he'd expected, at a point where the climbers were barely a third of the way down. He heard the sullen roaring of their shouts, and caught the menacing red glare of their torches bouncing off the branches of the elegant beeches that lined the road.

Ryan gestured to the others to flatten themselves against the damp face of the cliff, all of them drawing their blasters. But, as he'd hoped, the mob continued on toward the mansion without a glance in their direction.

He waited a couple of minutes, then, waving for the others to stay where they were, Ryan climbed carefully up onto the side of the trail. He peered through a screen of stunted bushes, seeing the last of the men from Bramton vanishing around the next gooseneck in the track.

He called down to the others, and they made good time along the trail toward the ville, not seeing another living soul.

THE BRIDGE OVER THE RIVER wasn't guarded, and the ville seemed deserted.

"Seems like most of the men have gone marching up the hill," J.B. said, glancing at his chron. "Wonder how long before they figure we're not up there and they come running back down the hill again?''

Ryan looked up into the darkness. "No sign of any lights coming back again. And no sign of Melmoth, either.''

Mildred stooped to retie the laces on her boots. "Have to say that Melmoth looked much the sickest of them all. Despite his strength and special powers, he still looked like a single puff of wind could've blown him from this world into the next." She straightened. "Probably sounds stupe, but in some ways I feel kind of sorry for the Family. Made by scientists and forced to carry on such an endless, painful, pointless existence, depending on the DNA samples of others to keep them half-alive.''

Doc nodded. "I can see that, Mildred, my dear. Living and partly living. Bleak, bleak. Oh, the horror of dragging out your days and years like that.''

"Mebbe shock of others being dead'll freak out Melmoth and he'll drop off the log, as well," Dean said.

"Could be," his father agreed. "Yeah, could be.''

THE MOON HAD VANISHED behind a thick bank of cloud, and the rising wind tasted of rain. The seven friends picked their way along toward the redoubt, passing through a section of the bayou where the villagers had been logging.

The path grew narrow, twisting between patches of muddy swamp. The overhanging trees were draped with the white fronds of Spanish moss that brushed damply at the faces of the companions.

Ryan was still leading the way, into a small clearing, when J.B. shouted a warning.

"Look out, left!"

The SIG-Sauer was already drawn and it swung around, almost of its own accord. Ryan glimpsed someone coming in at him on his blind side, carrying a weapon that glinted silver. It was a tall, skinny figure, wearing black, with a shock of white hair.

"Melmoth," he breathed, and squeezed the trigger on the blaster.

The bullet smashed into the dark shape, sending it skidding sideways and backward, with a muffled cry of pain. Ryan leveled the SIG-Sauer again, ready to put several more rounds into the skull of the vampire and pulp it beyond redemption, when Krysty grabbed at his arm.

"No, lover!"

"Why?" He saw the answer to his own question, lying still in a brief pool of moonlight, like a crumpled toy.

It was a young woman, thin, wearing a long black skirt and a white cotton head scarf. A short-hafted kindling ax lay on the ground a couple of yards away from her. The 9 mm round had been fired with extreme accuracy, hitting her just above the breastbone, tearing through lungs and heart.

A classic killing shot.

"Shit! Never saw her properly." Ryan walked over to look down at the dead girl, seeing that she was barely into her teens. "Came at me with the ax. I couldn't have..."

A violent gust of wind blew through the trees around them, almost as if some vast night-flying creature had soared overhead.

"Couldn't help it, lover," Krysty said. "She gave you no chance not to chill her."

"Even so..." He shook his head, remaining behind a few moments as the others filed out of the clearing. "I'm really sorry," he said. To himself.

THE REST OF THE WALK through the swamp was more or less uneventful, though a big bull alligator lumbered along the path toward them, tail swinging like an armored pendulum. But he made so much noise that there was plenty of time for everyone to get safely out of his way.

It was still dark when they reached the entrance to the redoubt.

Ryan paused, holding up his hand. "I'll go ahead. Make sure there's no sign of Melmoth. Soon as I think it's safe, I'll call you."

It took him only a couple of minutes to reassure himself that the outer sec door was still firmly locked. Unless someone knew the code, it hadn't been touched.

"Let's go!" he shouted.

Chapter Thirty-Eight

All of them felt uncomfortable, knowing that the oldest of the vampires might still be swooping around, somewhere behind them. They moved at a brisk walking pace along the corridors, past the numberless locked doors, until they reached the part of the redoubt that was familiar to them. Once they were close to the gateway entrance they all began to feel that they could finally relax.

"Nearly there," Ryan said.

Doc holstered the gold-plated commemorative Le Mat, rapping on the floor with the ferrule of his swordstick. "Well, my dear companions, we have once again fronted the forces of evil and come through successfully. And I do not believe that the dark powers have been so dark or so powerful, ever before. Certainly I can recall no precedent for such wickedness."

"Then again, Doc," Mildred teased, "most times you have trouble remembering what you had for breakfast."

"Door's still open, Dad."

The heavy vanadium-steel sec door had jammed three-quarters of the way up and it still hung there.

Ryan ducked under it, pushing away a momentary vision of the faulty catch giving way and the entire weight tumbling on himself and the others, crushing them to smears of blood and pulped bone on the concrete.

But they all passed through safely and crossed the control room, where the faint smell of damp still lingered, through the anteroom, with the armaglass sec door of the gateway directly ahead of them.

Everyone bustled through, all of them following Doc's lead and holstering their blasters. Dean had recovered all his sharpness and was back to his old self.

"Can I close the door, Dad?"

"No, I'll do it. You sit down with the others and get ready for the jump."

Krysty looked around, turning to stare behind them, across the deserted comp-control area, with its monitor screens showing endless, ever-changing fields of data.

"Anything, lover?" Ryan asked.

"No. Don't think so. Just got that odd feeling of there being something. And nothing."

"Well, if it's Melmoth, then he's too late. Another few seconds we're out of here."

Doc went in first, laying his swordstick at his side, stretching his long legs in front of him, knees cracking. Mildred sat next to him, her beads fluttering against the dark brown wall of the chamber.

J.B. stepped in third, avoiding a dried-up mess on the floor. "Could've cleaned up your puke, Ryan," he admonished. "Sloppy housekeeping."

Ryan grinned. "Remind you of that next time you throw up during a jump."

"That'll be the day, pilgrim." He settled himself beside Mildred, laying his weapons at his side, taking off his spectacles and carefully folding them, placing them in a top pocket of his coat. He took Mildred's hand in his.

Jak went in silently, sitting with the grace of a cat in front of a hearth.

Dean looked at his father. "Are you sure I can't do the door, Dad?"

"No. Sit down, quickly." Despite the security of being snug in the heart of the redoubt, Ryan still felt a little uneasy. The Trader used to say that an enemy alive meant always checking the shadows. It was true.

Krysty patted him on the cheek. "Let's hope we find a nicer, kinder place next time," she said, sitting beside Dean and waiting for Ryan to join them.

He took a last look behind him.

The air was still, though he thought for a moment he heard a whispering of wind.

He set that thought away and walked into the chamber. "Everyone ready?" A chorus of "yes" greeted him. "Then here we go." He closed the door and sat cross-legged beside Krysty, reaching out to hold her hand.

"To a good jump," she whispered.

"I'll drink to that, too, lover, when we got something to drink."

The disks in floor and ceiling of the armaglass chamber were beginning to glow, and a faint mist was gathering at the top of the hexagonal room.

"You see that the notice is gone off the wall of the little room, Dad?" Dean asked, his voice already echoing from far away.

"Notice?"

"Boy's correct, you know," Doc said, his voice booming like a bittern at sunset across a salt marsh. "About a show they were putting on here. Before skydark. It's vanished."

Ryan felt his brain beginning to scramble. Dean mentioning the note was somehow important. But how and why? Perhaps it didn't matter at all. Though it had to mean someone had been down in the gateway section since they jumped to the bayous.

"Who could...?" he said slowly, his voice distorted.

Krysty's fingers squeezed his hand very hard, painfully. She was telling him something, shouting. But the jump was almost under way.

Almost.

A silhouetted figure appeared outside the heavy door, someone tall and skinny.

Wearing black.

Ryan's grip on the present had almost gone, and he was clinging to consciousness by a ragged fingernail.

Door opening.

Closing.

Dark figure.

White hair.

Face close against his, with eyes that leaked bright blood. Skin like paper.

Old, immeasurably old.

Hissing words. "...what you did..."

As blackness finally swallowed him up, and his eye closed, Ryan Cawdor's last sentient thought was that his nostrils were filled with the acrid stench of decay.

Of death.

It's the ultimate battle between
good and bad—Made in Mexico

THE Destroyer

#102 Unite and Conquer

Created by
WARREN MURPHY
and RICHARD SAPIR

Not that things were so hot before, but when a huge
earthquake guts Mexico, nobody wants to hang around,
especially with all sorts of demonic doings by the barbaric
gods of old Mexico, released from hell when the earth
ruptured. It's god versus god, with the human race
helpless trophies for the victor.

Look for it in March, wherever Gold Eagle books are sold.

In January, look for Gold Eagle's newest
anti-terrorist weapon

MICHAEL KASNER

BLACK OPS

UNDERCOVER WAR

America's newest strike force, the Black Ops commandos operate
beyond the reach of politics and red tape. No rules, no regulations,
just results. Objective: retribution against U.S.-directed terrorism.

Don't miss UNDERCOVER WAR, the team's first Black Ops
mission: to save Cuba's fledgling democracy from Communist
hard-liners and the Mafia.

Look for it in January, wherever Gold Eagle books are sold.